# DEPTHS *of* REMEMBRANCE

## BOOK THREE OF THE ATLANTIS CHRONICLES

# SUSAN MACIVER

Cover Design by Monica Haynes; thethatchery.com
Interior Graphic Design by Colleen Sheehan; ampersandbookinteriors.com

Susan MacIver
Visit my website at
www.susanmaciver.com
Instagram@susan.maciver

Printed in the United States of America
First Printing: 2018

Published by MacIver Publishing, LLC

MacIver Publishing

ISBN: 978-0-9991782-2-5
Ebook ISBN: 978-0-9991782-3-2
Library of Congress Control Number: 2018958869

# DEDICATION

For my mom,
my very own Na-Kai

Y MOM, KAY Barnett was a funny, fearless, irreverent, politically incorrect, woman. Her joie de vivre touched everyone blessed enough to know her. As kids, she taught us to swim, dive, ski, play tennis and golf, try anything once and if it didn't kill us…maybe try it again. She played the piano by ear and if you could carry any kind of a tune, she would pick up the notes and play the hell out of the song.

As a private pilot instructor, she once had a student who froze at the controls of a single engine plane. In a stall and after repeating the phrase, "I've got the controls!" twice, she simply grabbed the man by his unmentionables and said, "If you don't let go, I'm twisting it off!" You can only imagine how quickly he relinquished his hold!

She took us hot potting in Yellowstone, scuba diving in Cayman, dolphin riding in Florida, skiing in Ruidoso, hiking in Montana and golfing in Roswell. Snakes were the only pets she refused us. Because we grew up with dogs, kitties, guinea pigs, goats, a monkey (who was meaner than a snake), horses, cows, and yes…even an alligator (Ralph was nicer than the monkey!) we developed a love for animals, for nature and for this beautiful earth.

In the stage play, *Auntie Mame*, Mame's famous line "Life is a banquet, and most poor sons-of-bitches are starving to death!" sums my mom up perfectly. To say that she lived life to the fullest paints an almost impoverished image…About the only thing she didn't get to do was go white shark cage diving off the coast of South Africa.

I remember she had a T-shirt that encapsulated her entire life's philosophy. On the front, in bold letters, it read, "If they can't take a joke…" when she hoisted the shirt up, the inside finished…"F@%# em!"

A combination of Scarlett O'Hara, Auntie Mame and Amelia Earhart, she taught us all how to live, love, laugh and be happy.

That was my mom and I miss her,
she would have loved this story
January 15, 1934 – March 31, 2018

# ACKNOWLEDGMENTS

OUR FORMATIVE YEARS are always with us. No matter how we choose to let our past shape us, it is the bridge to our present selves. Depths of Remembrance is about…well, remembering. In honor of the loved ones that have transcended before me, I would like to remember and acknowledge:

Thelma and Oscar Gilbert
John Barnett
Roger Lidman
&
Kay Barnett

Thank you for all you have been to me and all you continue to be…I am blessed beyond measure to have had you in my life, no matter how brief a moment in time.

Susan
8/19/18

# PRONUNCIATION

ARIS – AIR/iss

CLEITO – klee/ATE/o

DARIA Caiden – DAR/ee/uh KY/den

ENNAEL – uh/NEEL

EUMELUS – Yoo/mue/les

KAI-DAN – KY/dan

KALLI-DAN – KAL/ee/dan

KYLA – Ky/la

MARIK – MAIR/ik

NA-KAI eva Evenor – na/KY ee/va ev/uh/nor

NI-CIO evaw Azaes – NEE/shee/o ee/va UH/zays

OIA – EE/ya

OOMI – OO/me

PELTOR – PEL/tor

POSEIDON – PO/sy/den

ROGERT – RO/jer

TRAVLOR – TRAV/lor

YLNO – IL/no

# Synopsis for
# Currents of Will

In *Tides of Change*, Book One of *The Atlantis Chronicles*, the wrath of Travlor was loosed. Returning to Atlantis with a well-trained mercenary army, he makes good on his promise to avenge himself against the Atlanteans. With overwhelming numbers, Travlor oversees the complete destruction of Atlantis, leaving the underwater sanctuary in ruins.

*Currents of Will*, Book Two of *The Atlantis Chronicles*, finds our heroine, Daria kidnapped by the megalomaniac, Travlor, as the last of the Atlanteans flee to Travlor's abandoned military compound on the island of Santorini, Greece.

As Ni-Cio tries to re-establish his people "topside," Daria now pregnant with Ni-Cio's child, is held against her will with no way to break through the stranglehold Travlor maintains over her telepathic abilities. Utilizing Daria's healing powers, Travlor initiates an incident aboard ship whereby one of the cooks is severely burned. "You have done well, topsider. Better even than I had hoped. This little foray into all things miraculous will do much to help fuel the religious fervor I require."

Taking credit for Daria's secret healing of the injured cook, Travlor assumes the mantle of savior as the hardened men on board his freighter behold him as the new Messiah.

Arriving at a deposed drug lord's estate in the jungles of Columbia, South America, Travlor uses Daria's healing powers to continue to spread the word about the healing 'miracles' of the new Messiah. Soon a new religion springs into being with thousands of people flocking to join The Armies of the New Messiah. South American countries bow before the religious coups staged by Travlor's followers until Travlor is placed at the head of a theocratic rule whose grip extends far and wide.

Unable to break Travlor's hold over her and her baby, Daria finds herself drawn into a dangerous game as her brutal kidnapper initiates his plans for world domination.

Meanwhile the romance between Evan and Kyla deepens as they recognize each other as lifemates. Once Evan feels that the Atlanteans, under Ni-Cio's guidance, are able to carry on at the compound, he flies to Boston with Kyla where he divests himself of his assets as well as his main company. While in Boston, Evan and Kyla hear news of the rise of a new "Messiah" in South America. Believing that the news article is referring to his father, Evan and Kyla, fly back to Santorini in order to join Ni-Cio and a few of his select men in a desperate attempt to locate Daria and bring her back into the folds of the dispossessed Atlanteans.

Meanwhile, governments the world over are becoming more threatened by Travlor's growing armies, his untold wealth, and his dominance on the world stage. As threats are exchanged, countries spiral out of control as battles rage between believers and non-believers.

At Travlor's vast estate, he and Daria test their wills against each other with neither truly able to get the upper hand. The longer Daria is trapped in Columbia, the further along her pregnancy develops. Carrying a very special child, Daria must see to her own health as the supernatural powers of the baby place a severe drain on her energy.

At last, due to a breach in Travlor's hold over Daria's telepathic abilities, she is able to give Ni-Cio clues as to where she is being held. Flying through the seas in their biospheres, the Atlanteans, led by Evan and Ni-Cio, rip through the oceans toward Columbia. Their mission: Save Daria and the baby and prevent all out nuclear war as Travlor continues to subjugate the world's populations.

During the rescue, events go horribly wrong. Travlor is mortally wounded by friendly fire and Daria is thrown into premature labor when she tries to heal Travlor's injuries. Collapsing on top of Travlor's lifeless form, Daria, her baby and Travlor hover near death as Evan desperately attempts to save them. Holding both his father's and Daria's hands, Evan taps into an unknown yet powerful healing energy he never realized he had. Holding Daria, the baby, and his father in a type of suspended animation, Evan finds that he is drawn into the depths of his father's vast memories. Forced to follow his father's life, Evan and Ni-Cio realize that their only chance to save Daria, the baby, and Travlor, is to get them back to Atlantis.

And thus begins the final chapter; *Depths of Remembrance*, Book Three of *The Atlantis Chronicles*.

# The Canons

### ✦ I ✦

*As children of Poseidon you are granted the paradise that is Atlantis*
*In the purity of your actions will it remain thus*

### ✦ II ✦

*The healing power descends through my lineage*
*Live that you flourish*
*Attend not and you will surely weaken*

### ✦ III ✦

*No matter the form*
*All life is held sacred*

### ✦ IV ✦

*Whether in the heavens or the earth*
*We are bound by the same essence that creates life*
*Hurt another and you ultimately hurt yourself*

### ✦ V ✦

*Behold the miracle that is You*
*Cherish this offering*

### ✦ VI ✦

*The sacrament of love is inviolate*
*Written in the heavens before your time*
*Heart, mind and soul will bring you into awareness of your life mate*
*Act not until they speak as one*

### ✦ VII ✦

*Love is manifested within the smallest detail*
*Living thus will your life be enriched*

### ✦ VIII ✦

*Let your essence be filled with the joy of life*
*And spread that joy to those you touch*

# CHAPTER

*1*

NI-CIO'S THOUGHTS FLEW to his men: *"Aris!
Rogert! Get everybody to the front lawn, now!"*

His frantic orders were met with a quicksand
silence that sucked away all sound. Something was horrifically
wrong. He flew down the last flight of stairs and tore through
the cavernous rooms until, scrambling into the front foyer, a
ghastly tableau opened before him.

His mind recoiled, refusing to acknowledge what his eyes
starkly beheld. His body became leaden, and he couldn't move,
didn't want to move. Finally, willing his body to obey, he shuffled forward. However, like the space between the earth and
stars, the last ten steps became a distance too great to cross.
Ni-Cio faltered and stopped. He couldn't make it—wouldn't
make it. Those last precious feet had become an unfathomable
distance, something to ignore, as though they didn't exist.

Frozen in the thrall of a living nightmare, Ni-Cio watched
Rogert leave the press of men. Shaking his head, he tried to
back away, but the formidable Atlantean hurried to his side
and grabbed his shoulders. Rogert did what he could to steady

their leader. "His shield effect failed. There was nothing we could do. He is dead, Ni-Cio."

Ni-Cio wrenched his gaze from the grisly sight and tried to focus on what Rogert was telling him. Yanking free, Ni-Cio staggered to the body of his friend.

Drenched in a pool of blood, Aris lay on the ground, deathly white and unnaturally still. Sinking to the floor, Ni-Cio heard his own anguished sob as he gently gathered Aris's shattered body into his arms. A torrent of grief ripped wide the scars that marked his heart. Blackened stripes of indigo crossed his face; agony poured from his soul.

Rocking slowly back and forth, Ni-Cio sluggishly searched for a reason to continue, but as Rogert bent down to join him, a scream erupted from somewhere inside Ni-Cio: "*No!*"

His naked cry rent the air like a lightning strike and Ni-Cio collapsed over Aris's lifeless body. With each gut-wrenching sob, Ni-Cio's body shook so hard that Rogert was afraid they would lose him, too. He clutched at their leader. "Ni-Cio! We must mourn later. We have to get Daria to safety."

The only word that made sense through the endless gauntlet of sorrow was "Daria." Ni-Cio looked up and blinked hard. He clung to the urgency in Rogert's voice and ran a bloodied hand over his eyes. He was ferociously tired. *Why does Rogert persist? Can he not just leave me alone?*

At his wit's end, Rogert knew he had to break through Ni-Cio's shock. Without thinking, he cocked an arm and struck Ni-Cio's cheek as hard as he could.

Reeling from the force of Rogert's strike, Ni-Cio saw nothing but red. Beyond reason and intent only on killing, his eyes blazed with purple savagery, and he surged upward, ploughing into Rogert. Both men slid across the floor in a deadly embrace. Rogert protected himself as best he could, and though he tried not to hurt their leader, he knew he was joined in mortal combat. If he couldn't stop Ni-Cio, one of them was going to die.

It was Evan's sharp command that finally blasted through the fog shrouding Ni-Cio's mind: *"Ni-Cio, we need the choppers, now! I don't know how long I can maintain my hold on Daria!"*

# CHAPTER
## 2

RAVLOR, DEEP INTO his vision, saw his mother and his heart skipped. She was as beautiful as he remembered, and he was young again. He didn't know how it had happened, but his whole life stretched before him. Thoughts burst brilliantly through his mind like shooting stars, but it was hard to examine them, and truly, at this moment, he could have cared less.

He studied his mother standing over him, hands on her hips. The sun created a corona around her body and she resembled a goddess descended from Mount Olympus. The fact that she was human made Travlor love her even more. One glimpse of her blond hair and fair skin and he could see why his father, god over the lands and seas, had taken her to wife. Clieto was the dream by which every man judged beauty.

"Atlas, are you daydreaming again? Poseidon awaits! Run, rinse your face and hands—your father needs to speak with you."

Atlas shook himself and stood up, brushing the dirt from his knees. Nearly six feet tall, he towered over Clieto's slender frame. Sheepishly, he reached into a pocket and retrieved his treasure.

With reverence and immense pride, Atlas opened his hand, revealing an innocuous, dirty piece of clouded quartz.

"Mother, the crystal I have sought!" Eyes glittering, he lifted the quartz toward the sun. A thin striation ran the length of the crystal. Barely the width of a hair, the line gleamed clear and bright, sparking an intense beam of sunlight that caught Atlas's eyes and made them water. Blinking to clear his vision, he handed the crystal to his mother.

She carefully lifted the quartz closer to her eyes and gasped. "It has to be the one! It is exactly as your father described!"

An exuberant grin spread across Atlas's face. He felt like he could fly! "It is exactly as father described," he repeated. "Do you think he will be proud?"

"He will be very proud." Clieto shifted her gaze back to her only son. "But if you keep him waiting much longer, it will not be your crystal that draws his attention. Go, and remember to clean up!"

Atlas hugged his mother, thrust the crystal into her hand, and, with her laughter ringing in his ears, turned and ran. His legs pumped effortlessly and his arms drove like pistons. Wind whipped his long, dark hair and blood thrummed through his veins. His heart overflowed with such love and joy that he thought it might burst.

At last, cresting the hill leading to his home, the sublime grandeur of Atlantis spread out below him. Appearing as though it was suspended in clouds, the city created by Poseidon—solely for his people—sparkled with a majesty that rivaled Olympus.

The supreme city of Poseidon's earthly domain lay draped in glistening hues of polished marble, quartz crystal, and alabaster. Set against the backdrop of the blue Aegean, Atlantis sparkled like a heavenly diadem. Atlas was certain that this one city, Poseidon's crown jewel, was the most beautiful creation in all the heavens or the earth.

Wildly passionate about architecture, his not-so-secret dream was to become Atlantis's most renowned designer. His earliest memories were colored with the many marvels of the homes and buildings leading to his father's temple. During important ceremonies, the noise and excitement faded as Atlas lost himself in the beauty of line and symmetry, the juxtaposition of color as it related to material, and the sacred marriage of form to function.

He remembered wanting to grow up so fast, the sooner to realize his dreams. Now, even though the reality of those dreams continued to fan the flames of his imagination, part of him yearned for the security of his parents' arms as well as their approbation.

Startled, his father's thought-form raced through his mind. *"Atlas! Where are you, Son? I will not wait all day ..."*

*"I am coming, Father! I am almost home ..."* He pushed himself harder.

His home quickly came into sight. Situated on a bluff overlooking Atlantis, its elevation offered a commanding view. Rushing through the golden gates of a protective wall, Atlas was greeting by a lavish courtyard. It was replete with verdant gardens, shade trees, and meandering streams; a fountain, in honor of his father, stood at the very heart of the sumptuous enclosure. Pausing to listen to the music of the falling water, Atlas's heart soared with the magical tones that permeated the very air he breathed.

Atlas loved his home. Everyone in Atlantis knew that this was the only place Poseidon resided when he visited. Shading his eyes against marble so white it gleamed like a polished crystal, Atlas's thoughts were drawn to the god who had sired him.

Standing six-feet-eleven-inches, the man was commanding even without his godhood. A smile spread across Atlas's face as he remembered his father's booming laugh; he could laugh so loud and so long that others could not help but join in and share in Poseidon's pure joy.

On the other hand, Atlas had witnessed the lightning and thunder that could strike when his father was displeased. It was frightening and awesome in its majesty. That his father controlled the land and the oceans was a concept that he still had trouble grasping. He didn't know, being a demi-god, what role his father had planned for him, but he hoped with all his heart that it had to do with his loves and passions: design and architecture. At his sixteenth birthing day, his father was to divulge his life's mission.

He started when he realized how long he had been lost in his thoughts. He broke into a sprint and sent his father a quick thought. *"I am home, Father!"*

Atlas approached the entrance where a servant draped in the family colors of white and gold held the immense, bronze-carved doors wide. He barely glanced at the man as he halted his rush long enough to grab the nearest pitcher of water. Splashing the perfumed liquid into a bowl, he ran his hands through the cool water and doused his face. He grabbed the proffered linen, then wiped his damp face and thrust the towel back into waiting hands.

Hurrying through a lengthy hallway, he found another servant waiting. As Atlas came closer, the man solemnly opened the doors to the main library and announced in a stentorian voice, "Poseidon awaits."

Atlas halted and took a moment to compose himself. He took a deep breath. He knew his father would not want to meet him when he looked like a wild thing. After a moment, he entered, spreading his arms. "Father! How good it is to see you!" Atlas hurried to the seated figure.

Opening his thick, muscular arms, Poseidon stood to meet his son. "Ahh, at last. Why do you insist on keeping me waiting?" He laughed to lighten his tone, and Atlas fell into his embrace.

They held each other tightly until his father released the warm hug. Poseidon sat again, motioning for Atlas to sit next to him. He clapped his hands with relish. "So, tell me, what you have been up to?"

"I found one, Father! I found the exact crystal!" Atlas excitedly regaled his sire with the result of his summer's excursions.

Poseidon's face split into a huge grin and his laughter echoed through the house. "Well, do you want to keep me in suspense or will you show me your prize?" He slapped his son's knee.

"Mother is holding it for me. She wanted me to clean up a bit and did not want me to keep you waiting any longer than necessary, so I ran ahead."

Poseidon's deep, blue-black eyes sparkled like dark sapphires. "No matter. I will inspect it when she arrives." The huge man settled back into his chair. "We must discuss the plans for your upcoming birthing day. It is not every day a boy becomes a man, and I have many friends who will attend the celebration."

The preparations for this momentous occasion had started well over two years ago. The Temple of Poseidon, at the very center of Atlantis, had been decorated for the festival. An esteemed list of guests from all directions was expected. There was even a persistent rumor that Zeus, Poseidon's brother, would make a special appearance. Atlas had never met him, and he was filled with anticipation. "The celebrations will have to be seen to be believed. I can hardly wait!"

Atlas knew that his father loved him almost more than the other children he had sired. Poseidon had spoken proudly of his infectious enthusiasm, his sense of adventure, his curiosity, and his intelligence. His father had told him that his attributes blazed from him like a beacon and because of that, when it was time, he would make a fine leader. It had made Atlas's heart soar to know how proud Poseidon was of him.

"You will be honored fully, as befits a son of Poseidon. But tell me, how far afield did you roam today? I fear that your wanderings could take you beyond the bounds I have set for Atlantis. I am told that you become so immersed in your adventures that you do not keep track of our borders."

Atlas earnestly shook his head. "Please, do not concern yourself. I am careful. I confess, I have been close to our western border, but I am aware, Father. I will never cross our lines; why, it is one of your cardinal rules that has been implemented for our safety."

"Remember, Atlas," Poseidon sighed, "it is not only for safety that we hold ourselves apart. The newly struggling tribes and emerging groups that are learning to survive as more than savages must not be tainted by our knowledge or ways. We have granted them the freedom to determine their own course. That is a sacred commitment, and so it must be."

Atlas furrowed his brow. "I am aware of the specific Canon, Father, and I am careful. I give you my word."

Poseidon glanced up as Clieto entered the room. The clouds that had crossed his great countenance fled, and his face broke into a huge, love-filled smile. He rose from his chair and shortened the distance quickly. He stood before his wife, his admiring gaze drinking in her pale beauty. Poseidon took her into his embrace and stroked her radiant face. "My love, I am overjoyed to have you in my arms again." He kissed her deeply, then looked into her shining eyes. "I understand you have a special treasure to show me."

Proudly, Clieto took Atlas's crystal from her shift and gave it to her handsome husband. "He has done as you requested."

Poseidon closed his large fist around the crystal and walked to the far wall, standing before the tall, rectangular windows. The sun was slipping below the horizon, but the rock's singular hairline striation was still clearly defined in the last light of day. Glacial in its purity, Poseidon could see an entire rainbow locked inside. He turned it all around, studying the crystal with admiration. "You have done remarkably well, Atlas. It is truly a new type of striation. Soon, I will teach you how to harness its power." He gazed at his beloved wife and held out his hand. "But now, let us retire to the garden and enjoy the repast that has been set."

Atlas joined his mother and father as Poseidon led them from the room. "When will you show me, Father? You know I have searched for this crystal from the time my birthday celebrations began. Will you be staying with us tonight?"

Poseidon's explosive laughter rang out. "Atlas, slow down, my son! All in good time. Before your birthday, I will teach you the ways of this particular crystal. That is my promise to you." He ruffled his son's hair. "As for staying, I must decline. I have business elsewhere, and I expect to be away for a while."

"But my birthday is only a few months away! How long will you be gone?"

As his father's large hand lifted from his head, he took with it the comforting warmth. "I will return before the new moon." He saw his son's look of disappointment. "Do not worry! Enjoy the time you have left. As you step into manhood, responsibilities invariably arise. With the little time left, be a boy with an excellent sense of adventure and no responsibilities!" Poseidon placed his arms around Clieto and Atlas, and guided them out of the house, into the gardens.

Like hundreds of winking fireflies, votive candles hung suspended in the trees and graced the low marble wall surrounding the veranda. Servants stood, awaiting their god's command. Holding the chairs so the small family could be seated, a butler indicated that the meal was about to be served.

Doors flew open and a line of men and women proceeded to serve every kind of food imaginable. The tantalizing aromas of freshly baked bread and steamed clams mixed with night blooming jasmine—the smells were intoxicating. Atlas's stomach awakened with a purpose, and he was ravenous.

Twinkling in the last rays of a dusky-gold sunset, candlelight filled the veranda with warmth and serenity as a gentle breeze wrapped the family in a loving caress. Atlas was home, and he felt marvelous.

# CHAPTER

*3*

ARLY THE NEXT morning, Atlas filled a flask with water and grabbed a satchel, throwing some leftover bread, cheese, and fruit inside before heading outdoors.

It took nearly an hour to reach the site he had discovered the previous day. Since it was the only place in all his wanderings that had yielded the sacred crystal, he hoped with all his heart to uncover more. Although he knew the chances of finding sister crystals were remote, he wanted to surprise his mother and father at his birthing day celebration. Two such crystals would be the only gifts precious enough to offer his beloved parents.

He had been at the site for a while and was randomly kicking some dirt mounds, hands in his pockets, when he was astonished to hear a female voice: "Eh, what are you doing?"

The accent was spectacularly unfamiliar, as was the young woman he took in at a glance. She seemed to be near or about his own age. Unlike anyone he had ever known, she was tall, just a shade under his own height, and her coloring was unfamiliar. Her skin was a dusky brown which looked to Atlas like the color of dark caramel. She glowed in the bright mid-day sun. Mesmerized by eyes of such a startling shade of light green, Atlas was uncomfortable beneath her careful scrutiny. It was as if she could see his inner most thoughts. He was so unnerved by her that he forced himself to continue to meet her gaze. Words spilled out before his mind engaged. "Who are you?"

"I am Alia. You?"

Atlas cautiously approached and opened his hands, palms up, to show that he held no mal-intent. "I am Atlas. Do you live nearby? Are you Atlantean?"

The girl cocked her head, and a questioning look clouded her hypnotic eyes before she shook her head. "I do not understand—what is Atlantean? I come from there." She pointed west.

Atlas studied the direction she indicated. "Then I am certain you do not live in Atlantis. How did you cross our border?" It was impolite to stare, but he could not wrest his gaze from her exquisite face. She was beguilingly different, and he was surprised to find that he wanted to know more about her. That had never happened to him ... ever. He had always been too absorbed in his own wishes and desires to be concerned about anyone else. He was quite intrigued.

She shrugged. "I have come here many times. I like to look at the beautiful structures. We have nothing like them where I live."

Atlas glanced westerly. "Where do you live?"

Alia licked her generous lips and considered his question. "I cannot say how far, but for me, it takes the better part of a morning to reach your lands."

With her reply, Atlas caught himself intently focused on those lips. He was suddenly tongue-tied, unsure of what to say. She made him feel ill at ease, and if he truly thought about it, he was almost a little afraid of her. He spouted the first thing that came to mind. "How is it you speak our language?"

She was surprised. "Does not everyone speak this tongue?"

Atlas shook his head, flummoxed. "I do not know. You are the only person I have ever met who is not Atlantean. Though I am still unsure how you got through our border." He hesitated; he didn't know how to describe the thought-form that surrounded their lands. "There is a thought … uh, an unseen barrier that was placed around our lands. It is supposed to keep us separate from others."

The girl clearly had no idea what to do with that bit of knowledge. She swiped her brow, and Atlas peered at the beads of moisture that sparkled across her brow. He didn't know why the unbidden thought came, but he felt like tasting those iridescent drops with the tip of his tongue. *Why would I think that?* He shuffled his feet and laughed to cover his nervousness.

Alia turned to leave. "I should go."

"Please, not yet." Atlas grabbed her hand, but it felt as though he had touched a hot coal. Alia gasped and, as one, they dropped their arms and took a step back.

Atlas was confused. He didn't know what had just happened, and he really wasn't sure what he was supposed to do. His gaze darted over the landscape as he tried to think of a way to detain her just a little longer. Then it came to him. "I have to show you what I found."

He grabbed his satchel and dug around until he found what he wanted, then proudly extended his hand, bringing the quartz up to her sea-green eyes. "A singular quartz crystal." He ran a finger over the clear line. "See this tiny striation?"

She gazed at him, perplexed. "Yes, but I see nothing that would make this special to you."

"I have been searching for two years for this particular quartz with this single, clear line." He couldn't help himself. He puffed his chest with pride, but she huffed gently, and her next statement punctured his inflated ego.

"Why, that is not so special where I am from. There are many of those ugly things on the ground. I have been to one place where the ground is covered with them. You cannot take a step without walking over just such a crystal."

Atlas's heart lurched. He couldn't believe what he was hearing. "How is that possible?"

The girl shaded her eyes and looked at him as if he was slow witted. "We do not use them for anything—but they are there. I can take you there, if you would like."

Atlas swallowed his excitement and tried to adopt a more worldly countenance, but his heart hammered against his chest so hard he was afraid Alia could hear.

The girl came closer and studied the crystal. Atlas's heart ratcheted up until he wasn't sure if he could take another breath. She bent close so that he detected her scent: an elusive blend of cinnamon and honeysuckle.

He inhaled deeply while trying to collect himself. She tantalized his sense of adventure and curiosity, but he found that, more than anything, he just wanted to be near her. He managed to stammer, "I, uh, I would love to see where you found the other crystals. Can we go now?"

Alia grinned. "No, it is too late in the day."

She liked the gangly young man, and was happy they had met. She liked the way he looked at her. It made her insides tingle. All the men in her tribe made fun of her height, and she felt awkward and ugly because of their taunts. Atlas didn't make her feel that way at all. She examined him for a moment and decided that—for a boy—he was quite handsome. However, as soon as that thought came to her, she felt herself blush. She had never even considered the men of her species as anything other than creatures to be avoided at any cost. She shook her head to rid such thoughts.

Atlas grinned back. "How about if we run?"

She interrupted, "No, I cannot." She thought for a moment. "If you come to this spot before sunrise tomorrow, I will meet you and take you there. We will have more time and more daylight ahead of us."

Atlas grinned even wider and then, unable to stop himself, nodded as though his head was about to detach from his neck. *I look like a fool.* However, the thought of seeing her tomorrow filled his heart with such joy that he forgot about appearances.

He swallowed hard, gathered all his courage, and took her hand again. As skin touched skin, another shock raced up his arm. He fervently sought her eyes, hoping to see that she recognized the mysterious connection, too.

Alia's gaze was riveted on his. It was clear that she felt something but was as unsure as he was as to what should be done. "I promise I will be here." With great reluctance, he released his hold.

There was nothing more to be said. Alia raised her hand in a shy wave, smiled, and turned away. Atlas watched her break into an easy lope. He prayed that she would look back before she disappeared over the horizon. When she stopped at the top of a gentle slope, he was overjoyed when she once again raised her arm and waved. The wind brought her words to him on a sigh. "Tomorrow, Atlas!"

The boy, on the threshold of inheriting tremendous responsibilities that accompanied the rites of becoming a man, forgot every trace of every warning he had ever received about leaving Atlantis and crossing the borders. The only thought tumbling through his churning mind was the endless number of moments he had to surmount before seeing Alia again.

He tossed the crystal into the air and snatched it on the downward spiral. Laughing with abandon, he regained his satchel, safely tucked the quartz inside, and followed the path he had trod earlier.

The rest of the day spread out like a long voyage; a voyage he was more than willing to span in order to see her again. It never occurred to Atlas to heed his father's admonition. In the youth's riotous mind, it was as though the Canons had never existed. He headed home, hoping for any distractions he could find.

# CHAPTER

*4*

LIA WAS BREATHLESS when she arrived near the campsite. Her tribe was a band of nomads who continually wandered the vast plains and lands. What they were looking for, she was never very sure. She loved where they had chosen to stay this time because she had found the gleaming city of white on one of her long explorations. She had never seen anything like the glittering city before, and she was drawn to it as a bird to a song.

She liked to imagine the people who lived there, and she would make up stories about their lives and loves. She was afraid to venture too near and had been content to gaze from afar, though she was always curious what the inhabitants looked like.

Meeting Atlas today had shown her how beautiful and graceful the Atlanteans were. She had felt awkward in his presence until she had seen the way he looked at her. It was almost like he had never met another living soul.

She had been schooled early in the mating rituals of her tribe members. The men treated their women as well as could be expected. But as far as she could tell, there wasn't much ritual other than that of convenience. I hunt, you cook; I eat, and if anything is left, you eat. Alia wanted nothing to do with any of them.

Atlas was so different from anybody or anything she had ever known that, against her better judgement, she was fascinated. That he had agreed to meet again thrilled her until she almost felt dizzy with anticipation. She wasn't sure how she was supposed to handle this sudden surge of feeling. She sighed; she hadn't wanted to leave but she knew she would be missed, and she didn't want anyone searching for her. She was ashamed of her people when measured against Atlanteans. She pronounced the word out loud, "Atlanteans." It tasted exotic on her tongue. She tried his name: "Atlas." His name lingered in her mouth like a heady wine. Not that she had ever sampled much.

Panting with effort, she reached the encampment. The tribe looked busy, and she noticed her mother's sorry attempt to clean their rudimentary tent. She ran to the haggard woman. "Mother, do you need my help?"

The woman shaded her eyes and grumbled, "Time you showed yourself. Where have you been, you lazy girl?" The woman stood and straightened her aching back. She despaired of teaching her daughter the traits needed to land a good husband. The girl was headstrong and too curious for her own good. She was also too tall; no one would want her. The woman let out a loud snort. "I am done. See if you can help your brothers; they are looking for firewood. These plains offer no help in giving fuel for our fires."

Alia backed away. She hated to help her brothers. They treated her even worse than the other boys. She didn't know any kindness from the men of her tribe. And if she'd had a father, he had left or died long before any memories of him could settle into her … except his rage.

Her mother was aging, and she always complained about how much her body ached. Alia had spent many nights rubbing her back or her legs. She was sorry her mother hurt, but she wished she didn't have to help her so much. The woman never seemed to care whether she was there or not, and her efforts, more often than not, were met with complaints, silence, or the occasional strike of a branch against her legs.

Alia left to locate her brothers. *Zeus only knows where they are!* Reluctantly, she followed the obvious path they had tramped. It wasn't hard; they were both clumsy.

In a way, being the oldest was burden enough. She couldn't remember a time when she hadn't had to watch the boys while her mother scouted for food. The people of her tribe shared when they could, but it was a hard existence. Some places were better than others, although some lands were so barren or so dangerous that the tribe ended up breaking camp too early to have foraged much. Then all of them went hungry.

Alia noticed a few errant sticks and snatched them up for their meager fire. Maybe the communal soup pot would hold something of substance tonight—her stomach was becoming more and more insistent.

Alia ran her hands through her silky, dark hair while scouring the area for sign of her brothers. Her hair was braided on one side and held into place so that her vision was never obscured. If her hair was flying in her face and covering her ears, she might not be able to see a predator in her peripheral vision or hear someone approaching.

She caught movement off to her right and found her brothers quickly. They had gathered some stray pieces of wood, but she could tell they had not been paying much attention to their task. They had some kind of rock that they were throwing and kicking with their feet, and they were engrossed in their game. "Hey!" Both Shema and Jaruth looked up, faces sheepish. They had been caught. They threw the rock down and approached Alia.

Two years older than Jaruth, Shema was the larger of the two boys. However, they often quarreled because they had both inherited their father's explosive temper, and Jaruth was always angry that he couldn't intimidate Shema physically.

They reached Alia, panting and whining their excuses: "There is nothing here!"

"The place is barren. These two sticks were hard enough to find."

Alia shook her head. She knew from their shared history that there wasn't anything she could do about their laziness. It was just better to move on; otherwise, they would take out their frustrations on her. "All right, we will try that side of the plain. Maybe the wind has blown something our way. Are the men out hunting?"

Jaruth sulked. "Yes. Lot of good that will do; this place is as barren as an old woman's tit."

Alia crinkled her face. "If Mother hears you talk like that, she will throw you in the pot and then everyone will have plenty to eat for quite a while."

Jaruth punched his sister—not hard, just enough to show his disgust. "I talk how I want to and you never tell me what to do, gigantus."

Shema joined in Jaruth's jibe; nevertheless, they raced off in the direction Alia had indicated.

Alia sighed, picked up a rock, hefted it to feel its weight, then cocked her arm and threw. The rock sailed through the air and then plummeted to hit another, larger stone—her target. She was the best shot of all the young tribesmen, and she was proud of her strength, even though most of the boys and girls made fun of her. Her thoughts shifted back to Atlas. There had been such kindness in his dark eyes, and she guessed that he was quick to laugh, although hopefully not at someone else's expense. She liked that he was secure in himself.

A deep sigh escaped along with her thoughts. She straightened her shoulders; if she didn't quit daydreaming, there would be no fire for the stewpot, and she could tell from the freshening breeze that the night would bring with it a brisk taste of fall. She hurried to catch up to her brothers.

# CHAPTER
## 5

ATLAS AWAKENED EARLIER than he expected. The richness of the dark crowding him told him that dawn had yet to make her appearance. He drowsed in the warmth and comfort of his bed, then his heart beat double-time with the thought of what this particular day was to bring.

He rolled toward the windows and smiled. Discovering a cache of crystals there for the taking was more than he could ever have imagined. But the girl … Alia …

Again, his mind drifted to the moment he had first seen her … the stunning shade of her sea-foam green eyes, set in a beguiling and fine-boned face, combined with her uncommon height created a vision of someone otherworldly. She would be a rarity in Atlantis. Just thinking of her beauty took his breath away and a sudden rush of blood caused an abrupt stirring in his loins.

Rather than lie about dreaming, Atlas jumped out of bed, rinsed quickly in the chill predawn air, threw on clean garments, and silently stole away from the house. He had primed the guards the night before, and so they looked the other way when he pushed open the gates and disappeared outside the walls of his home.

He surreptitiously made his way through the dark and entertained himself as he replayed the little he had gleaned of the strange girl. She exuded a quiet assurance and strength of character that was unusual in one so young. While her beauty seemed ethereal, Atlas felt that beneath the beautiful exterior lay a hidden well of strength to be drawn upon at any time.

He laughed aloud as the first stirrings of dawn began to drain the sky of darkness. Alia was more than special; she was a rarity, and Atlas found it interesting that he had discovered two jewels—the cloudy quartz and Alia—within a day of each other. A sure sign from the gods that he was blessed!

Russets and golds chased away the darker night colors, and Atlas picked up his pace. He shifted the pack on his back, glad that he had thought to bring enough food for both of them. A large wine skin, filled with his father's best wine, was nestled among the supplies, and he was excited at the prospect of sharing his carefully prepared picnic. His muscles warmed and loosened with each step, and as the sun returned to light his way, he increased his speed.

All was quiet. The only sound was the drumming of his soft leather sandals against the earth—even the birds had not yet greeted the morning with song. Pushing himself into a sprint, Atlas felt the rush of air parting with his passing. Blood soared through his veins. A multitude of mysterious and exhilarating possibilities lay before him. His heart beat like wild drums; he couldn't remember ever feeling so free or so alive … he was almost there! He pushed harder.

It never occurred to him that she wouldn't be there, for deep in the night, when he had tossed from lack of sleep, in the restless part of his soul yearning for his destiny to unfold, he had heard whispered intimations of a part she was yet to play. It had been long before sleep found him.

Atlas finally sighted the meeting spot and shouted a greeting. Alia was already there, waiting for him. Even from this distance, he could see the wide smile lighting her face, and his heart started another kind of dance. Beads of sweat broke out across his palms; his vision blurred as blood pounded his temples.

He refused to break stride and restrain himself. All he could think about was reaching her side. His breathing came in huge gasps, and he knew he should slow down and reorder himself, but he couldn't help it. He skidded to a stop, dust floating over his sweaty body, hair disheveled, with, despite his best efforts, a wild-eyed look that would have alarmed anyone.

However, Alia, taking in his bedraggled comportment, clamped down on a desire to laugh and took advantage of the moment. "You took your time getting here. I have been waiting well past the uprise mark."

Atlas, unable to catch his breath, bent over with his hands on his knees and inhaled air like a drowning man. He swiped at his brow, ran his palms down the side of his pants, and stood, attempting to regain some control of his windblown locks.

Clearing his throat, he teased, "I was not too keen on this morning's adventure, so I took a few more turns in bed. It was not until my conscience got the better of me that I decided to rise. Although I have been taught not to keep a lady waiting, I feel that you are a bit young to be considered a lady; therefore, I bided my time."

He couldn't keep up the charade when he saw the surprise in her eyes, and he let out a belly laugh that had her soon joining in. She playfully slapped his arm, then started like a colt and took off, looking back over her shoulder and taunting, "This way, and try to keep up!"

Atlas scrambled to follow, but deliberately slowed his pace so that he could admire the sight of her speeding form. He was captivated watching her legs and lovely rounded rump—however, when he stumbled over a rock and nearly went down face first, he increased his stride so that he could run beside her.

Running for the better part of an hour, Alia finally began to slow, and as they entered a small rift valley, she glided to a stop.

Atlas drew next to her and whooped. "By the gods, Alia, that is an enormous amount of quartz!" In the early morning light, the valley floor glittered as though strewn with precious jewels. He gaped in amazement. "How did you find this?"

She took a moment to appreciate some deep breaths, then said, "The tribe passed the valley on our way to find a camp-site." She pointed. "I marked it from that old tree on top of that ridge. When we were done setting up, I came back to see what it was." She glanced at her companion. "And no one has been interested enough to come with me, until you. Shall we?"

Atlas nodded silently. He couldn't believe his luck. This day had offered gifts beyond anything he had ever imagined. However, as he and Alia began to pick their way through the crystals, a niggling sensation arose in the back of his mind … but, he didn't have the time to examine it. He brushed the thought aside and followed Alia's lead.

There was hardly any place to walk other than over the crystals. Slowly, before moving on, he knelt to inspect the ones closest to him. He could hardly believe his eyes when he lifted the first piece of quartz. The glacial striation gleamed clear and clean in the bright sunlight, and his mind reeled.

Alia knelt next to him. "Is that what you are looking for?"

Atlas didn't trust himself to speak at first. He held the crystal for her to inspect. He tied his hair back with a thin length of linen, then stood. "That is exactly what I have been searching for for two whole years, and in all this time, I have only found the one I showed you yesterday." He laughed. "Now you have shown me a place brimming with crystals almost as far as I can see!"

He took Alia's arm and pulled her up.

Looking into her eyes, he rejoiced, "You have no idea what kind of present you have given me! I was desperately hoping to find even two crystals similar to the one I uncovered, in order to present them to my parents at my sixteenth celebration." He hugged Alia, then turned and surveyed the quiet valley. In awe, he whispered, "Now, you have given me an entire field."

Without thinking, he faced his beautiful guide and drew her near. With infinite tenderness, he kissed her full lips, tasting the salt and the sun that had kissed her long before he had.

Hearts beating hard, breaths intertwining and deepening, they parted reluctantly. Yet Atlas held her close. He caressed a strand of dark hair out of her eyes. "I want to share my world and everything in it. And I want to know everything about you."

Alia slipped out of his warm embrace and cast her gaze about. She didn't want Atlas to know how ashamed she was of her life and her tribe. She loved her mother and brothers, but they wouldn't understand, and there would be hell's own wrath to pay if she ever brought Atlas into their camp. "I think we should concentrate on finding the crystals that you need."

Atlas felt a sharp stab of disappointment but managed to hide his frown beneath a bright smile. "Well, there will come a time when I will show you Atlantis, and you will be amazed. For now"—he held his hand out to her—"let us gather the crystals I need."

Together, they shuffled through the field and found crystal upon crystal with the glacial striation his father had described.

In the sky, the sun rose higher and warmed the air. At last, Atlas stopped and opened his water flask. Offering a drink to Alia, he said, "Here, it will refresh you."

She lifted the flask to her mouth and took a tentative sip. Her eyes widened in surprise and delight, and she drank heartily until her thirst was quenched. Wiping her mouth, she handed the bottle back to Atlas. "It is like drinking air it is so pure!" She laughed and reached for his hand. "I know you have many wonders to share … possibly, one day, it will happen."

Atlas drank his fill and then recapped the flask, noting a small thicket of bushes. "Are you hungry?" Pointing at the greenery, he offered, "We could sit under the shade of those bushes."

Alia didn't want to tell him that she'd been without anything to eat since yesterday morning. And though the hunters had searched far and wide, they had been unsuccessful in their attempts. Last night's soup had been so thin that it was mostly warm water. She hadn't even taken the cupful that had been offered.

At the thought of food, her mouth watered so much that she didn't trust herself to speak. However, she managed a rather enthusiastic nod.

Atlas spread the lunch his servant had prepared, and when Alia saw the amount of food he kept pulling from his pack, she exclaimed, "Did you think you would have to feed my whole tribe?" She was hesitant to reach for anything afraid it was a mirage.

Atlas grinned and shrugged. "I know how hungry I get when I am exploring. I thought you would be famished as well."

Alia just nodded and waited anxiously for him to hand her some bread. She tried to be patient while he spread a blackish mixture on top of the thick, downy looking loaf. It took all of her willpower not to yank it out of his hands and stuff it into her mouth in one quick motion.

Finally, he broke off half and handed it to her. Not wanting to seem as depleted as she really was, she accepted his offer and tentatively bit into the soft bread.

Around a rather large mouthful, she mumbled, "Ye gods and little fishes, it is still warm!" To Alia, it was like manna from the gods; the bread melted in her mouth and the sweet taste of the topping was richer than honey.

Manners departed, and Alia savored and swallowed as fast as humanly possible. Between bites, she managed a garbled, "Wha's tha' toppin'?"

Atlas looked at the spread and back at Alia. "This? She nodded. "Jam made from blackberries. Do you like it?"

Alia rolled her eyes in pleasure. "It must have been sent by the gods; I have never tasted anything so wonderful." She almost cried with sheer happiness as the food reached her aching stomach.

Atlas quickly opened the other offerings. "This is a raspberry based soup, meant to be eaten cold." He gave her a spoon and encouraged her to try.

He continued to share more delicacies, food that was as foreign to her as the young man seated beside her. The choices!

If she hadn't been so hungry, she would have been overwhelmed, but the emptiness in her belly prodded her on.

At last, her hunger tamed, she lay back on the red earth. The thick dirt was like a velvety blanket cushioning her and supporting her back. Scooting next to her, Atlas propped his chin on his hand and studied her exquisite beauty.

Suddenly, Alia reached up and drew him to her. She kissed him deeply and passionately, her tongue encouraging his response.

When she started to part, he grabbed her shoulders and pulled her on top of him. In the breathless moments that followed, time ceased its forward march, and even the sun seemed to stop its journey across the sky. They were lost to each other with no other thought but the touch of sun-warmed skin and deep, wet kisses.

Atlas knew what to do, though he had only ever been with servants. Years ago, his father had schooled him in the mysteries shared between a man and a woman. And though he wasn't a virgin, he suspected that she was, and he was reluctant to let their passions follow the course open to them. He struggled to bring his desires under control. "Alia." His voice shook with restraint. "We must stop."

With a questioning gaze, she looked deep into his eyes and smiled. "But why? You want me, and I want you. Is there a better reason?"

Atlas pushed himself up and studied her. Her green eyes had darkened and blazed with desire. Her lips were parted, inviting more exploration. "Am I right to suspect that you have not been with a man before?"

Alia sat up and brushed her hair away from her face. "I have not, but that means nothing. I am as ready as I will ever be, and I choose you to be my mate."

Atlas was taken aback. He had never imagined that he would be attracted to someone outside Atlantis … Atlantis! By the gods! In a flash, all his father's warnings, admonitions, counsels, and Canons flooded into his mind. He was stunned to realize that he had forgotten everything he had ever been taught. *What is wrong with me?* The sheer magnitude of his transgressions surged through his veins with such a terror that a heavy shudder ran through his body.

He stared at Alia with something akin to panic and grabbed her hand. "I do not expect you to understand anything I am about to say, but a union between us is forbidden. We must not see each other again."

Alia straightened up, yanking her hand away, eyes ablaze. "What are you saying? This bit of knowledge is apparently not new. Did it escape your mind so that you did not think to tell me before? What has changed so suddenly?"

Atlas felt like his heart was tearing apart. So much blood pounded in his head that he could hardly hear her protests. He turned away from Alia and quickly lost the contents of his meal. His body shook as though it was being lashed by a strong wind. Wiping his mouth on the back of his sleeve, he had to admit that he had become so enchanted with Alia that he had forgotten everything. He ran some water over his hands and face and dragged his fingers through his hair. "I did not mean for this to happen." Alia snorted and scrambled to her knees. Desperately, Atlas grasped her hand and pulled her back to his side. "No, please, do not go." She waited, anger and hurt pouring from her in waves. Atlas frantically searched his mind for the right words. "You are exotic beyond imagination, and by every holy word ever uttered to all the gods, I want you and only you as my mate." He swallowed hard. "Alia, I love you."

Alia scrutinized him with such an accusatory glare that he knew he had to choose his next words with utmost care. He placed her hand over his heart. "I love you as the wind loves the air that carries it across mountains and valleys. I love you with the breath that sustains my life; I would give my very life to love and protect you always. And if I could, I would take you with me now and I would never let you go."

Drifting back to earth, Alia didn't say anything, but her eyes softened, encouraging Atlas to continue. "Our ways are unfamiliar to you, but as an Atlantean, I live by a strict set of laws laid down by my father long before my time."

Alia shook her head; her mind careened. Atlas was right. She didn't understand anything that was happening. Stiffening her spine, she took her hand from his heart and let it drop. "That makes no sense. I don't even know my father. How is it that your father can set forth such rules so long before you were born?"

Struggling with his own sense of guilt, Atlas rushed to explain. "My father is" —his tongue stuck to the roof of his mouth, and he stammered— "he is a ..."

"A what? A mean, ugly-tempered man like my father?"

Atlas tentatively took her hand again and was relieved when she didn't pull away. "Alia, I am trying to make you understand how different we are." He looked steadily into her beautiful eyes willing her to hear his truth. "My father is a god."

Alia couldn't have looked more surprised if he'd punched her in the nose. "Now you truly are spouting nonsense." She glanced at the horizon considering his words. "How can anyone's father be a god?"

Atlas took a deep breath, but Alia barged on, disdain dripping from her words like candle wax from a hot flame.

"Men are men, and there is nothing between us and the world … nothing exists but what we can make with our own hands and scrounge with our own hearts and minds. I should know: my tribe harbors us, but if people no longer contribute to the welfare of the tribe, then we are cast aside without contrition or backward glances. We are ruled by the strongest and the meanest. It has been that way since I can remember." She stared hard at the young man facing her. "And it is so with any and every other tribe we have encountered in all our travels."

Atlas cleared his throat. "Alia, I cannot think of a satisfactory explanation because, at times, it is hard for *me* to understand. But believe me when I tell you that my father *is* a god. He is imbued with special powers, powers that give him control over all the lands and the seas. I have witnessed terrible destruction when he is displeased, but at the same time, he is a very loving father. Atlantis flourishes under him … but he implemented a strict set of rules long before our time. While he is a fair and just man, he does not deal lightly with the transgression of any of his laws."

Atlas could think of nothing else to say, and Alia was lost in thought, pondering the details he had shared. He stood, brushed the dirt from his tunic, and offered his hand. "There is nothing for it but to show you. You have never seen the like of Atlantis, and maybe by showing you, it will help you understand our ways. Then my life and my father will make more sense to you."

Alia was mystified. Atlas was vastly different from any other human that had crossed her path. His words had frightened her, but she decided to follow him anyway. Her feelings for him ran deep, and if there was truth to his story, then she owed it to both of them to see where their paths might lead. "All right. When will you show me these marvels?"

Atlas tried to think of a time that would be the most beneficial. It would be best if she met his mother first so that she could smooth the way for an introduction to his father. Setting his course, he said, "I will figure this out. And I will make sure that you are introduced very soon, well before my birthing day celebration occurs."

Alia reached for Atlas's hand. She drew him to her and kissed him tenderly. "Then I will be ready to understand your life, because I want to understand you."

They shared another tender moment before Atlas broke away. "How will I know where to find you when I am prepared to take you to Atlantis?"

Alia had started gathering crystals for Atlas's return journey. She glanced up. "I will know when you are ready. Return to the first place we met, and I will be there."

Atlas bent down, pulling her close. Regarding the sun, he kissed her one last time. "In three days' time, I will be there."

Alia nodded solemnly. "In three days' time, for good or ill, we will both be there."

# CHAPTER

## 6

NI-CIO ABRUPTLY RELEASED his death grip on Rogert and pushed away. Rogert stumbled, but quickly regained his footing. Ni-Cio turned wildly about the room, trying to order his thoughts. His deep voice shook. "Are the choppers en route?"

No one answered, but Evan's thoughts ran through his mind: *"They are coming in for landing. I have ordered more men to help move Travlor and Daria ... We will be down as soon as we can ..."*

Upstairs, Evan bent over both comatose forms, maintaining a fearful grip and continuing the healing tones. He was terrified. *If I lose focus ... we lose all three.* He sucked in a deep breath and tried to exhale, but the air was stuck in his lungs just as Daria, his father, and the baby were stuck in some netherworld.

Suddenly, a picture formed within his mind, and Evan gasped. Enthralled, he watched as the baby slowly opened her eyes and smiled. Another picture followed. Small hands lovingly stroked his neck, and he felt rather than heard, *"You can do this ... we will help ... cease not ..."*

With one loud exhalation, Evan's breath left his body, and as it did, a suffusion of love and light filled the emptiness, chasing away the remains of fear and uncertainty. His heart, mind, and body relaxed at once, and his breathing returned to normal. Glancing at his father and then at Daria, his grip tightened; the healing tones gathered strength. He had not expected a response from either of them, but both Daria and Travlor seemed less tense than before.

The door flew open, followed by the heavy tread of boots crossing the floor. Hope ignited in Evan's heart. Orders circled him as men brought their stretchers into position. In seconds, moving in syncopation—their movements perfectly mimicking each other—they reverently and gently lifted the comatose forms onto the stretchers. They were ready.

Evan nodded curtly. Without releasing his precious charges, the unit, moving as one, carefully navigated out of the house until, followed by Ni-Cio and his remaining men, they made it safely to the front lawn.

Ni-Cio cradled Aris's body in his arms. He had refused help because he couldn't stomach the thought of anyone else touching or holding Aris. Because of him, his brother was dead, and the burden of that knowledge, along with the weight of Aris's lifeless body, was his to bear. He sent one anxious thought, *"Daria ... she lives?"*

Evan's reply was quick. *"Yes, don't worry ... do what you have to do ..."*

Helicopter blades chopped the air and people moved aside as if encased in mud. Everyone was tired to the bone, and the believers were destitute without their savior. Evan, carefully leading the men holding the stretchers, approached Ni-Cio. The sorrow—evident in his violet eyes—kept him from speaking.

As it was, there was nothing either of them could say. Ni-Cio nodded once, and the loading began.

Daria and Travlor, with Evan maintaining direct contact, were loaded carefully into the cabin and strapped down. Ni-Cio followed, carrying Aris's body. His men gathered round to help, but Ni-Cio again refused, issuing a blunt order, "I will do it!"

With grim respect, the men stood aside as he gently placed the body onto a sheet that had been spread on the cabin floor. He gradually wrapped the body of his friend. Once he was done, he situated himself onto one of the benches and donned the harness.

The rest of the men loaded quickly, giving Ni-Cio a wide berth. Wrapped in their own mournful silence, they honored their leader's need to grieve alone.

Once everyone settled, Rogert took charge and commanded the pilot, "To Barranquilla—now!" The chopper lifted into the air and quickly gained altitude. The miles passed below, supplying a panorama of mind-numbing green, and time ticked slowly by.

Evan's thoughts were drawn to Travlor and, once again, he was pulled into his father's memories with no desire to disentangle his thoughts from the man whose life hung in the balance.

# CHAPTER

## 7

HE CRYSTALS WERE beautiful beyond compare—each containing a glacial striation so clear that they glowed as though lit by an ice-blue fire. After returning home with a dozen of the finest crystals, Atlas had finished secreting them under his bed. He didn't want them discovered until he was ready to present them to his parents. Still, his joy upon finding these treasures had diminished to the point of becoming nonexistent. Tired, he settled himself on top of his covers and put his hands behind his head. He needed to think, but his mind recoiled when he thought how fast his father's admonitions had escaped him. Such aberrant behavior puzzled him. Alia had invaded his entire being! He tried to admonish himself, and yet, thoughts of her quick intelligence, her stunning beauty, and the depth of her curiosity left him spinning.

He knew to what extent his father, as well as the other gods, were worried about changing the course of development for burgeoning tribes. Since his youngest memories, it had been drummed into him that those people—savages, they called them—had to forge their own way toward civilization, no matter the struggle.

However, he couldn't comprehend why Alia couldn't remain with him in Atlantis. It wasn't as though she would ever want to revisit her old life. She was so different from any of the other people about whom he had read or studied: intelligent, resourceful, and beautiful. Surely, his parents would understand and allow him his own judgment?

He rubbed his hands over his face. Well, he could hope anyway. Try as he might, Atlas couldn't remember any time the laws had ever been broken. He had no idea the punishment following such a transgression. He had never even thought to ask because it had never been a concern.

Both parents had always encouraged him: "Follow your heart; your heart will lead you to your joy." He had done exactly that, and Alia was his joy. He loved her with his entire being and couldn't imagine a life without her. He slapped his hands down on the bed and sat up. His decision was made: he wasn't going to let some ancient rules laid down way before his time get in his way. He had always been able to reason with his father, so why should it be otherwise, now?

He would bring Alia into Atlantis first. While he suspected that she would have no problem, he wanted to make sure that she liked his home and would feel comfortable leaving her tribe. Once he knew, then he would worry about telling his parents.

Atlas looked out his window and saw the sun beginning its descent. He smiled. He went to the door and stepped into the hallway, shouting, "Mother! Mother, will we be dining on the veranda again?"

He could hear her muffled voice somewhere deep in the house. He knew without hearing her that she would be chiding him to lower his voice and come find her before loosing such a bellow throughout the house. He grinned. He loved his mother, but she had her rules, too. Shaking his head, he left the comfort of his room and his churning thoughts to find her. He was hungry and ready to eat.

# CHAPTER
## 8

THE DAYS DRAGGED, but at last came the dawn when Atlas was to meet his beloved.

He was already at the original site, but Alia had yet to arrive, and he was anxious that she should show. The sun was peeking over the horizon, sending streams of color into the clouds. Rather than enjoy the sight, he continually scanned the horizon, hoping to see her approach. Nothing stirred in any direction. Feeling uneasy, he wondered if something had happened to detain her. The possibility existed that her tribe had found that she wanted to leave and rather than lose a hard worker, they had kept her from coming. He ran his hands through his hair, and as the wind picked up, he grabbed a leather tie and secured the errant strands.

He had started walking in the general direction of her encampment when he heard a distant shout. He turned toward the sound and was overjoyed to see Alia's running form. His heart leapt in his chest, and his stomach suddenly filled with its own percussive beat, like the wings of hummingbirds. He waved excitedly and broke into a sprint.

Bodies colliding, they fell into each other's arms, their elated laughter soaring into the cool morning air. Their embrace was fierce, their kisses longingly deep. The flames of passion leapt higher until they were almost overcome. Atlas wrenched himself from her embrace and, panting with desire, clasped her shoulders tightly. "Where were you? I was worried. And I have no idea where to find you …"

Alia reached up and placed her fingers on his full lips, halting his questions. "I am so sorry to worry you, my love. I had to finish not only *my* chores but my mother's before she would let me leave. Her suspicions are aroused because I have been so happy the last several days."

"Then show me where you are camped. I will not let this happen again." Atlas was adamant that he would never again be at a loss as to where to find her. "I must be assured that I can find you—only then will I take you to Atlantis."

Alia stroked his cheek, placating him. "Come, I will show you. But I hope you will not be too disappointed."

She motioned for him to follow, and they took off at a comfortable lope. After the better part of the morning was behind them, they came upon a tribe that looked to Atlas like they were on their last legs. The tents were tattered and hanging in sad disarray. A miserable campfire struggled weakly against the daylight while one bent, old woman tended a pot suspended between two poles. Her sparse, gray hair was stirred by a breeze and lifted in worse tatters than the tents. All in all, it was a slovenly, disordered group that greeted Atlas's eyes. He glanced at Alia and saw that she was regarding him silently. "I told you it would not be much."

He hadn't known it was possible for anyone to live so close to death. Where did they find food? The plains were barren and water was so sparse as to be nearly nonexistent. Atlas didn't know why Alia hadn't grabbed his wineskin and gulped every precious drop.

Questions bombarded him; however, he was more concerned about Alia. He dare not let her see how shocked he was at such bedraggled conditions. He sighed in quiet sympathy for the hardscrabble life she had experienced. At least he knew where to find her now. "How long do you stay in one place?"

She shrugged. "Depends on the area. If there are other tribes near that threaten us, we leave in a hurry, as we are weaponless other than the sticks and slings we use to trap and find food. Other times, when we are alone and we have found a place that allows us to exist for a time, we try to stay longer. Every situation differs, but we adapt."

Atlas scratched his head. She was so naïve to the ways of his world. He couldn't imagine what she would think of Atlantis. He took her hand. "Come, let me take you to my home."

# CHAPTER

*9*

DELAYING THE MOMENT until he escorted Alia through the gates of his home, Atlas chose to bring her into the city another way. He wanted Atlantis to open before her as a flower opens its shy face to the sun. She would be awestruck by the many different sights and sounds, so the slower he could introduce her to his way of life, the better. Hopefully, it would grant her enough time to compose her senses.

Entering the west gates, Atlas took Alia's arm and led her through the streets, explaining details and pointing out interests as they passed. After a while, Alia had not uttered a sound. Atlas halted and faced her. "Are you well enough? I am worried that you remain so quiet."

Alia didn't know how to respond. She had never seen such sights, could never have begun to imagine such a place could be real. She was dumbfounded. Shaking with nerves as she was, she was sure to disappoint Atlas. Gingerly reaching for his hand, she swallowed hard. "I am at such a loss for words that I can scarcely breathe. Our differences were manifest from the moment we met, but I never thought to be in a place such as this. I … I feel so small and anxious, like a mouse trapped in the overhead shadow of a soaring hawk."

Atlas led her to a carved marble bench and, beneath the deep shade of a spreading laurel tree, they sat. Silently, Atlas held her hand and gave her time. *It is possible that she could never adjust.* The thought annoyed him, and he banished it quicker than it had surfaced.

Finally, turning to Atlas, she whispered, "I am ready to continue." Alia took a deep breath and exhaled slowly. Her eyes met his with a steady gaze. "I have decided the only way I can proceed is to suspend all I have ever known and just *be*." It was Atlas's turn to feel overcome. Now, he was at a loss. Her statement was so remarkable on so many levels that all he could do was gape in open astonishment. He doubted anyone in Atlantis would have been able to make such a leap. A grin spread across his face and, completely forgetting their surroundings, he pulled her close, kissing her face, her cheeks, and her lips with every ounce of joy that pervaded his being.

At length, his own senses returned, and Atlas reluctantly moved away. "I cannot speak for you, but I am starving. It would be my honor to show you a place nearby where we can procure excellent food and drink."

"It is a suggestion that already invites the rumblings of my stomach." Returning Atlas's smile, she happily let him lead her through the laughing crowds until they stood before a lovely, whitewashed house with striking blue shutters.

Sheltered from the glare of the noonday sun, a pergola rife with the heavy growth of colorful bougainvillea shaded a tangle of people seated at all sizes of many tables. The patrons seemed to be enjoying a bounteous repast, and Alia could hardly wait to sample more of Atlantis's magical foods.

Atlas guided her to an empty table backed into a secluded corner. Holding her chair, he helped her sit, then seated himself. He leaned back and watched as Alia scrutinized every intimate detail of the restaurant.

A young woman wound her way to their table, and while Atlas ordered, Alia studied the people surrounding them. She was amazed that there was a place that not only let you choose whatever food you wanted, but prepared it and served it for you as well. Eventually, satisfied that she had taken in every detail that she could, she took Atlas's hand and gazed lovingly into his eyes. "You are an amazing man, and I never want to leave—you have to show me everything!"

Alia felt almost too excited to eat even a bite, but when the food arrived, she inhaled the exotic aromas and found that she was truly hungry. Atlas explained the different dishes and showed her how to use the utensils that were provided. She glowed with pride as she mastered the pronged instrument.

Wrapped up in each other and trading stories between bites, they didn't hear a boisterous group of young men enter the restaurant. Suddenly, Atlas heard someone address him. "Atlas! Where have you been?"

Atlas was surprised to see his best friend, Jaron. Their time together had grown less and less as they both seemed to have discovered separate agendas, so Atlas was glad to see him again.

He stood and, with a huge smile, wrapped the other youth in a strong embrace. Jaron was tall, like most Atlanteans, but Atlas towered over him. Swarthy skinned and muscular, Jaron prided himself on his prowess in the different competitions held around the city. His love of all sports drove him to excel, and he walked with the easy, assured gait of a finely tuned athlete. He clapped Atlas heartily on the back. "I have not seen you in weeks. What have you been up to?"

Atlas pointed to his table and offered, "Come sit with us and we will talk."

Jaron threw a questioning look at his other companions. His friends seemed dubious, and he could tell that Atlas would have preferred time alone with his friend. Gallantly, he offered, "I am only in for a small libation, so we will find our own table. However, we would be honored to be introduced to your beautiful friend."

Atlas didn't want to share even a moment of Alia's time, so without hesitation, and secretly remembering to thank Jaron for his consideration, he laughed good-naturedly. "Please, come meet Alia."

It was evident that Alia was very different from anyone they knew, and the group of young Atlanteans were fascinated. In an attempt to withstand their worshipful scrutiny, Alia tried to continue the stalled conversation. "Do you eat here often? I find the food quite amazing."

The companions guffawed as though she had said something highly amusing. When Jaron regained control of his group, he asked, "Where are you from?"

Alia lowered her head and mumbled something unintelligible. Atlas felt her discomfort and broke into the conversation, regaling his friends with his latest jokes. It wasn't long before their curiosity had been quite forgotten.

Once his friends had acquired their own table, Atlas wiped his mouth with a linen cloth and took Alia's arm. "It is time to meet my mother."

Alia's senses heightened, and her nervousness returned. After everything she had experienced, she wasn't at all sure that the idea still held merit, but she didn't feel it was her place to counter his offer. She tried to look happy. "If you feel it is the proper time, I am ready." As they exited the restaurant, Alia couldn't help herself: "Do you really think your mother will like me? Have you ever brought anyone home before?"

Chuckling, Atlas shook his head and squeezed her hand. "My mother will love you. Although she will be quite surprised, as I have never cared about anyone enough to introduce them to my parents."

Alia grew vastly more uncomfortable and felt the sweat beading at her hairline. Her palms were too moist, so she dropped Atlas's hand and swiped both hands down the front of her rough shift. She had to believe that Atlas knew his parents and had a good idea as to whether they would accept her or not. She wasn't sure what to expect from a "god," but she was quite curious to find out what his father was like.

Circumventing the main thoroughfare, Atlas led her through a maze of streets until they stood before a single stretch of road. Alia had noticed that most of Atlantis was flat and very spread out. To her untrained eyes, the city seemed to stretch into forever. The lone structure that Atlas had indicated was his home graced the top of a steep rise, as though apart from the rest of the world. Alia could tell that Atlas's family was wealthy beyond belief. Her heart pounded in her chest, and she was reluctant to begin the first anxious step.

Atlas hesitated, too; she heard his quiet intake of breath. He turned to her and, as much to reassure himself as Alia, said, "Do not worry, it will be fine." It was all Alia could do not to grimace. Hand in hand, they started up the rise.

Upon reaching the top, Alia gasped and slapped both hands over her mouth. The house sparkled in the afternoon light like the crystals she and Atlas had gathered. In the entirety of her life, she had only known tents or makeshift dirt hovels. To stand before the grand entrance to Atlas's home was mind-numbing. She rubbed her eyes in disbelief, when all she really wanted to do was turn and bolt.

Atlas felt her fear quickly getting out of hand, so he stroked her arm in an attempt to soothe her. "Take a few deep breaths. We will rest until you indicate that you are ready to proceed."

Alia tried his advice, but her lungs didn't want to work. She was starting to feel light-headed, and hoped she wouldn't make a fool of herself and faint the moment she met Atlas's mother.

Glancing at her beloved, she had no doubt that she wanted him above any other. So, summoning every shred of willpower she possessed, she straightened her shoulders, stiffened her spine, and gave Atlas a shaky smile. "I am ready."

Leading her through the courtyard and beyond the statue of his father, he opened the entry doors and escorted Alia inside. They were immediately approached by a servant, who inquired as to whether they needed anything. Atlas shook his head. "We are fine, thank you, Seral. Can you tell me where I might find Mother?"

"She is in the gardens, sir." The man pointed toward the largest veranda.

Grasping Alia's hand, Atlas progressed through the house until they passed through a set of tall, leaded glass doors. The view from the veranda was breathtaking. Alia had never seen such a riot of rich, beautiful colors. Trees, shrubs, flowers all flourished under the touch of a loving hand. "Your mother takes great pride in her gardens, they are like nothing I have ever seen."

"Hardly a day passes that she is not outside tending her plants, she loves them almost like children." Atlas scanned the grounds but couldn't see his mother. "Mother, I am here! Where are you?"

"Atlas, must you always yell?" He heard her exasperated snort even from where they stood.

Clieto pulled off her work gloves and hurriedly approached the veranda. Peering out from under the deep brim of her sunhat, she stopped so abruptly that her gloves flew out of her hands and landed with a thud on the top step of the veranda. The sight of a young woman standing at her son's side was not what she had expected. Tales of another adventure, yes, but she had never expected to meet the actual result of one of his adventures. She steadied herself and took the stairs slowly, allowing time to calm herself. Stopping before the blushing girl, Clieto held out her hands, palms up in the traditional greeting. "Welcome. I am Clieto." Not knowing what to do, Alia grasped the woman's outstretched hands and squeezed.

Clieto couldn't hide her wince and Alia hurriedly released her grip. "I apologize. I should not have grasped so hard." She tried to be brave and looked straight into Clieto's thoughtful eyes before she said quietly, "I am Alia."

Clieto was instantly charmed. She raised her eyebrows and questioned her son, "Where did you two meet?"

Atlas shrugged nonchalantly. "We both happened to be exploring." He extracted a handful of crystals from his pocket. "Look! She showed me where to find more."

His mother took the crystals and looked at each one. Carefully, she handed them back to Atlas and glanced sideways at Alia. "And where were these crystals?"

Atlas shifted his weight and ran his hands nervously through his hair. Alia looked terrified. Atlas knew she was unable to help, so he took a deep breath and forged ahead. "Alia showed them to me. She found them a long time ago."

Clieto studied Alia. "Are you from Atlantis?"

Alia couldn't offer a response—she didn't know what to say, and a fleeting look at Atlas for help showed that he was at a loss as well. Clieto dusted her shift and took the hat from her hair. As she shook her hair loose from its binding tie, her heart sank. She didn't need to be told that Alia had come from somewhere outside Atlantis. She fiddled with her clothing until she was certain that her voice remained calm. Gesturing at the table, she asked, "Shall we enjoy some lemonade? It would seem that you have quite a story to share."

Atlas surreptitiously swiped his brow when he realized sweat had been trickling down his face, neck, and back like rainwater. He flashed his mother a hearty smile. "Excellent idea." He ushered Alia to a seat and tried to look at her with what he hoped was reassurance. "I knew she would like you."

"That remains to be seen," she whispered as she studied Clieto's regal bearing.

The woman seated herself at the head of the table and poured each of them a glass of yellowish liquid. After offering a glass to Atlas, she handed one to Alia and carefully eyed the stranger. Clieto leaned her elbows on the table and asked gently, "Alia, at the risk of appearing rude, can you tell me where you are from?"

Alia took a small sip of her lemonade in an effort to stall. She savored the sweet but sour taste, then drank deeply. When she had wasted as much time as possible, she faced the inevitable and plunged into the conversation. "I am from a tribe that is settled west of your amazing city. I cannot say how far away we are camped, but it does take from early to late morning to run the distance."

Clieto sat back. She closed her eyes against her rising anger in order to spare Atlas and his guest. She shivered at the thought of how Poseidon would respond to this news. With no graceful way to continue, Clieto took a direct tack. "Atlas, my only son ... although it is patently obvious to me, just what is your intention in bringing her to us? Are you prepared to explain to your father why it is that you have wandered outside the boundaries of Atlantis?"

Atlas gulped hard. His heart pounded so hard that he thought it would beat its way out of his chest. He couldn't fool himself anymore. His mother was highly upset. She was exerting tremendous will power in an attempt to maintain civility. He tried to calm her with his carefully thought out explanation. "I was well within our boundaries searching for more crystals like the one I had found. I heard a noise, and when I looked, Alia was standing near."

His mother was so still that it seemed that she had turned to stone. Any hint of kindness had fled, and her mouth was set in one of the grimmest expressions Atlas had ever seen. He hurried on: "She was exploring, and wandered away from her encampment into Atlantis. We struck up a conversation. Before she turned to go, I showed her my crystal. It was then she described a valley that contained an entire floor littered with the exact same kind."

Atlas paused, hoping his mother had calmed somewhat; instead, her face was turning a ghastly shade of red, a shade he had never seen on another human being." I—I ... wanted to get some crystals for you and father so that I could present them to you at my birthing day. I wanted to give you something special." His words trailed off as he finished. His eyes narrowed, and he sent a quick, pleading thought, *"Please, you must understand!"*

Her thoughts seared through his. *"Atlas, you have no idea what you have done! Your father will be irate when he finds out about this ... do you think there will be no consequences?"*

It was apparent that some kind of silent communication was transpiring between Atlas and his mother, and Alia shifted uncomfortably. She hadn't thought it would be as easy as Atlas hoped. It was time to take her leave.

She stood, and mother and son looked up. Wiping her mouth, she clumsily folded the napkin and placed it next to her glass. "Thank you so much for the refreshment, but it is past time for me to be going."

She opened her hands and held them out for Clieto. The woman hesitantly placed her palms on top of Alia's. "I will offer my goodbyes, and then I will leave you both alone."

Atlas sprang from his chair and raced to Alia's side. He placed his arm around her small waist and pulled her tight. "Mother, we love each other. I want her as my lifemate!"

Clieto lost all semblance of control. She threw her napkin down and pushed away from the table. Shoulders back, head held high, her eyes burned bright and her lips drew into such a tight line that they turned white. With all the patience she could muster, Clieto intoned, "I will say this only once. Please guide Alia out of our house and show her to the border. You are not to cross again under any circumstances. Have I made myself clear?"

Without waiting for an answer, Clieto exited the veranda, dignity wrapped around her like a cloak. She had proven formidable in her resolve. That she was wife to a god had never been more apparent.

When her figure had receded into the shadows of the interior rooms, Atlas looked sorrowfully at Alia. "I had no idea it would be like this. My mother has never hurt anybody. I do not understand. Please, wait, and let me talk to her."

Alia adamantly shook her head. "No, Atlas. Her wishes are clear. We would do well to follow them. It is time for me to go."

She looked at him with such sadness and despair, he thought his heart would break. He didn't want her to go—he needed her in his life, he loved her! Did that count for nothing? How was it that his father could bed any woman he pleased? His anger increased, and he muttered, "I will not put up with this, either. If we are not welcome here, then I will come with you. Surely your tribe would not be so hostile?"

Alia almost laughed at the preposterousness of his idea, but she loved him for even thinking it. "Atlas, you were born here. I was born over there. The obstacles that stand in our way cannot be overcome, no matter how much love we share. If your father is as powerful as you say, then we were done before we even started."

She dropped his hand and started toward the entrance. Her heart felt like it was ripping apart. No matter what they tried, it was obvious that their love was not meant to be.

Desperate, Atlas followed her to the door. He took her hand one last time. "I will come to you, I promise. If your tribe will not accept us, then we will find someplace that does. I love you and I will not let you go."

Alia stroked his handsome, determined face. She knew he meant every word, but she also knew how difficult it was to go against parental decisions. Nevertheless, she couldn't leave without giving him some hope. "If you come to me, I promise we will go somewhere where we will be accepted as we are."

Atlas sighed. "That is all I need—some sign that you will wait, because, my love, never doubt that I will come for you."

Alia kissed him on his lips and stroked his face. "Do not follow; I know the way. I have come closer to Atlantis even than I told you. It will hurt more to leave you in the dark and know that you are walking away from me. Stay in your beautiful house where I will be able to see you in my mind's eye."

Before he could respond, Alia ran down the steps. In no time, she had vanished from sight. Atlas swiped at his eyes. He was ready for the battle of his life. He would make his parents understand.

# CHAPTER
## 10

O EVERYONE IN the chopper, the ride to Barranquilla was interminable. However, wrapped in his own
thoughts, Ni-Cio had not noticed the miles slipping
by. It was only the change in engine noise as the pilot prepared
to land that snapped him back to reality. Seeing Evan bent
over Daria and Travlor, he sent a thought. *"Evan ... are you
holding up?"*

Evan gazed at his friend, a bewildered expression on his face.
*"Ni-Cio ... I can't explain what's happening, but I'm experiencing
Travlor's younger life ... it is definitely not memory based ... I'm
actually watching his life playing in real time... have you ever
heard of this?"*

Ni-Cio was just as puzzled as his friend. He knew that the
healers passed down genetic memories to each succeeding healer,
but this sounded like something else entirely. Before he had a
chance to respond, the pilot brought the helicopter to rest and
turned the engines off. The blades wound down, and everyone
readied themselves for the transfer to Rogert's requested boats.

Soldiers raced to the helicopter and helped the Atlanteans pile out. Other soldiers stood, waiting to help with the stretchers. Ni-Cio started to cradle Aris's body, but Evan stopped him. "Ni-Cio, let the others take Aris, please. I need your help with Daria and Travlor."

Ni-Cio nodded and let Rogert pry his hands from his friend. He stood reluctantly and jumped from the chopper, then turned to help Evan. He was bewildered to see how dazed the topsider looked. It was then that he realized it was becoming harder for Evan to separate from Travlor and rejoin the present.

Evan held as tightly as he dared to the lifeless forms, but he felt his strength waning. Just as he thought he would falter, another image flowed into his mind: the baby, resting peacefully, slowly opened her eyes. Love sparkled within the depths of her knowing gaze, and Evan was overcome with such powerful feelings of courage, strength, and hope that it took his breath away. He stopped in order to appreciate the gift he had just received.

Alarmed that something had gone horribly wrong, Ni-Cio halted and looked inquiringly at his friend.

Evan squared his shoulders and sent him a quick thought. *"We are alright ... but let's don't waste time ..."*

Aligned next to the concrete pier, three large Zodiacs, motors idling, waited for their passengers. The drivers had been briefed on the critical nature of delivering their passengers safely and quickly to their final destination.

However, before allowing anyone to board, the captain in charge, loyalty severely strained, demanded everyone's attention as his men drew their weapons. "Where are you taking our messiah?"

Ni-Cio eyed the soldier and tried to explain. "We are taking him back home, at his request." A look of innate stubbornness crossed the man's features, but Ni-Cio refused to hear him out. "Captain, please, do not delay us any longer. If we are able to help him, it is the only place we can take him."

After hesitating for the blink of a heavy-lidded eye, the man accepted the explanation and stepped aside. His men lowered their guns and helped the Atlanteans board. As soon as everyone was seated, the boats started slipping from the pier.

The captain raised a hand and shouted, "You will get word to us?"

Ni-Cio sent him a thumbs-up as the boats opened up and headed in the direction of the tethered biospheres.

Rogert studied their leader. The noise of the motors precluded conversation, so he sent a thought-form. *"Ni-Cio, the pilot shared news that you will not want to hear, but you must listen … war is upon us … nuclear proliferation has taken on a life of its own … fingers are poised and people around the world are demanding action from their governments … as soon as news gets out of Travlor's condition, bombs everywhere will start flying …"*

Ni-Cio rubbed his eyes. *"Then we must act first to quell any rumors …"* He turned towards Evan and shared what he had just learned, *"My friend … how do we reassure Travlor's followers as to his health? If people think Travlor can be healed, maybe it will buy some time and encourage hope … it might even help stop the ground wars that have broken out …"*

With an effort, Evan cleared his mind and focused on the issue at hand. He ran through alternatives before it occurred to him, *"We need to get the word out quickly … an international news agency is what we need … as soon as we are back we'll issue a release … if you are right, it will help …"*

He just hoped that ruse would work. His father had single-handedly driven the entire world to the brink of nuclear war. He shook his head and tried to clamp down on his own impending sense of doom as the crafts slowed and pulled up.

Rogert signaled for the biospheres' retrieval. Four Atlanteans slipped overboard and quickly resurfaced with the three 'spheres. Hatches dematerialized and everyone helped load Evan so that he wouldn't lose his grip. Daria and Travlor were gently handed into Evan's craft while the body of Aris was placed into the arms of the men waiting in another craft.

The biospheres adjusted to fit the extra bodies, and Rogert motioned the Zodiacs to be moved. The Columbians watched in stunned awe as the hatches closed and the 'spheres glided silently under the waves.

# CHAPTER

## 11

IN THE NORTHERN section of Atlantis resided a young man by the comical name of Heedrow. He was a strange fellow in that he was not particularly strong, nor was he particularly fast. He was a plodder. He was steady and sure, and his thought process reflected his physicality. He was big for his age. While not able to pass through school easily, the youth had realized early on that he had a passion for digging, and when he was not busy with studies or helping his mother, he would dig. During an extended dig, Heedrow discovered that creating tunnels had, for him, become an art form. He discovered he had an innate talent for knowing the best direction to tunnel and how to keep his excavations from caving in. His tunnels were wonderful to behold, and his mother was proud that he had found something at which he excelled.

Heedrow didn't have many friends, but that didn't bother him. He was always a happy boy; however, he was happiest in his world of underground tunnels.

On his sixteenth birthing day, he had told his mother that all he ever wanted to do was dig tunnels. His mother, loving him completely, didn't discourage him, but she wasn't sure where his skills could be used. Other than the canals and waterways and ditches that curled through Atlantis, there had never been a big call for tunnelers.

So, even though she didn't discourage him or try to dissuade him from thinking about that type of work, she didn't know how to help him find a job that would welcome his unique talents. She was getting older, and Heedrow had never been on his own. She worried that he wouldn't learn to be independent, so, she was determined to help him find his place. If she could do that, she could transcend once her time came, secure in the knowledge that her son would be able to take care of himself.

To that end, she traveled far and wide in an attempt to locate someone, anyone, who required a young man with Heedrow's specific skills.

It was during one of her side trips that she was delighted to find out about a man who lived near the city of Atlantis. She was told that he was the preeminent tunnel expert, and that he had designed and overseen the building of most of the tunnels that now connected Atlantis in an underground maze.

She visited the expert and was overjoyed when he agreed to take her son as his apprentice. She hadn't thought her search would end in success, and she excitedly returned home to share the news that she had found something that suited Heedrow perfectly.

The following day, she helped pack Heedrow's few belongings. They threw some supplies in the back of their handcart and Heedrow grabbed the handles. He gladly took the first pull. He pulled steadily, pace never wavering, until his mother told him it was time to stop for lunch.

They rested while they ate, enjoying the picnic his mother had packed. When it was time to resume their journey,

Heedrow's mother took her turn and pulled the cart close to the outskirts of Atlantis. Heedrow could see that she was tiring and that her hands hurt from pulling the handcart. "Mama, you stop now." Heedrow took both her hands in his and gently rubbed them in order to encourage circulation back into her aching fingers. When his mother felt a bit better, Heedrow took the cart and pulled it the rest of the way. He looked forward to meeting his future mentor, and he didn't want to waste any more time. Heedrow was anxious to learn any and all of the fascinating secrets his master had to impart.

Heedrow had never told his mother, but he could envision an entire underground city. In his imagination, his city rivaled the beauty and majesty of Atlantis. He had dreams of people living freely and happily under the earth. Now that he would receive the instruction he needed to learn such a craft, he knew that, one day, he would be able to make his vision a reality—he would create that exact city.

He pulled the cart up to his master's house and dropped the handles. He studied the place he would be staying. His mouth fell open, and even though his mother had warned him against that very thing, he couldn't help himself: he gaped unabashedly. The house in which the master resided was nothing like Heedrow had expected. Compared to his mother's tiny house, this place resembled a palace. "It has to be huge, yes, Mama? For him to teach me, it has to be huge, yes, Mama?"

His mother took his hand and stroked his innocent face. "Yes, Heedrow … he has many apprentices, and so it has to be big."

Heedrow looked puzzled. "Will I get lost inside?"

His mother smiled. "No, Heedrow; you will figure it out very quickly. It is like one of your tunnels. You know how fast you got to know the rooms of your tunnels?" Her son nodded. "It will be just like that, so do not worry."

She guided him up to a large covered patio. The structure wrapped around the whole house, giving it a warm, welcoming feel. Heedrow's mother took his hand and knocked on the door. Sounds of footsteps hurrying through the hall echoed and faded, and then the door opened. Before them stood a diminutive man.

With hair white as a cloud, he sported a close-cropped beard, also very white. His voice was kind, and his eyes sparkled as he stood to one side. "Please, come inside." His voice was so gentle that Heedrow had to listen hard to understand his words.

Heedrow and his mother entered the master's home. When he closed the door, the old man offered his hands, palms up. "I am Ranol. Welcome."

A voice from another room called out, "You have to be hungry! Food is ready." A woman stepped out of the kitchens and came forward. She and her husband could have been twins, they looked so much alike. Her hair was white as goose down but terribly thin. As the light shone through, her hair created a nimbus around her head, giving her the look of a fantastical creature. Though smaller than her husband, the woman was truly quite beautiful. She guided the tired visitors to the eating area. "Come, I have been preparing for your stay—my name is Mellor." She glanced at Heedrow's mother, eyebrows raised. "And you are …?"

"I am Hana. Forgive me, I am overwhelmed by your display of generosity."

The women exchanged a look, both of them silently acknowledging that Heedrow was in good hands. Hana was relieved to find that her son would be well taken care of during his five-year apprenticeship. Both Ranol and Mellor were kind and caring people, and Ranol had taken many young men under his tutelage and trained them well. At the present time, the usual numbers of students had dwindled because many of them had graduated to master status and were now making their way out in the world. With only a handful of students left, Heedrow would receive the special attention his mother felt he deserved.

The meal was a festive occasion, and it gave Heedrow and Ranol a chance to get better acquainted. Master and student liked each other immediately, and were able to fully appreciate the complex passion they shared.

Once they were finished dining, and Mellor and Hana were cleaning up, Ranol showed Heedrow the path to the tunnel entrance. "This is where to come after your morning breakfast. Come, I will show you to the room you'll occupy during your apprenticeship."

As Ranol made Heedrow comfortable, Mellor showed Hana to her room. "Your son is in the room adjacent. The baths are down the hall to the left." Before closing the door, she suggested, "Once you have seen to your things, you are welcome to join Ranol and me for a bit of wine on the patio."

Hana blushed. It was not that she didn't appreciate the offer, it was that she had never had the money to spend on such luxuries, so consequently, she shook her head. "I think I will remain here. It has been a long journey, and tomorrow will seem even longer without Heedrow. Thank you again for all you have done for both of us."

Mellor smiled. "You are welcome to visit anytime. It is always wonderful when parents look in on their child's progress. Sleep well."

Everyone but Heedrow slept soundly that night. Heedrow was too excited. Visions of underground cities crowded his thoughts, so he tossed and turned until the dark began to recede before the beginnings of first light.

Upon rising, Heedrow and his mother found that Mellor had already prepared their morning meal. Happy to spend their last moments alone, they enjoyed the sumptuous repast outside, under the deep shade of the covered patio. Heedrow's mother set her spoon down and gazed lovingly at her only son. "It will be a long walk home, but in my heart, I am so happy that you have a chance to make something of yourself. I have done the best I can for you. Now it is up to you."

Once their meal was over, she didn't linger. Grabbing the handles of her old cart, she took one last look at her son and said, "Work hard, do good, and you will succeed."

Heedrow waved at his mother. He was sad that she was leaving, but he could hardly wait to begin his first lesson. He watched her figure get smaller and smaller, and when he could no longer keep his mother in sight, he left for the tunnels. Ranol was already underground. He was preparing the day's lessons for his older apprentices, and Mellor had left to shop in town.

Hurrying to the entrance, Heedrow laughed out loud, pulled open the door, and began his descent into Ranol's breathtaking tunnel. He hoped with all his heart that he would actually get to dig today!

# CHAPTER

## *12*

HE TRIBE WAS packing when Alia got back to the encampment. Her gaze darted from tent to tent, and she could see the bleak desperation on each face as they loaded their scant belongings. She ran to the area where they had constructed their tent and could see that her mother and brothers were ready to leave. Her brothers were standing together, jeering, "Are you in trouble!"

"Where have you been?"

"No one could find you!"

Her mother reached over and wacked both boys on their heads. Her strength was still enough to make them squirm under the weight of her slap. "This is between your sister and me."

Her mother's grizzled form lumbered slowly to meet her. From beneath her hooded gaze, her mother took in her appearance, the blush of her skin, and didn't have to ask where she had been. "So, you have found a boy."

Alia flinched. Atlas was no mere boy, but her mother didn't need to know that. She stood silent, willing to take whatever punishment her mother deemed necessary. "Well, answer me! You have been with a male!"

Alia scowled at her mother's venom-laced words. She raised her head and stood with the same dignity that she had witnessed in Clieto. "I have not *been* with a male. I have been exploring with the man I have chosen to be my lifemate."

The cackling sound of her mother's laugh grated on her ears. "So, where is this fine, strapping man? Is he so near that he is just waiting for the right moment to ask for your hand?"

Alia swallowed hard and eyed her mother. "He is coming for me."

Another bark of disgust. "Bah! Men have trouble keeping to the truth, much less keeping their promises. But take heart, you worthless girl … at least you have his word. It should be such a comfort in the dark of the night as you wait." She gestured at the bundles. "There is nothing here with which to sustain ourselves. We are on the move. Pick up your share of the load."

"But if we move, he will not be able to find me!" Alia protested.

Her mother refused to listen. Turning quite deaf, she ignored any more argument and plodded to the small pile of belongings. Standing over them, she motioned the boys. "You two, over here and grab what is yours. There is no time to waste; we dare not lag behind. Now go."

The boys hoisted their packs, and Alia's mother grabbed what she could. As frail as she looked, she was still a tough old woman. Alia went to her allotment. Bending down, the tears started to come. It was infuriating that no one would listen to either of them. She had half a mind to sit down and never move again. To think of never seeing Atlas again was more than she could to bear. She'd loved him at first sight, and she wouldn't give him up without a fight. But even though she was strong and brave and could use her throwing arm for protection, she would be risking nothing short of death if she chose to stay here alone.

She groaned, picking up the bundle. It seemed as though a new path had opened to her and Atlas was the bright star, shining the way toward a better life. But between their two mothers, that star had been stamped out. She could see nothing for the rest of her life but darkness, and an endless struggle to survive stretching beyond the horizons.

Atlas would never know which direction they had gone. The tribe could travel long distances, and by morning, they would be so far away that he would never pick up their trail. She dropped her head and let the tears flow freely. There was nothing else to do.

# CHAPTER

*13*

ATLAS WOKE WITH a start. He tried to make out the shapes in his bedroom, but it was the darkest hour of the night and the darkest time of the moon. He felt cast adrift, alone in the vast space of a black void. His surroundings reflected his dismal mood; in his room, as in his heart, not a glimmer of light could be found. Huddled under warm covers, he relived the awful clash between his mother and him. It had gotten so bad that he could hardly believe the hurtful words they used to bludgeon each other.

He had gone to Clieto's bedroom, hoping that he could reason with her, but it was as though his mother had turned into someone he had never known. After parrying several of her objections, their voices escalated until they had found themselves in a terrible row.

At length, Clieto had turned her back to him and quit responding. It was like addressing a stone wall. There was not the slightest chink in her behavior, and it was then that Atlas gave up. She would never back down. Searching her inflexible countenance for a hint of compassion, he had to step away from her as she woodenly began reeling through the list of his transgressions. He was startled so many infractions rolled so easily off her tongue. Exhausted, sad, and silent, his mother finally invoked his father's name. She instilled such fear in him that he had backed down and gone to his room.

Sleep would not come, and sometime during the night, he had made up his mind to leave. Rolling over with a deep sigh, his last thought before he drifted into a fitful slumber was that he refused to lose Alia because his parents couldn't see reason.

Now, throwing the covers off, he felt his way through the gloom, stuffed a few garments into his canvas bag, and then silently descended to the kitchens. He grabbed what he could from the counters and the storage chambers. He quietly filled only one canteen, then thought better of that and filled a second one.

He drew his robe close against the cool of the nighttime air and shivered. In the dark of the night, it wasn't as easy to leave as he had thought, but he was determined that Alia should be his lifemate. He knew in his heart and in his soul that he would never find another like her. Never.

Silently closing the door behind him, Atlas made his way out of the front gate. He waved to the guards and the guards, accustomed to his nighttime explorations, waved back.

Atlas surreptitiously found the path that would take him back to Alia. It helped to know that the woman he loved waited. He would change the scurrilous conditions in which she lived. He was determined that they would make their own way. Surely, they could find something, somewhere, someplace that they could call home. He shouldered his bag and strode into the night.

# CHAPTER

## 14

HERE WAS NO one there ... not even a scrap of evidence that an entire tribe had camped in the area.

Had he chosen the wrong direction? He had studied the way with great care and was certain he was in the right place.

Atlas turned in a slow circle, as if that would make Alia reappear. How could they have packed up and left so quickly? Where had they gone? He looked for any signs that Alia might have left for him to follow, but he found nothing.

The dirt was so disturbed that without superior tracking skills, it was impossible to tell which way they were headed. Atlas searched in ever-widening circles, trying to pick up some kind of trail, but in the intense gloom, he saw nothing. It was as if they had vanished into thin air. Scrubbing his face with both hands, he looked up at the dark sky and shouted his frustration. "Where are you? Where have they taken you?"

He could think of nothing else he could do, so he sat on a rock, grabbed a small stick, and traced nonsensical designs in the dirt. Resting his chin in one hand, he pondered his stark dilemma. If he attempted to find her and chose the wrong direction, she would be lost to him forever. If he did nothing, what kind of man would that make him? The more he wrestled with alternatives, the only one that made sense was to find his father, throw himself on his mercy, and ask for his help.

The man had been young once—surely, he understood the yearnings of the heart. After all, how many wives did he have, and how many maids had he bedded? It was well known that Poseidon was a man of hearty appetite. So, how could he fail to understand the love for one woman that consumed his son?

Atlas got up and dusted the back of his robe. He re-shouldered his pack and started back. The light stretched and the sun peeked over the horizon, illuminating the world in a deep reddish-gold glow. As the earth warmed, so did Atlas. He took off his robe and pushed it into his pack. He would be home soon.

He glanced at the horizon and noticed that a line of men had appeared and were running towards him. Yelling and gesticulating, their fear was immediately communicated to him. Just then, the figure of his father materialized, bringing up the rear. Atlas shook his head. He felt like a leaf waiting for the onslaught of a rising tsunami.

He was surrounded before he could do anything—two men grabbed his arms and clapped them in chains. Unable to watch his father's blistering approach, Atlas lowered his head and stared at the ground. If Poseidon was willing to have his son escorted back in chains, then all was lost. Despite his best efforts to hide his dread, Atlas's hands shook, and his knees trembled uncontrollably.

His father's heavy tread shook the ground, and men scurried to give way at his approach. Though he was terrified of facing his father's wrath, Atlas nevertheless swallowed hard and raised his head.

The man before him no longer resembled the father he knew. The man before him didn't even resemble a man. Atlas fell to his knees. Towering over him, in the full force of his majesty, stood the supreme god of the lands and the oceans. Arrayed in all his glory, menace poured from Poseidon like lava from a volcano. One word from the wrath-filled god and Atlas would cease to be. There was no doubt in his mind that his life was coming to an end.

He waited for something to happen or for his father to speak. When no one stirred, he ventured an upward glance. Although no sound issued from Poseidon, the ground began to shake, and black clouds raced overhead, gathering into the beginnings of a massive storm. Thunder and lightning crackled in the darkened sky; everyone grew restive.

Atlas cleared his throat, but before he could utter a sound, his father held up a finger and shook his head once. It was then that reddened flames erupted from Poseidon's countenance. His eyes danced with fire while flames licked his hair and engulfed his shoulders and head. Atlas waited to be consumed. However, without a word, Poseidon turned and strode over the landscape, each step accompanied by the terrible crash of thunder and blood-curdling lightning strikes. Men scrambled to follow. Hauling Atlas off his knees, they coursed after their god as though their very lives depended on it.

Atlas was summarily left in a spare cell inside one of the city's containment centers. He had known of them, but had never visited one. The facility was where lawbreakers were held while awaiting sentencing. He shuddered. He had started to realize how serious his transgression had been after he and his mother had gotten into such a vicious fight. However, her anger was but a drop in the ocean compared to his father's rage.

Taking stock of his surroundings, he saw that the only light to find its way into the room was through a long slit in the roof. The single skylight let a bit of sunshine fall onto the floor, but the stones refused the light. They retained their own murky sense of despair and darkness. All night, he had sat upright and unmoving, but it was not until he wriggled his arms that he realized his chains had been removed.

The one piece of furniture in the room, a chair, which he occupied, was hard and uncomfortable. Obviously, people were not here for comfort. He didn't know the hour but wondered how long he would have to wait. His father had to talk to him sometime, but, he admitted, it could be a long while.

He had resigned himself to a lengthy wait when the thick wooden door was shoved open and his father walked into the room. Poseidon resembled the father Atlas knew and loved, but the flames of anger that seethed just below the surface were quite evident. Atlas was on dangerous ground, and he dared not risk stirring anything up. He waited for his father to speak.

Pacing the room, Poseidon stopped before his son, trying to find the words. He had never before experienced such fury toward one of his own children and last night, before the full force of his violence erupted, Clieto had calmed him enough that he followed her suggestion and ascended to Olympus for a night of determined debauchery. He had evidently succeeded far beyond his own immense capacity because, today, he was disturbingly hung over. He grumbled abruptly, "How was your night?"

"As intended, uncomfortable, cold, and lonely." Atlas could not look his father in the eyes.

"Hmmm." Poseidon stepped into the corridor and signaled for a chair to be brought. Once it had been deposited, he closed the door and gingerly settled himself to face Atlas. Suddenly, he reached over and, grabbing his son, shook him like a rag. "What were you thinking, Atlas? Have you lost your mind?"

He pushed his son from him, causing Atlas's chair to tilt crazily. Just when he thought he would tumble to the ground, the chair slowly found its equilibrium and righted. Exhausted and heartsick, Atlas didn't know where to start. What could he say that would make this man understand?

Poseidon clamped down on his temper, crossed his arms, and glared. "Explain why you ignored the warnings I gave you regarding our boundaries. Did we not have a discussion on that very subject not two weeks back? Did you expect the laws to change just because you found a crystal source?"

Atlas remained silent, head down, defeat showing in the slump of his shoulders. Poseidon felt no sympathy. He continued, "Have I not given you clear reasons we remain separate? The purity of this city and my people depends upon adherence to the very first Canon. I did not create this world in order for you to pollute it! How is it that you feel so entitled that you dare bring this girl into Atlantis?"

At last, Atlas peered at his sire. "Father, I was not trying to disobey you or your Canons."

Poseidon was jittery, and blood pounded in his temples. He stood, rubbing his arms, and again paced the small cell. Stopping in front of the door, he leaned back and rested one foot against the wood. He waited for Atlas to be more forthcoming. When his son remained quiet, he closed his eyes and raised his face to the ceiling. "Why, of all my children, did *you* do this? I trusted you the most. I had great plans for you, but you have deliberately gone against all my teachings." He lifted his palms up in a gesture of supplication and repeated mournfully, "Why?"

Atlas had trouble gathering his thoughts. He was drained from the rampant emotions of the last several days, and he was bereft that he no longer knew how to find Alia. He cleared his throat and looked his father in the eyes. "Father, I have no defense for my actions. I met Alia when I was looking for the special crystals and fell in love with her before we even spoke." Atlas shrugged his shoulders and rubbed the back of his neck before he continued. "I willingly followed her to a place where, as far as the eye could see, the ground was littered with the crystals you specified." He hung his head and mumbled, "Because I chose her for my lifemate, I thought if I could introduce you, you would see how special she is … was."

Atlas stood and looked at his father accusingly. "I no longer know how or where to find her."

Poseidon shifted and walked back to his son. Hurt had replaced the anger, and he motioned for Atlas to reacquire his seat. Once Poseidon had taken his, he leaned toward his son. "You are not yet sixteen—how can you know your mind at such an age? Do you know how many girls and women I have been infatuated with? Why, I have lost count."

When he received no response, he stood. "I have brought your birthing day gift."

Atlas looked up, startled. "Why would you bring this now?"

Poseidon sighed deeply. "I would have you understand the responsibilities I ask of you before your birthing day arrives. I am willing to give you a chance to decide what you want to do with your life. If you choose to accept what I offer, then there will be no more talk of this young woman. However, if you decide to repudiate your birthright, then you are free to go. I will even locate this missing girl, and I will see that you have safe harbor somewhere outside Atlantis."

Shocked out of the depths of his despondency, Atlas beheld his father with awe. "Where am I to receive this gift?"

Poseidon held up his hands. "Do not think I am allowing you out of here that easily. You will stay through another night." He crossed his arms and studied his son carefully. With his next statement, he tried to impart the seriousness of his offer. "Consider what you are asking. It is crucial that you fully grasp the consequences of your choice. Neither choice will lead to an easy life; however, one choice offers immortality."

Atlas frowned. He couldn't imagine anything that would make him change his mind. He stood up and approached Poseidon. "I love you, Father. You know I do."

Poseidon beheld his son. "Atlas, I have always loved you. You are the son of my heart, but you have placed me in an untenable situation. I urge caution. Do not make your choice lightly, as you must never have regrets." Poseidon went to his son. "Now, come into my embrace before I depart."

They hugged long and hard, neither wanting to be the first to draw away. Finally, Poseidon disentangled himself. "Your gift will be forthcoming. Food and drink will be brought later. You are not to be offered anything else in the way of comfort. You are here to think, not sleep."

A couple of men entered with candles that they placed around the room. The lighting was not the best, but Atlas knew better than to ask for more. Curiously, he gazed at the man who had sired him. "I do not know how to thank you for this chance. No matter what, I am honored to be your son."

Poseidon opened the door. "Once you have made your decision, you will be released. We will see then if your mind has changed."

"Thank you, Father, I could not ask any more."

Poseidon stepped out as the two men reentered the cell. They bore a seal and a book. Reverently placing the book in Atlas's lap, they positioned the seal on the floor next to one of the candles. Leaving without a word, Atlas heard the lock turn. With a heavy sigh, he bent to his task. He had no idea what the book was or what it contained. He opened the cover and was surprised to find that his hands were trembling.

# CHAPTER

## 15

POSEIDON RETURNED HOME where Clieto stood, awaiting his entrance. She ran into his embrace the moment she saw him. Stroking his face, she was surprised to find wetness where tears had flowed over his cheeks and beard. "My love, why do you cry?" He looked so sad, Clieto's heart lurched. "Has something happened to Atlas?"

Her god shook his head and led her to a deep couch. He settled himself then pulled her onto his lap. "Although your suggestion goes against everything I have ever known, your counsel was sound. I have allowed Atlas his choice."

Clieto kissed her husband deeply—she knew what that decision had cost him. When they parted, Poseidon continued.

"He will discover his true destiny, and sometime during the night, he will choose to ignore it and leave it all behind ... or it will be as I desperately hope, and he will make the right choice and assume his birthright."

Clieto stroked the worry lines of his strong, handsome face. "Come, I have prepared a special supper. One that will help distract you from what promises to be a very long night." She stood and held out her hand. "Have faith in our son. He will do the right thing."

A sigh rumbled from the depths of Poseidon's soul. "I hope you are right, Clieto. I hope you are right."

Atlas read until he felt that his eyes would roll out of his head. Bone tired, he straightened his back, joints grumbling. With great care, he closed the book and placed it next to his chair, then stood and stretched his stiff, aching limbs. He tried to massage his eyes but his lids felt as though they were filled with salt.

Walking around the small cell, he saw that the candles had melted down to their bases. The flickering light bleeding from each drowning wick barely lit the stones upon which they sat. He couldn't read another word. He shivered and reached for his robe. The hour before dawn had always seemed the coldest to him, and he was glad to have a small measure of comfort.

He had read through the night, pausing occasionally to consider all that was being revealed. The heavy book traced the genealogy of his parents and their parents before them, winding back through the ages. History came alive on the pages as he read of great wars between the old gods and the new. He learned how capricious the gods truly were and how carelessly they used humans as their ultimate distraction from lives wild with drink, debauchery, treachery, and death. It was the unarguable duty of every son and daughter born of a god to honor their remarkable birthright and accept a position of importance and prominence within the hierarchy of their lineage. Any child resulting from the coupling of a god, no matter how far removed from the supernatural bloodline, stood to gain talents, wealth, and privilege well beyond their human counterparts. Duties were meted out according to each child's inherited talents. Even the lowliest son or daughter was considered welcome in Olympus, albeit as servants to the gods in residence.

It was as he neared the end of all the stories and accounts that Atlas discovered the gift his father was offering him. He felt as if he had been struck in the heart with his father's trident. Poseidon, god of the lands and oceans, was presenting him with nothing less than responsibility for the world itself. Atlas was stunned.

It had never entered his mind that he was being groomed for such a position. It had certainly never occurred to him that he would be honored in such a deeply humbling manner. Why, he hadn't known a duty such as this would ever be offered to a half-god. He circumnavigated the small space, pondering the responsibility he was being offered. In his heart, he knew the architecture needed to separate the earth from the sky had not even been created.

Rolling his shoulders, he was besieged by questions. How was this to happen? Who would teach him all that he needed to know? How much time would it take to accomplish his bequeathed task? Was he to have a life outside of this tremendous responsibility? Overwhelmed, he tripped over a raised stone and had to catch himself before he fell.

He resumed his seat and attempted to compare the ramifications of accepting his father's gift against finding Alia. He loved the beautiful outsider beyond anyone he had ever known, but, again, he never imagined his father would offer him such a post. His brothers and sisters had been given domain over forests or animals or other such things, but to hold the entire world separate from the sky? How was that even possible?

Glancing at the lone skylight, he could see that the dark night was losing its grip to the coming day, yet suddenly, he felt small and lost and alone. He slumped over, elbows resting on his knees. He had seen enough, and he had examined his options until his mind no longer functioned. However, one thing was certain: without a single doubt, he had made his decision.

Dawn was creeping through the black, bringing the first colors of daylight. Atlas stood and shook himself. Inhaling deeply, he realized a weight had fallen from his shoulders, and he felt good. Uncertainty cast aside, he knew what he had to do.

# CHAPTER

*16*

POSEIDON AWOKE WITH Clieto wrapped securely in his arms. He marveled, after all their years together, that she was still the only woman he could sleep with through an entire night. Where most women clung like leeches until he felt suffocated under the weight of their need, Clieto was a delight to him in every way possible.

Inhaling her warm, sleepy scent, his mind wandered back to the day they had met. He had been with friends who had spent the better part of a sunny morning torturing travelers with their antics. He'd stifled a laugh at some of the stunts they had pulled—oh, nothing bad, just boyhood pranks.

Although, if he really thought about it, he couldn't blame it on being young any longer. He, too, had celebrated his sixteenth birthing day, and during the ceremony, he had solemnly accepted the gift his father, Cronus, had offered him. While surprised at such an offering, he had accepted readily. Poseidon loved everything about the ocean, and truly, he couldn't wait until his twenty-first year when he would actually assume the responsibilities from the previous god. But until such time, he was determined to enjoy the intervening months as much as possible. So, it was with his companions that he spent most of his time, playing tricks on other gods and wreaking havoc among the humans.

That singular day was when he met Clieto. Her family had been some of the travelers he and his band of ruffians had harassed. She had laughed to see their idiotic antics, and he knew it was at that moment that he had fallen in love with her. However, his father had interrupted his plans to woo and bed the beautiful girl. Cronus brooked no argument and insisted that the next years be spent honing his skills and knowledge of the deep. Poseidon had reluctantly followed orders so that when the day came for him to take over, he would be ready.

He shifted in order to appreciate Clieto's exquisite countenance. He smiled—she had been well worth the wait. He had taken many wives and loved most of them well, but Clieto was special. She retained an air of mystery that he still hadn't been able to fathom. She fascinated him, and he was proud of their son. All things considered, they had done well.

That thought brought with it the realization that Atlas was still detained. Their son had spent the night in a cold, inhospitable containment center. Poseidon closed his eyes and sighed. If he could have sent a request to his father, it would be that the boy make the correct decision.

It made no sense to lay abed, wondering. There was only one way to find out, and that was to get the day started. Poseidon leaned over and kissed his wife. She nestled closer to his warmth and reached for him. Even in sleep, she was the only woman whose passions reached the heights of his own. She was insatiable and always ready to love him. But today was different. He couldn't think of making love until he knew Atlas's decision. He kissed her again and gently removed her hand.

Rolling onto his back, he yawned until his jaw popped. Ruffling Clieto's golden hair, Poseidon threw back the covers. "We must get up and make ready for the day. It is time to find out what our son intends to do with his life."

Clieto roused herself and slid on top of her husband. Looking deep into blue-black eyes, she reiterated, "Our son will do what is right. Do not worry, my love." With that, she shoved her way out of the fluffy bedding, wrapped an errant sheet around her waist, and headed to the bathing room. Before she disrobed completely, she looked back at her husband. "You will see."

Poseidon groaned and sat up. He wished he could feel as certain about Atlas's decision as Clieto. He knew too well how strongly passion ran in a young man's veins. He had been young once, and the memories were never very far.

He got out of bed, feeling older than he should, and went to join his wife in the baths.

Atlas was standing with his back to the door as his parents entered the room. Turning, he was surprised to see his mother, but then he realized that his decision would affect her, too. He was glad she had come.

Poseidon and Clieto, wreathed in portentous silence, awaited his decision. Without a word, Atlas reached down and respectfully picked up the book and the seal. He crossed the uneven floor and stood before his father. After handing the seal to his mother, he placed the book in his father's hands and opened it to the last page. He then loosed the seal and very firmly stamped his mark in the allotted space.

Tears stung the edges of his eyes, and Atlas blinked rapidly in order to clear his swimming vision. Clearing his throat, Atlas placed his hands in prayer attitude against his heart and solemnly bowed his head. "Father, you have placed such an extraordinary responsibility before me that I cannot turn away. From the depths of my soul, I thank you for this honor. I just hope I am worthy of such a charge."

He looked up at his father's face, and it was as if the sun had come out after years of darkness. Poseidon and Clieto went to their son. The joyful laughter that echoed off the stone walls of the containment room had never before been heard—it was a sound the guards would never forget.

# CHAPTER
## 17

ITH DIZZYING SPEED, the biospheres whipped through the Atlantic and Mediterranean seas. Faster than any topside transport, the 'spheres began their gradual descent to Atlantis in less than three hours' time.

Ni-Cio piloted the craft and concentrated on the voyage; however, he was concerned for Mer-An's health. Conjoined by thought-touch, the minute Aris had succumbed to his attackers, Mer-An knew her mate was no more. Ni-Cio was racked with guilt that all he could do was send Mer-An his love, his heart, and a sorrowful apology that he hadn't been there for his friend.

Mer-An's compassionate reply still echoed in his mind. *"You know Aris was my life, but I am blessed to carry our child … in that, I will find a measure of comfort … you did all that you could … come home, Ni-Cio, and bring his body to me … all will be well …"*

Unable to think of anything else to say, Ni-Cio had sunk into his memories, particularly the time Aris had made him

venture closer to topsiders than even he had ever dared …
*"Aris, no! We must not!"* Ni-Cio's adamancy poured into his
impish friend.

Aris halted his forward momentum and laughed. *"You know
you have done nothing but dream about seeing them up close!"* He
motioned Ni-Cio to follow. *"Come, my friend … this is the time!"*
Aris swam away, protected by his bioskin.

Ni-Cio blinked and swallowed hard. He tried to think, but he
had to admit, Aris was right: he was fascinated by topsiders. He
had longed to see them with his own eyes. Curious in nature,
he wanted to know everything about them. The crystal-based
processors they used to gather information and learn about
topside ways were only as good as the knowledge they acquired
… what the processors couldn't do was give any Atlantean a
firsthand feel of topside life.

In all Ni-Cio's wanderings, he had studied how volatile and
young all the different cultures were, and he had to admit that
he envied their lives above the vast oceans.

He glanced up to see Aris waiting impatiently. Although
his friend floated in neutral buoyancy, he looked to Ni-Cio as
if he was tapping his foot and looking at the hands of a clock.
He smiled and threw Aris the OK sign. Topsiders were the
forbidden fruit, but for Ni-Cio, the temptation was too great.
Aris had flashed that lopsided, trouble-making grin and led
the way.

They swam close to one of Santorini's rocky beaches. They
had chosen Santorini as it seemed to be the busiest island in
the entire Greek chain. If they were to swim among the topsiders, unimpeded by biospheres, then this particular beach
would give them an incredible glimpse into their actual lives.

The young men surreptitiously broke the surface water and found that they were blinded by the intensity of the harsh Greek sunlight. Ni-Cio remembered that they had tried to shade their eyes, but even then, they could still barely see ... their eyes streamed tears, and they blinked uncontrollably. Finally giving up, Aris had slipped beneath the waves, sending Ni-Cio a sardonic thought. *"Your idea, not mine ... I will watch from here ..."*

Surprised to find topsiders as ungraceful in the aquatic world as fish were out of the water, Ni-Cio still enjoyed their squeals of delight and laughter as vacationers frolicked in the waves.

Using his coloring as camouflage, Ni-Cio got close enough to touch some of the swimmers. Intently, he studied the different groups of friends and families until Aris laughed and prodded him. *"Not so different from us, eh?"*

Ni-Cio, fascinated, hardly dared breathe. *"Aris ... it is better than I imagined!"*

With great reluctance, Ni-Cio finally let Aris tug him back toward the open ocean. *"We must leave, our time grows short, and we must not risk discovery ..."*

It was later, when they had gotten back to Atlantis, that the young men had found out just how much trouble they were in - Ni-Cio hadn't thought he and Aris would ever be freed from kitchen duties.

He laughed at the trouble Aris had always stirred up. Softly, he murmured, "By the gods, Aris! We faced the consequences together, and I would not trade our adventures for anything." He bowed his head. *"Thank you ... for all of it ... if not for you, I would never have saved Daria ..."* His thought-whisper was lost to the sea.

Evan stirred. "When we dock, we'll have plenty of help. Rogert has sent word, and half of Atlantis is waiting poolside. If you and Rogert can lift Daria out of the biosphere, Peltor and a couple of his men will lift Travlor. So that I don't lose my connection, I have asked to be carried as well. I am losing strength and I am terrified of losing my grip."

Concentrating on bringing the 'sphere easily into the docking pool, Ni-Cio just nodded.

Once they were secure, the hatch disappeared, and Ni-Cio lifted Daria into Rogert's waiting arms. Peltor and three other Atlanteans approached Evan and lifted Travlor's body with gentle hands. Evan let himself be lifted out last.

Once everyone was in position, Ni-Cio took a moment to study Evan. He was astonished to see how pale the topsider had become. Dark circles ringed both eyes—the strain his friend was under was evident in the weighted lines of his body. It was nothing short of a miracle that they had gotten this far without breaking Evan's connection. Ni-Cio sent a quick thought to his men. *"Take them to my quarters ... then go to the compound ... load the 'spheres with extra provisions and bring Kyla and whoever else she needs to help prepare meals ... get back here immediately ..."*

Assiduously, the Atlanteans wound through the hallways, hurrying as quickly as was prudent. Once inside Ni-Cio's rooms, they settled the bodies on either side of Evan in Ni-Cio's large bed. They made sure everyone was comfortable, then most of the men left without another word.

Ni-Cio regarded his friend. "I will be back as soon as I see to the news release."

Evan lacked the strength to respond, but it didn't really matter; his mind and thoughts were sinking back into Travlor's life.

# CHAPTER

*18*

ATLAS SPENT MOST of the time prior to his twenty-first birthing day studying his chosen path. Rarely did his thoughts return to Alia; however, sometimes, when the light outside looked a certain way, he would remember the girl who had spoken to his heart. It would be during those times that he would wonder what had become of her. Most times, he refused to let himself dwell too long. It never did any good—his thoughts just looped endlessly. When that happened, he drove himself even harder; he had too much to learn before the keys of power were handed to him, and time didn't stop its forward march for anyone … not even a god.

The extravaganza that had crescendoed with his sixteenth birthing day had bordered on embarrassing. Gods and goddesses poured from Mount Olympus like the heady wine accompanying their arrival. Their gaudy display of wealth, power, and glory was duly impressive, and with the amount of pomp and circumstance surrounding the acceptance of his birthright, it was thought by most of the attending Olympians to be the best party in eons. However, when Zeus made his grand entrance riding across the sky in his chariot of fire, pulled by six white-winged offspring of the mighty Pegasus, the party had devolved into one of the wildest bacchanalian feasts anyone had ever witnessed. Most of the major attendees had barely made it back home in one piece.

Some of the lesser gods and goddesses had provided their own debased form of entertainment by changing unsuspecting mortals into animals and back to humans. For additional ribaldry, they left some of their terrified prey in the awful state of being half human, half animal. The wails of the mortified semis provided days of unbridled hilarity.

It had been a celebration to end all celebrations. Standing proudly in the temple with his father, Atlas was acknowledged as the supreme child in the pantheon of children sired by gods. When the mantle of his birthright was formally announced and accepted, all of Atlantis looked upon Atlas with a new sense of awe. The gangly youth had blossomed, and his muscular physique attested to his athletic prowess. Atlanteans appreciated his powerful strength, his quick mind, his compassion, and his unfaltering loyalty to Poseidon and to Atlantis. The people were secure in the knowledge that he would never let their world falter. He was accepted fully and with love.

Three months later, the party had finally splintered, and the last of the celebrants took their leave. Though it had been a memorable celebration, once it was done, Atlas put his life on hold, put his head down, and studied every book, tome, and scroll his tutors provided. In the field, his father had him accompany different gods so that he could learn their tricks and their traits. Ultimately, he discovered that separating earth from sky, while taxing his strength, was not too difficult when his thoughts adjusted to the sheer scope of effort needed to accomplish the unending task.

He closed his current book and considered the next milestone. Looming near, his twenty-first birthing day was the day his father would actually bequeath his rightful inheritance. He felt strong, and powerful, and knowledgeable, and he was proud he was no longer daunted by his special designation.

He stared out of the windows of his father's study and reviewed his lessons in thought transference. He felt he had done well. Learning to harness the power of thoughts and make them manifest came easier than he'd initially thought. It was a remarkable skill to have in his repertoire.

Kai-Dan, Atlantis's Most Sovereign Healer, had summoned the very best healers from all over the land to teach him the healing arts. He was now able to tap into the same power they possessed, should he ever have need. At no time was the teaching of a skill or an art denied him. Even though Atlas was not a full blooded god, he was treated as such, and so received the most intensive instruction possible to help him harness the powers he possessed.

That Atlanteans could read each other's thoughts was something every toddler learned almost as soon as they could talk. However, there were learned men and women from all over the realm who came and went. Some of their teachings were easy to master and were quite magical; however, there were other skills that he would never master. In this, he was hampered only by his half human bloodline. For the most part, though, Atlas was as skilled as any other young god, and he was poised to take over his responsibilities with aplomb.

It was on a particularly rainy day that Atlas had been studying in the field when, running back to his house, he decided to take a break and stop for something to eat. He hadn't consumed a very substantial breakfast, and it was a fact that his studies quickly drained his already formidable metabolism.

He shouldered the door open and entered the restaurant. It was filled with people enjoying a break from the rain. The air was close but the place was abuzz with happy patrons. Atlas jostled his way through the throng, wending his way toward a vacated table. As he passed through the crowd, he felt someone reach out and grab his hand. He looked down, thinking to upbraid the person for their impertinence, when he was caught short.

Gazing back at him, with a pair of the most beautiful emerald green eyes he had ever seen, was Alia. Atlas's knees gave way; the only reason he didn't fall was because Alia had caught his arm and was helping steady him.

Atlas was struck dumb. He couldn't remember even one simple word. He just stared and exerted tremendous effort to keep his mouth from falling open. His eyes devoured her beauty like a starving man relishing his first meal in years. She had barely changed. While her figure had filled out a bit and she seemed taller, he would have known her anywhere. The charged silence escalated until Atlas felt he would explode. Still, the words would not come.

Alia finally broke the spell. Her nerves showed as words tumbled out in one breathless heap. "Atlas, it is so good to see you. I wondered if we would ever bump into each other. I have heard about your studies ... You are making everyone jealous with the speed with which you are learning ..."

Her words trailed away—she was embarrassed that she could think of nothing else. It finally registered in Atlas's brain how much her speech had changed. It had deepened, and she had taken on the Atlantean cadence.

At last, Atlas found his tongue. "Wh—What are you doing here?" he stammered. Still unable to comprehend how it was that she was in this particular restaurant, at this particular time, on this particular rainy day.

A shy, shaky smile appeared, and she pointed to the man still seated at the table. "I would like to introduce you to my husband, Inolde." The man nodded but held his seat.

Atlas just looked stupidly from one to the other. "How did you come to be in Atlantis?" He wrenched his gaze from Inolde and stared at Alia. "And why didn't you find me?"

It was Alia's turn to fall silent. She knew why she hadn't sought Atlas, but she doubted he would agree with her reasoning. She motioned for him to take a seat. Once everyone was settled, she gazed into impossibly blue-black eyes and tried to explain. "Inolde found me and brought me here. We have been together for four years."

Although Atlas had transgressed several Canons himself, he hadn't expected to find anyone else who so blatantly broke the laws. The wrath of his father started to rise, but he stopped short. *Am I really upset that the man has transgressed the laws of my father? Or am I upset because of whom he has married?* He shook his head to clear his roiling thoughts.

Falling back on his manners, he offered his upturned hands to Inolde. The man returned in kind, while Atlas studied the man who had captured Alia's heart. "You are fortunate; she is truly a treasure. I wish you success in your endeavors. Now, I will excuse myself."

Holding himself as straight as possible with as much decorum as he could muster, he bowed woodenly, then turned and walked toward the empty table. Before he took his seat, a tentative touch on his shoulder halted him. He sighed and turned around.

Alia's face was drained of all color. It was apparent that she was struggling with her own dormant feelings. "Join us? We have yet to order, and it would give us a chance to talk."

He hesitated—not because he didn't want to be close to her, but because he wanted it too much. She overpowered his senses. He started to decline, but she quickly interrupted. "I want to share some things with you and ..." She bowed her head and stared at the ground. Inadvertently, she touched his foot with hers and the shock was immediate; it gave her courage to continue. She looked into his eyes. "For all we meant to one another, I would appreciate it if you would listen."

Helpless to resist, Atlas followed Alia back to her table.

After their orders had been taken, Alia leaned forward and placed her elbows on the table. Gazing at Atlas with ill-disguised admiration, she began. "I would like to answer your second question first. You wonder why I have not sought you out." She pulled her chair closer and once again leaned close. "You have been selected to take responsibility for separation of the earth and sky. Of all the young gods, you are more special than I could ever have known." She touched Atlas on the wrist to invite his gaze. "I do not want to be known as the woman who took you from your path. It is not a burden I could easily live with."

Atlas nodded and looked away. He couldn't trust himself to speak yet. His heart and soul were filled with too much sorrow. It was as if the intervening years had never happened.

When he did turn back, he knew what he needed to say, so he took her hand. "You need to know that I did come back for you. I searched your campground, but I found no trace of the direction in which you had been taken." His thumb rubbed the small space between each finger as he continued. "My father's men found me. He ordered me clapped in chains, and I was taken to one of our containment centers."

Tears glistened in Alia's eyes, and as Atlas reached to brush them away, he caught himself and placed both hands in his lap. "I was held overnight. When my father came the next morning, he left me a book and a choice."

"Oh, Atlas. I did leave a trail, but my mother must have covered the tracks. It was hopeless from the start." Her heart sank to her stomach, and she was no longer hungry. She shook her head sadly. "Too many forces … too many parents preventing the way."

Inolde sat quietly throughout the exchange, but he found the anger rising in his chest. Although Alia had been honest with him from the start, and he knew she wasn't in love with him, he'd never had reason to doubt that she cared for him. Until now. He had never considered himself a jealous man, but watching her reaction to Atlas was more than any man should have to stand.

Before he could say anything to dishonor himself, the food was served, giving him a reprieve and giving everyone a chance to focus on something else.

When they had finished and the table had been cleared, Inolde excused himself. He had decided that valor and trust would win the day. He needed to believe in Alia's loyalty, or their marriage didn't stand a chance. "There are things I must attend to, and I know that you still have questions." He bent to kiss Alia, then muttered, "I will see you back home." To Atlas, he placed a hand over his heart. "I am glad to meet you at last. I wish you well with your studies." With that, he was gone.

Suddenly alone, both Atlas and Alia felt uncomfortable, and neither ventured to speak. The time lengthened until the silence seemed insurmountable. Neither knew what to say or how to start. Too many feelings swirled too near the surface. However, it was clear that neither of them wanted to leave. Atlas finally signaled the server for more wine and took a chance.

He leaned toward her. "Do you like your life in Atlantis?"

Alia considered his question. She waited until the wine was served, then took a sip and glanced at Atlas. "Life in Atlantis is so much better than what I knew that I have no cause to be unhappy or complain. My husband is a fair and loving man, and I am content in the life we have created."

Atlas studied her profile as she gazed out the window. He spoke his heart. "You will never know how profoundly sorry I am that we were kept from being together." He took a sturdy gulp of wine and continued as gallantly as he knew how. "Knowing that you are here and safe and that your husband is a good man gives me a small measure of comfort."

His heart ached so that he felt that he was being torn apart all over again. However, he refused to spare himself. He had to know everything. "Do you and Inolde have children?"

Alia couldn't help but admire his strength of character. He was trying to make it easy for her, so she swallowed her longing and shook her head. "No, we have been unable to conceive. I have visited a healer and she assured me that everything was normal." She finished lamely, "We will probably keep trying." The sadness lining Atlas's face was almost more than she could stand, so she tried to change the subject, but morbid curiosity got the better of her. "Have you not found anyone?"

Atlas looked away in attempt to rein himself in. He wanted to tell her that there would never be anyone else, but he bit his tongue and shook his head. "No, I have been immersed in my studies." He quirked a sideways grin. "It is not easy studying to be a god."

Alia closed her eyes. She could sense that he was on the verge of leaving, but before that happened, she gathered her courage and brought her hand to her heart. "I never stopped loving you. I will always love you."

Atlas stood. He stayed his response because he could not torture himself any longer. And the longer he was in her company, the more tempted he was to intervene and take her as his woman. As a god, it was well within his right. However, as much as it cost him, it was a right he was unprepared to force. She had found a good life and it was not in him to present an obstacle to her happiness.

Outside, the rain had ceased, and the granite roads smelled fresh and clean. He followed the way back home and found pleasure in the blessings of his life. He refused to think about his one great loss.

He approached the road leading to his house and turned to survey his city. Awash in sunlight, Atlantis looked surreal. He took a moment to thank the gods that Alia was safe and well, then turned to begin the climb. It was not until he heard his name shouted that his heart beat wildly against his chest and the passion he had quelled for so long rose up with a furor.

Running with the grace of a gazelle, curves well defined as her garment pressed against her body, Alia reached his side. Barely out of breath, her eyes shone bright as stars, and the smile she shared was meant for him and him alone.

Out of control, they collided, bodies joining at every juncture. Their breath mingled with their kisses and they were again one heart, one soul. Atlas's senses swirled. Her honeyed scent wrapped around him in heady abandon, and the warmth of her was more than he could take. He wanted her more than he had ever wanted anything in his life. When he dared look into her eyes, he saw her answering response and took her hand.

They ascended the hill and, upon entering the house, he swept her into his arms and carried her directly to his rooms. The door closed behind them as he lowered her onto his bed. Divesting himself of his clothing, he sank onto the cushions next to her. Slowly, achingly, he wound each of her garments from her until she lay revealed before him.

She was life, she was breath, she was love. He needed her more than he needed air. He pulled her beneath him. Lowering his weight onto her, he plunged home. One being, sharing one breath and one heart, he covered her with kisses. In his soul, he knew that this one night would have to last them an eternity.

# CHAPTER
## 19

THE WEEKS PASSED, and for Atlas, each moment had become a constant struggle to stay focused on his studies. The night he had shared with Alia colored his days and his nights, and now it was impossible for him to push her from his mind or his heart. He wanted her, and he wanted a life with her. However, he had not attempted to find her; he had made his choice and he was determined to leave her alone.

He didn't know whether he was relieved or not that she had not tried to reach him. He sighed and leaned back in his chair. *It seems we both know that our paths must diverge.*

He was more resolute than ever to be worthy of his father's love and trust. They had never spoken of his transgressions again, but Atlas knew that the fragile bond of trust between them had been broken. It wasn't that his father didn't trust him anymore, it was that the foundation that had existed for that trust had been destroyed. And now, even though he had not done anything to betray that trust, Atlas recognized that his father watched and listened more intently than he ever had.

Three weeks before his birthday, Alia came to him.

After finishing a full day's lessons in the temple, Atlas stepped outside to enjoy the cool air and he felt her before he saw her. She waited beneath the shade of a grove of olive trees. His heart skipped several beats; his blood raced. He slowed his steps so that he could fully absorb her beauty. When he reached her, he touched her face and felt her trembling like a newborn foal. "You are shaking—are you cold?" He started to offer his robe, but she shook her head. Perplexed, he asked, "Why have you come?"

She carefully reached for his hand and inhaled deeply before she shared his gaze. "I am with child, and he is yours."

Atlas gasped. The news was like a thunderbolt. He had never considered that there might be a lasting result to their lovemaking. His mind swirled with wonder while joy washed over him like a tidal wave. *I am going to be a father!* Atlas grabbed Alia and lifted her in his arms. "Alia, tell me it is true!"

She raised her eyes to the heavens and then looked down at the face she loved more than any other. "Yes, love, the healer confirmed it today."

"How far along?"

"Three months." She saw his face fall and rushed on. "I hesitated to tell you until I was certain—we are having a boy!"

Atlas was filled with so much love, he thought his heart might burst. He twirled her around and then set her gently back to earth. "But what shall we call him? Have you thought of a name?"

Suddenly feeling quite shy, Alia lowered her gaze to the ground and nervously raked her fingers through her hair. "I thought that would be something we could do together."

Atlas's thoughts raced with possibilities as he gazed at his beloved. It was then that reality set in and the dream started to fade. "Alia, I may be the father, but I am not your husband." He grasped her shoulders as though that would keep her from slipping away. "Have you told Inolde?"

A look of confusion crossed her face, and she hesitated. "No, of course not. I wanted you to be the first to know." An obdurate look crossed her beautiful features, and she stubbornly crossed her arms over her chest. "He is not the father."

"Inolde must be told, but have you thought about how he might react to this information? I mean, how is my presence to play in all this? Have you thought of the outcome?" Atlas didn't want to be the doom sayer, but he couldn't see how this was going to end well.

The happiness lighting Alia's eyes dimmed, and she grasped both his hands in hers as though he had already denied her. "I cannot be with him. I have never loved him. I love you and you are the father of my child!"

Atlas was torn. He loved this woman more than life itself and the thought of her being with anyone else made him sick to his stomach. However, he had taken an oath and forsworn all but the path he now traveled. He released her hands, straightened his shoulders, and stood before her, palms held in supplication. "I have … responsibilities, and you are not among them."

As though a knife had just ripped through her insides, Alia couldn't seem to take in enough air. Her heart contracted so that she didn't think it would ever beat again and she thought she might faint. Her eyes swam with tears; her head spun crazily.

It never occurred to her that Atlas would deny her. She only knew how happy he would be that, because of the depth of their love, they had conceived a life together. She suddenly felt unsteady, and she grabbed Atlas before her legs gave way.

"Alia!" He gathered her in his arms and held her as a drowning man holds to a lifeboat. "Forgive me … I do not know what I am saying." He pushed the hair back from her face and kissed away her tears. "We cannot go through this again. I promise I will never leave you. We will be in Atlantis together or we will leave."

Clinging to each other, the hardships awaiting them faded into nothingness, and it seemed that through their love, anything was possible. Neither of them were remotely aware of the devastating consequences their actions would unleash.

# CHAPTER
## 20

NICO RACED HIS biosphere through the murky deep, and as soon as he sprinted into Evan's compound, he enlisted Kyla and Mer-An's aid in releasing a statement to the international press. The news spread through cyberspace like lightning; all over the world, TV anchors, along with the largest syndicated columns, reported that the Savior, mortally wounded by friendly fire, remained in capable hands and stood an outside chance of surviving his injuries.

Word of the Savior's critical condition caused church coffers to swell. But as a direct result of Travlor's plight, new recruits besieged church offices in every country, expanding the ranks of Travlor's righteous armies to unheard of levels. The current headcount numbered in the hundreds of millions. As calls flashed around the world for prayers and donations, Travlor's church exploded like a firestorm.

World tensions ebbed by infinitesimal degrees when the governments of the United States, Russia, and China, agreed to pull back from DEFCON One. The three superpowers with their eyes in the skies, documenting troop movements, cautiously downgraded their status to DEFCON Two. Missiles, however, still remained at the ready.

Once assured that the crisis of nuclear war was no longer imminent, and the world had dragged itself back from the brink of an atomic holocaust, Ni-Cio left the compound and raced back to Atlantis. When he had docked, he hurried to his quarters. Although he knew that Evan still cultivated the link that held his beloved and their child to life, his concern did not extend to Travlor even though all their destinies seemed to be intertwined. Why that should be, Ni-Cio had no idea, and he was afraid to venture a guess. It was enough for him that Daria continued to hold to life.

Upon his arrival, the door to his rooms dissolved, and he entered to find Evan propped up, a mountain of pillows at his back. Ni-Cio studied Evan's sunken eyes and his thinned out frame. He was afraid for his topside friend. He had no idea how much strength Evan possessed, but it was apparent that the drain on his energy was tremendous.

Kyla had instituted round-the-clock feedings to help supply the nutrition that enabled Evan to continue his healing attempts. Even so, Ni-Cio could see that the topsider's breathing was labored. Nevertheless, his color remained, and if there was any indication that he was nearing the extent of his abilities, he was not showing it.

Carefully lowering himself to Daria's side, Ni-Cio took her free hand and leaned in to kiss her brow. *"I am here, beloved ... cling to Evan and come back to me when you are ready ..."*

Daria stirred slightly, then slipped back into her suspended state. Even that small response helped hearten Ni-Cio, and he glanced at Evan. "How do you fare, my brother?"

Evan's eyelids opened to mere slits. He was finding it hard to focus on present reality as he was pulled more and more into Travlor's younger years. He was cognizant of Ni-Cio's presence, but it was becoming increasingly difficult for him to disengage. It was with concentrated effort that he wrenched his thoughts from his father. "I am well enough."

"Is there anything you need that we can provide?"

Evan shook his head. "Kyla is bringing all the nourishment I could possibly ask for." He sank lower into the pillows. "Ni-Cio, it is becoming more difficult to separate myself from Travlor. Is there any way to figure out why I am so tied to his memories and what good any of this will serve?"

Ni-Cio feared for Evan, but he had no clue as to why his friend should be so immersed in Travlor's past life. He didn't want Evan to despair, so he tried to alleviate his concern. "I will do what I can to research this manifestation. When I find an explanation that makes sense, I will let you know."

Kyla entered, bearing another tray loaded with food. She smiled at her brother, but she saw the fear in his eyes, so before feeding Evan, she set the tray down and crossed to Ni-Cio. Leading him from the bed to a nearby couch, she motioned for him to sit, then settled herself next to him. She spoke quietly so as not to disturb Evan. "How many times have I heard you say, 'All will be well?'"

Ni-Cio frowned and shrugged. Kyla continued, "So many times I have lost count." She took his hand and urged him to look at her. "I tell you now that all *will* be well." When Ni-Cio didn't respond, she squeezed his hand. "You cannot give up hope. Daria needs you and your child needs you and Evan needs both of us most of all. It is through his love and endurance that he sustains everyone's life. You and I must stay strong or we stand to lose everything."

The truth of her statement stung. Aris's death had affected him so deeply that it had become impossible to remain optimistic about anything. The outcome of Evan's courageous attempt to help his small family only provoked more feelings of helplessness.

Kyla snorted her disgust. "You, of all people, know that life is fleeting. Do you think Aris would want you to fall into a quagmire of depression because of him?"

Ni-Cio almost laughed at that thought. "No, Kyla, you are right. If he were here, he would probably punch me in the face."

A small smile crossed Kyla's features. "Not only that, he would upbraid you for your negativity. He lived life fully and without reservation, and I know that he expects you to do the same."

Scowling, Ni-Cio eyed his sister. "I have not been a very good leader."

Kyla relented just a bit, tone softening. "You have had insurmountable odds placed in your path, but you have always risen to the task. Do not cease now. Your resolve will buoy Evan which, in turn, buoys Daria, your child, and Travlor. Wherever this leads, we are compelled to follow, and we must help to the best of our abilities. If we fail Evan, we fail everyone."

# CHAPTER
## 21

THE FESTIVITIES FOR Atlas's twenty-first birthing day were to be substantially more subdued than those of his sixteenth. Once a young god or goddess acknowledged their inheritance, the twenty-first year was but an addendum to the original celebration. Although not quite an afterthought, the twenty-first did not carry the same importance. It certainly would not be the same riotous celebration that had brought the residents of Olympus out in force. Nevertheless, Atlas's twenty-first would commence in the city and swarm to the countryside as festivities ran throughout the month.

From all over the land, chefs and bakers came to share their wares, wine merchants traveled from far and near bringing their most excellent vintages, and Atlanteans hung decorations from every balcony, post, and rooftop. The city was in a flurry of preparations.

Two days had passed since Atlas had learned he was to become a father. In that time, he had secured a small room in town for them to share. Before involving Inolde, they wanted time to plan the best route open to them. However, before their discussions could reach any concrete solutions, they had rapturously fallen into each other's arms, the world forgotten as their lovemaking soared to unexplored heights.

Locked in each other's arms, awash in the afterglow of their lovemaking, Atlas couldn't remember being so happy or so fulfilled. He wished with all his heart that they could forget about obligations and stay in their little room forever. But the boisterous noise of celebratory preparations intruded on his thoughts, causing his mind to cloud over as reality entered.

He kissed Alia's jasmine scented hair and pulled the sheets around her. "I will talk to Inolde. Surely, he will listen to reason and step aside."

Alia ran her fingers lightly across the line of his collarbone, trailing down to the hard ridges of his stomach. When he was this near, it was hard to think of anything or anybody else. It was with difficulty that she diverted her attention to the matter at hand. "I do not share your certainty, love. While it sounds easy enough, he loves me, and I do not think he will step aside willingly just because your arguments are so persuasive."

"If Inolde refuses to relinquish his station as your husband, then we will go before the courts. It will be through the courts that you could possibly dissolve your marriage and be reinstated to single status. Once that is done, there will be no more argument."

She blanched to think of Inolde's reaction. But she couldn't think of another solution. She didn't want to hurt her husband, but she would never again give up Atlas. It was their destiny to be together. They had to face Inolde, no matter how hard it might be. They would find a way.

Sighing into Atlas's strong shoulder, she acceded. "All right, my love; go and seek him out. Although I believe you will be very disappointed."

Atlas settled deeper into the cushions and pulled Alia on top of him. He nuzzled her neck and whispered, "I will seek him out tomorrow. He cannot escape logic—of that, I am sure. Together, we will change the course of our lives."

As his hands roamed her luscious curves, all thought of the morrow was cast aside and they sank into the realms where dreams actually come true.

# CHAPTER

## 22

YESTERDAY, INOLDE HAD received a note requesting a meeting between himself and Atlas. He didn't think the visit boded well. He hoped Atlas wasn't playing him for a fool, because he was quite aware of the attraction his wife and the young god held for each other. By Zeus, he wasn't blind! From the moment Alia had reached for the man as he walked by their table, it was clear that what had been between them when they were younger had not diminished one whit.

He had imbibed in a few drinks prior to their meeting, thinking it would calm his nerves and help rein in his rising temper. At this point, he was more upset with himself than anyone else. He reasoned that, by letting them alone, he would be giving Alia the freedom she needed to come back to him. But with this afternoon's visit looming, he had decided that that was not going to be. He had awakened with a distinctly bad feeling, and it certainly didn't escape his attention as to how unapproachable his wife had been as of late ... *And if I am honest with myself, I noticed her behavior change when Atlas joined us in the restaurant.*

He shook his head and took another long swallow of the potent brew. He swiped his mouth with the back of his sleeve and stared out the window. *The insufferable man will be here any moment.*

Inolde went to the kitchens to leave his drink for later. As he sat the cup down, he heard the staccato beat of Atlas's knuckles rapping against his front door. His anxiety ratcheted up, and his hand inadvertently jerked, spilling the contents of his drink across the table. Too nervous to clean it up, he left it and approached the door.

Taking a moment to prepare himself, he gripped the handle firmly and stood aside, inviting the man to enter his home.

Atlas was nervous, too, but he was well within his rights, and the child was his, after all. He nodded at Inolde. "Thank you for seeing me."

Inolde stared at the man and blinked. He didn't remember Atlas being so big or so muscular. It was quite irritating. With as much civility as he could muster, Inolde beckoned Atlas to be seated. "Please, may I offer some refreshment?"

Shaking his head, Atlas declined. "This meeting will not take long, so we will not stand on ceremony and I will be brief."

Inolde steeled himself. "Then, by all means, get to the point." He crossed his arms over his chest and waited.

Clearing his throat, the young god stared at Inolde for the space of a few heartbeats, then began. "You have been a good husband to Alia; however, her heart has always belonged to me, and now that you have so conveniently brought her to Atlantis, it is my right to take her as my own. I am asking you to step aside and do what is best for Alia."

The man towering over him was speaking, but Inolde had ceased to hear anything beyond "her heart has always belonged to me." Try as he might to make sense of the situation, all he could think about was what a donkey's ass he had been.

Heat rose from the bottoms of his feet and surged into his being with the force of a cyclone. He wanted to hate Alia, but every ounce of anger came spewing out at the hulk standing before him. Any pretense of civility fled, and Inolde lost control, shouting, "You come to *my* house, draped in your presumed right as a god, to take *my* wife?"

Inolde hated the man! He tried to choke back his rage, but he watched his hand rise and strike the man across the face—and even then, what he really wanted to do was beat him to death.

Inolde, beyond reason, wild-eyed and out of his mind with jealousy, ran to the bedroom and scrambled to retrieve a sword his grandfather had given him. It had been smuggled into Atlantis by the old man, and Inolde had kept it hidden beneath the bed. He had never mentioned it to Alia, as weapons were not allowed inside Atlantis, but it would serve its purpose now.

His rage-filled scream resounded through the house, and Inolde flew into the sitting room, attacking without notice. Caught unprepared, Atlas was driven back against a wall. It took every bit of his strength and cunning to withstand the man's enraged onslaught.

Atlas ducked and parried, thinking Inolde's strength would fizzle out quickly. However, the infuriated Atlantean continued his advance like a super-charged bull. Relentlessly, he attacked and attacked and attacked again. He narrowly missed striking Atlas's chest, swinging wildly, but when the sword glanced off his right shoulder, Atlas began to lose his temper.

He issued a powerful thought-form, forcing the man to cease and back away. Atlas thought maybe then he could talk sense to Inolde. But the man struggled against the restraint like a maddened Minotaur. Spittle flew from his mouth, and his eyes flamed with hatred. "Preventing me from killing you does nothing! By the gods, I will bring you down any way I can!"

Before Atlas could react, the man raised his sword and, with all his strength, rammed it into his own stomach. Eyes glittering with revenge, Inolde pushed the blade in until it came out his back. He coughed thickly as blood gurgled from his mouth. Choking on the black liquid, he staggered forward. As he fell, he grabbed Atlas around the waist and, trailing blood the length of his body, slid to the ground, lifeless eyes staring accusingly at the young god.

Atlas couldn't believe what he had just witnessed. This was not supposed to happen—the man was not supposed to take his own life!

He backed away, panic surging through him. He would be held accountable for this treachery and the consequences for his actions would be swift and merciless. He would be banished from Atlantis forever. "How could you?" He grabbed the slack body and shook it as though he could bring the man back to life. "Why? You have ruined everything!"

A sob escaped Atlas, and he ran from the house. Blinded by his tears and fury, he didn't know where to go. He stopped in an alleyway and bent over. With hands resting on his knees, he tried to get his bearings along with his breath. He couldn't comprehend what had just happened. He had honestly thought he could reason with Inolde, right up to the moment the man had lost all control and run to the bedroom. Atlas had had no idea that he harbored a weapon, and he had not been prepared for such a ferocious attack. There was not a doubt in his mind as to whom they would find guilty.

He groaned and put his head in his hands. "Everything is ruined. I have dishonored my family, and by the gods, my father will never get over this."

He stood up, his only thought being to get to Alia. They had to leave before this mess unraveled even further. He couldn't stand the thought of being banished by his father. The rift between them would never be healed.

Atlas did the only thing he could: relying on pure animal instinct, he ran off into the night. He had to get to Alia and get them out of Atlantis before his father found out. There would be such hell to pay that he didn't want any part of it.

# CHAPTER

## 23

IN MORTAL FEAR for their lives, Atlas and Alia feverishly gathered necessary items they could carry in a few canvas bags and escaped under the cover of darkness. Although Atlas knew his father to be a fair man, he also had experienced the man's hair-trigger temper. When his anger was unleashed, it always got the better of his sound judgment. And there was no doubt in Atlas's mind that this was one of those times.

He couldn't remember his father actually killing anyone before, but it was not beyond the realm of possibility. An enraged god was not somebody anyone—other than another god—trifled with. He didn't want Alia to be anywhere near Poseidon when his father learned of his duplicity, and he wasn't about to endanger the life of their child. So, on they ran.

Atlas had never ventured outside of Atlantis except for the time he had followed Alia to the crystal grounds, and he was as clueless as a young child. When they stopped to rest, he looked expectantly at Alia. "I have no experience outside the bounds of Atlantis, and though I apologize with all my heart, I must trust you to shoulder that burden. If at all possible, you must lead us to another life, another city, another country."

"Do not worry; we will find a place."

Atlas nodded. He didn't know how far they had to run in order to escape Poseidon's wrath, but deep in his soul, he feared no place would ever be far enough.

He took Alia's hand. "Come, we must try to find somewhere to wait out the night. It is getting far too dark to travel much farther."

Hand in hand, they walked until the stars shone like precious jewels and their legs started to tire. At length, they passed a deserted home that had burned down. While Atlas knew they had to find a place with more people and more life, the abandoned structure would afford them a bit of protection against the night.

Carefully picking their way through the fallen timbers, Atlas located a corner, walls intact, and spread a blanket on the earthen floor. As he helped Alia sit, his concern was evident. "Are you well enough?"

Alia grasped his hand, pulling him down beside her. "I am crushed by the actions of Inolde. He was always so kind to me, I had no idea he would react in such a manner. While I mourn his passing and wish things had turned out differently, you have to know that I am always well with you, my love."

Atlas unwrapped the paltry amount of food they had procured. Breaking off a larger portion for Alia, he handed her the dried bread and crumbly cheese and opened the wine skin that she might drink first.

Once their hunger subsided and they were wrapped in their robes, they huddled into each other for warmth. Soon, they found that the horrors of the day slipped away against the longing explorations of their bodies, and the heat of their passion warmed them throughout the long night.

Without fail, the sun rose, bringing with it the sounds of morning. Opening their eyes to a new day, they were greeted with the knowledge that sometime during the night, they had been surrounded. Poseidon's men hadn't made a sound, and Atlas reeled with the thought that they had been located so quickly and so easily. He groaned, closed his eyes, and shook his head.

"You are to come with us." There was no argument, there was no discussion. It was a direct command handed down from a god. Atlas despondently helped Alia stand, then wrapped the warm blanket around her. He guided her through the desiccated house and stepped outside. Shocked to see more soldiers than he realized resided in Atlantis, he looked out over their numbers and marveled at the massive search their departure had precipitated.

It looked like an entire army with men spread out on horseback, soldiers in racing chariots and foot soldiers dedicated to a thorough ground search. It was obvious that his father had not spared anyone from taking part in the search. His father! Atlas shivered, suddenly cold and clammy. He ran his hands up and down his arms, but nothing could stir warmth in his bones.

Poseidon had been upset last time, but Atlas knew that what he and Alia were about to face would make the consequences of his earlier transgressions look like a leisurely stroll on a sunny day. He didn't know how he was going to accomplish it, but he had to shield Alia and their child from Poseidon's wrath.

Glumly, the couple was escorted to one of the larger chariots. When they had been properly restrained, men saddled up, whistles were exchanged, and everyone turned towards Atlantis.

Curious, Atlas addressed the driver. "Where are you taking us?"

The driver glanced over his shoulder. A deep look of concern shone from sharp eyes. Atlas felt the man understood his reasons for wanting to know where they were being taken, so he held his breath and hoped for a response.

The soldier was quiet for a bit, then changed his mind. "We are to take you to the temple. That is all I can tell you." He looked back at Atlas. "We are not supposed to talk to you at all." He whistled three high-pitched bursts, and the horses took off at a high gallop.

Secured tightly to the chariot, Atlas had been allowed to put his arms around Alia. With her back to him, he used his body to shield her and hold her securely against the stanchion. With her balance already shaky from the pregnancy, the last thing he wanted was a mishap.

The road back proved faster than the way they had come last night. When Atlantis came into view, Alia glanced back at him, a worried look furrowing her brow. Atlas kissed her forehead and hugged her tighter. "I do not know what will happen." He grimaced as the chariots raced over the main road leading to the city. *No good will come of this.*

It was as if that very thought caused the earth to shift, but as Atlas watched the riders attempt to rein in their frightened mounts, he knew it wasn't his thought that had caused the earth to move. Their chariot driver slowed, and it was then that the ground truly began to writhe. Atlas swallowed hard. His hands shook and his breathing escalated so that he almost hyperventilated. The blood battered his eardrums so that he could no longer hear the horse's hooves pounding the ground, and last night's skimpy meal was on the verge of coming back up.

Alia looked up at him, tears streaming down her cheeks. He wished he could do something or say something to comfort her, but his own soaring fright precluded any talk. What else was there to say?

In the little time left before arriving in Atlantis, Atlas wracked his brain to think of some way to mitigate his father's wrath. If he didn't choose his words with the utmost care, there would be hell to pay. If he were brutally honest with himself, there was probably nothing he could say to divert his father's ire. Even now, they remained alive only because of Poseidon's mercy.

With just a few miles to go, Atlas sent a thought-form to his father. *"We are coming … will I be able to speak to you alone?"*

He realized his father's answer when the ground began shaking so hard that the men driving the chariots were forced to stop while the riders on horseback tried to settle their mounts. The earth undulated so that the broad expanse resembled waves on the ocean rather than solid ground.

Terrified horses reared and bucked, and men scurried to hold to anything that felt solid. Atlas's chariot rocked back and forth like a crazed pendulum, and Atlas held to Alia with all his might; still, the earth roared its pain.

Just as Atlas thought the ground would crack apart, the rolling quake subsided. Men scrambled to their feet, dusted themselves off, and regained their mounts. They were ready to finish their mission and divest themselves of the prisoners. But, because of aftershocks, their progress slowed considerably. Resigned, Atlas thought morosely, *We just delay the inevitable.* His arm tightened around Alia.

Entering the city, the party found Atlantis to be unnaturally quiet. Far and wide, Poseidon's wrath was well known, and citizens had fled to places they hoped provided safe shelter.

Random thoughts swirled through Atlas. *How did he find us so quickly? I thought he was away.*

Making their way carefully through the main thoroughfare, people ventured out to watch them pass, but no one dared make a sound. Eyes wide and rigid, fear glinted in petrified faces. Not one Atlantean had ever heard of a betrayal such as had been perpetrated by Atlas. Surely not Poseidon's son! Certainly not Atlantis's favorite son! It was as if a collective breath had been drawn in and would not be released until sentencing was passed.

The oldest citizens remembered a time long ago, when Poseidon had been upset with one of the rules passed down from his brother Zeus. The channel had rocked for days. No one could take their boats out of harbor for the winds and high seas that pummeled the coast. During that time, people kept their doors and windows securely shut and waited, fervently praying that the storm would soon pass. No one had ever prepared for something like this; no one knew what to expect.

At last, the army reached the heart of the city and pulled up in front of the temple. A magnificent structure, it was meant to evoke awe and fear and wonder. Looking at it through new eyes, Atlas admitted that it did all of that and more. Even as his tremendous ordeal continued to unfold, he couldn't help admire the carvings adorning the entryway arches. The artisans had done a superlative job. The carved statues, a tribute to the gods and goddesses, looked real. Atlanteans swore they could see them breathe.

The polished white granite gleamed, as light and airy as windswept clouds. However, the temple had been built to last. The domed roof was held in place by twelve soaring columns. The columns themselves were massive and it took ten tall men, all holding hands, to encircle the largest one. Their fluted tops resembled palm trees and gave the impression of fluttering in the lightest of breezes. White and gold marbled stairs rose upwards like water seeking its own level, and into the riser of each step, the artisans had carved one of the Canons. The top step held the last and most sacred law: *Fill your life with joy and share that joy with those you touch.*

Orichalcum, Atlantis's most cherished metal, had been applied throughout the structure. Even in the darkest night, the temple glowed with lustrous reddish-gold hues, a beacon from any part of the city.

Atlas shook himself as he and Alia were helped from the chariot and escorted up the stairs. Even the sea birds had ceased their usual cacophony and remained silent, watchful. If a newborn had sighed, Atlas thought he would hear it.

Alia clung to her man, fear coursing through her faster than the blood throbbing in her veins. Breaking out in a cold sweat, she shook so hard that she didn't think she could ascend the stairs without several strong men holding her upright. She was more afraid of meeting Atlas's father than anyone she had ever encountered in her life. She was a pariah, and Poseidon would not look upon her with anything but aversion and antipathy. She feared for her life and was terrified for the life of her child.

The one she feared for the most was Atlas. Where his son was concerned, Alia had no idea what his father was capable of doing. If the god was angry enough, banishment wouldn't even serve. She clung to Atlas's strength, but she sensed that he was just as frightened—this was all new to him, too.

At the entrance to the temple, the soldiers halted. Atlas and Alia were motioned to continue. Atlas took a deep breath and squared his shoulders. They entered the temple and Atlas wrapped a protective arm around Alia before guiding her through the vestibule and into the main room.

While the outside of the temple was magnificent, the throne room had been designed to intimidate. With no adornments other than the gleaming white of the granite and the bright glow of gold and orichalcum, the room was frightening. The golden throne floated ten feet above the floor. Wreathed in drifting clouds, it was impossible to look directly at Poseidon. Mirage-like, it was evident that he was too glorious to be gazed upon.

Atlas stepped in front of Alia in a poor attempt to shield her from his father. Poseidon's voice boomed through the temple and rolled out into the city. "Let her come forward, that I may see the woman who has crafted the downfall of my beloved son."

Atlas started to object, but Poseidon held up his hand, and that was enough. Atlas closed his mouth, but he didn't move. Alia came from behind him, shaking like a loose sail in a stiff breeze. She tried to look strong, but she didn't think she fooled anyone. "I am here, god of the land and oceans." She bowed deeply.

"Rise!" Alia stood upright. Poseidon didn't move for the longest time. He glared at the two lovers as if he was trying to recognize his own son. While his countenance was sorrowful and not quite as threatening as Atlas had imagined, lurking just behind his aspect was the power that initiated earthquakes and incited tidal waves to towering heights. Destruction of imaginable proportions was this god's domain.

Atlas and Alia did not move or speak; they barely dared breathe. Waiting for Poseidon to speak was torturous. Time ticked away slowly, and Atlas was uncertain as to what was expected of him. Usually, Poseidon dealt swiftly with transgressors, so that he could get back to his amusements. Atlas had never seen his father so silent for so long a time.

Finally, Poseidon stood. His eyes reddened like a wildfire. Slowly raising his arm, he held his trident high overhead. Three times, he solemnly struck the end of the trident against the throne. With each blow, the noise rebounded through the atmosphere like the crash of thunder. Alia and Atlas covered their ears, but managed to stand their ground.

The last echo died to nothing. It was then that Poseidon issued his proclamation in a booming voice: "My son, for the first transgression, you are to be held in Atlantis until the end of your days. With your second transgression, you relinquish all rights pertaining to the gift given to you upon your sixteenth birthing day. The designation 'Bearer of the Heavens and Earth' is no longer yours. Atlas, my son, because of your third transgression, you will work the rest of your days as a common laborer."

Atlas screamed, "No!"

"*Quiet!*" The word nearly flattened him, so great was its power. The temple rocked under the thunderous vibrations of his pronouncement; water sloshed in the harbor; the earth groaned in agony.

Atlas looked at his father in desperate supplication, but, eyes glowing like coals, Poseidon was not to be denied. His stare raked the couple cowering before him. He took a deep breath, then turned the force of his gaze to Alia. Menace radiated from every pore as he glared at the outsider. Atlas's heart stopped beating. Would his father smite her right then?

"As for you!" Poseidon raised his great finger, pointing at Alia. "How you circumvented our barriers in order to reside in Atlantis remains a mystery. One I do not care to understand. I will fix the error so that it never happens again!"

His wrath descended upon Alia. Doubling over as if she had been physically assaulted, fire raged through her insides. Screaming in agony, she gripped her stomach and fell to the ground.

Atlas grasped her arms and roared. "You are killing her! Stop! Father, you cannot do this!"

Atlas still possessed all the powers of a highly educated god, and his father was brought up short. Alia relaxed somewhat, and Atlas threw himself across the floor to the foot of the throne. Prostrating himself before his father, he pleaded, "I beseech you, do not kill her—she bears my son!"

"What is this?" Poseidon didn't trust what his ears had heard.

Atlas dared to raise his head, although he avoided his father's eyes. "Alia carries my son."

Poseidon brought his fiery gaze to rest on the woman. "Is this true?"

Alia blinked hard and, after a few deep breaths, staggered to her feet and faced the wrath-filled father. "Atlas speaks the truth."

They felt a slight tremble under foot and watched the temple walls begin to shake in earnest. Bells clanged wildly around the city, and observers fled the square. Buildings swayed until they looked dangerously close to collapse. People's terrified screams reverberated throughout Atlantis, and still Poseidon's anger continued to boil.

"So, you lay with another man while married to a husband that you conspired to kill after you found you were with child!"

The ground convulsed so that Alia lost her balance and pitched forward. She would have fallen had not Atlas rushed to her side. Wrapping her in his arms, he yelled, "No, Father, that is not what happened!"

The earthquake subsided somewhat, and Atlas leapt at his only chance.

"Please, release her from Atlantis—she has done nothing wrong. Give our child a chance to live!" Atlas fell to his knees, head bowed. "I throw myself on your mercy and your love!"

Poseidon looked at Atlas as though he had turned into a creature too repugnant to contemplate, and he snorted, "Love? You talk about love to me!"

At the sound of his father's fury, the seas began to boil and the earth rose up in revolt. Atlantis was on the brink of being destroyed, yet Atlas dared one more try; he screamed, "Yes, love! I have transgressed laws, but I *still* love you!"

The ground ceased its movement and the seas settled. Heartened, Atlas barged on. "Father, I did not kill Inolde. He attacked me, and when I compelled him to desist, the man turned his sword on himself!" His father made no comment, so Atlas dared continue. "I will abide by your decision, but Alia and our child must be cared for. I beg you, let them stay with me. I will gladly take care of them, and I swear that we will live our lives as you demand."

Poseidon shook his head sadly, the fire in his eyes dimming a bit. "It is beyond me why even now, you do not understand the severe consequences of your actions. The only choice open to me is to discontinue her existence or banish her from Atlantis. She and the child cannot stay here. It will not be allowed."

Atlas carefully approached his father. "Banishment is death! How will she survive? Let me go with them!"

"*Silence!*" Poseidon pounded his trident once and the skies parted; lightning and thunder slashed the land, and the earth heaved in pain. At the height of the cacophony, Poseidon roared, "I have spoken the only judgments allowed! Which is it to be? Speak now, or I will decide for you both!"

Alia pushed Atlas aside and screamed, "I take banishment, my lord—let it be so!"

Atlas felt like his body had turned to marble. He didn't think he would be able to draw another breath. Painfully, he forced air into his burning lungs. "I agree to her banishment." His only hope was that banishment might give them an outside chance of surviving.

Atlas choked back tears, his voice hoarse from trying to make himself heard; hate blossomed in his heart. He rose to his full height.

The menace lacing his voice cut the distance between himself and his father like a knife. "You are dead to me. I am no longer your son, and I will never again seek you out. For what you have commanded of us, I give my undying hatred, and if there is ever a time I can avenge myself, it will be done!"

Grabbing Alia's hand, Atlas raced from the temple, but before they reached the street, the stairs rolled violently and seemed to turn into water. Thrown to the ground, Atlas watched, horrified as the skies darkened and storm clouds unleashed a god's fury.

Trees, bridges, and fountains broke apart. Buildings swayed, loosening stones and tiles until it was impossible to tell which was more life-threatening, the debris or the downpour pummeling Atlantis. The havoc wrought by Poseidon lasted for what seemed like days, but at last, the carnage quieted.

Atlanteans knew who was responsible for the devastation, but no one dared say anything. People were just relieved that Poseidon's ire had finally calmed. Citizens dragged themselves out of the dirt, dusted themselves off, and tried to go about their lives as if nothing had happened. People avoided Atlas as though he was a leper.

Atlas guided Alia through streets with the least amount of debris. They entered an abandoned market and picked up some loose linen bags. Winding through the rubble, they searched for food, clothing—anything that would help sustain Alia once her path took her out of Atlantis. Atlas stopped his search and went to Alia. Fervently, he kissed her, then held her close and whispered into her hair, "You have to survive! Otherwise, I have nothing to live for." He pulled away and declared resolutely, "If at all possible, I will leave Atlantis and I will come to you."

Alia smoothed the hair from his face, kissed his lips, and murmured, "My love, I will survive. I have done so before, and I am not afraid." They parted, and she studied Atlas intently before she spoke. "The only thing I am afraid of is losing you. I do not think it possible for you to escape imprisonment. You may be part god and possess powers in your own right, but your father has just proved his mastery." She shook her head sadly. "If you deny his judgment again, he will destroy all of Atlantis before letting you leave."

Atlas withdrew from her embrace and continued searching through the rubble. "I do not doubt your words, but I cannot survive without you."

Alia decided to let him believe that the possibility of escaping Poseidon's judgment existed. It made her love him more than ever, that he would remotely consider escape an option. She knew that he would never be able to break away from Atlantis. Poseidon was too powerful and would have him under constant surveillance.

She feared for Atlas's own life. Should Poseidon be tested again, it was not beyond the father to kill the son. However, she kept her thoughts to herself. "Come, love, let us gather what we can before I leave you."

Atlas frowned. "I am accompanying you to the border."

Alia shook her head vehemently. "Your father will be watching, and I am afraid that if you come near the border, you will try something rash." Atlas started to object, but she rushed on, "That will do neither of us any good. Please, you must trust me on this. Accompany me to the edge of town, but not the border."

Atlas felt like he was dying. He had never been able to understand the despair that caused people to take their own lives. Now, he knew. He couldn't speak; his lips could not form the sentences he wanted to say. Tears slid over his cheeks and dripped from his chin. His breath came in huge gasps, and it was all he could do not to break down and sob.

The darkening gloom slid over them like a cloak. They decided they had rummaged for provisions long enough. As Atlas placed the last apple in her bag, he remembered the sword. "Inolde's sword." He hurried Alia outside. "We must go to your house—maybe it will still be there! It would afford you some protection."

Alia shook her head. "I think I would only harm myself. It is time to stop searching. I must leave before night is fully upon us."

Shuffling through the streets, Atlas felt like he was caught in the throes of a never-ending nightmare. The thought occurred to him that if he closed his eyes and went to sleep, he would awaken in Alia's arms, relieved to find that it had all been a bad dream. He hoisted the bags higher on his shoulders and tried to imagine that possibility as true, but it did him no good. He wasn't a child anymore, and he couldn't tease his mind into believing it had all been just a terrible game. The end was near.

If his father had just banished him, he could have lived with that decision. He never dreamed that Poseidon would separate him from Alia forever. It spoke to his heart of a brutal, vengeful being who gave no credibility to matters of the heart.

They trudged through the deserted thoroughfare where the damage was not as widespread. It helped them travel easier, so they made good time to the edge of the city.

Reaching the city's border, they heard a soft snort. Atlas left Alia's side to investigate, darting behind a screen of flowering bushes. Alia called out to him, but received no response. She had started to drop her packs when she heard Atlas's reassuring voice: "Do not worry."

As he stepped from behind the thick brush, Alia was shocked to find that he was leading a horse. "He must have gotten free during the storm. There is nothing to identify his owner." He held the harness firmly, relieved at this bit of luck. "This animal will ease your journey, and should you need money, you can offer him for sale."

He led the horse to Alia. She stroked his soft nose, and when he whinnied, she offered him an apple. The horse took it and munched loudly until there was nothing left.

It was time. The couple gazed at each other but there was nothing else to say. Alia dropped her bags and let Atlas help her settle on the horse's back, then she leaned down to kiss his lips one last time. Atlas finally regained some control and before they shared their last kiss, he reiterated, "I will make it out of Atlantis or die trying. If I am to leave this existence without finding you … then I swear to you that I will find you in another life." He kissed her tear-drenched lips and tasted the salt and the warmth. "You are my lifemate, now and forever."

Alia wiped her eyes and face with the sleeve of her robe and coughed to clear her throat. "I love you more than life itself, my Atlas. I swear that I will survive, and once I find a place, I will raise our son to be strong and good and just. I will tell him stories of his brave and handsome father, and we will wait."

She bent down once more and took his hands in hers. Kissing both his palms, she lifted her face to him and looked deeply into his eyes. "Should we not meet again in this life, I promise I will look for you in the next, and the next, and the next, until I find you again. You are my lifemate, now and forever."

They kissed, then she released him and took the reins. Atlas tied the straps of the bags together and slung them across the horse's withers. With one last look, Alia turned the horse around and headed toward the border. It would be dark soon, and she needed to find shelter quickly.

Atlas watched until she reached the edge of the woods. He waited and hoped that she would turn and look at him, and his heart leapt when she turned the horse around and waved. She placed her right hand over her heart and gave a slight bow. Atlas did the same. When he glanced up, Alia and the horse had disappeared into the forest.

# CHAPTER
## 24

LIETO WAS SO disgusted with her husband that she didn't think she could even stomach his appearance in their house. Never, in all her memories, had she ever seen him so upset. He was out of control, and though she loved him with every beat of her heart, the man, when he reverted back to his godhood, had a fearsome temper when he was crossed. He had caused so much damage to Atlantis that even Clieto was hard pressed to understand such wrath. And the extreme measures he had imposed upon their son was, in a mother's mind, unforgivable. Clieto was enraged and paced the entire house until Poseidon's return.

Upon hearing his entrance, Clieto stopped pacing and waited for him to come to the study. Once the door was secured behind him, she flew at him like a banshee. Slapping his face with all her might, she railed at him and beat his massive chest with her fists until her energy was spent. Then, falling into his arms, she cried herself out until her breaths came in huge gasps.

Poseidon held her through it all and never uttered a word. It was as though he wanted to be punished, so that his actions could be somewhat ameliorated. He took her anger and swallowed it. Once her sobs quieted and her shoulders no longer shook, Clieto stepped from his embrace and looked inquiringly at her husband. "Why? Why did you treat our son in such a fashion?"

Poseidon shook his head. With all of his heart, he had not wanted to proclaim the judgment that he had. If he could have seen any other way, he would have taken it, but there had been no other choice. The laws had been set long ago. "My dearest, if I absolved our son of his transgressions, then when would I ever be able to uphold my laws again? There must be order. If we have no order, then we devolve into chaos. It is from chaos that I have created this city that we call home. What would you have me do?"

Clieto dried her eyes with the tails of her husband's soft linen shirt, then looked up at his massive frame. "Why could you not have banished him, so that at the very least he could be with Alia and our grandchild?" She felt the heat rising in her face and found that her anger had far from abated. "That is what I do not understand!" She tried to dam the flow of vitriol, but she was helpless against the loss of her only beloved child. "You could have sent them both away!"

Weary of explaining his actions, Poseidon lunged for his wife as she jerked away. Grabbing her shoulders, he spun her around. "I do not owe you or anyone a reason for my decision! That you have reacted thus would provide all the rationale I would ever require to have you executed. Because you have been a treasured wife is the only justification I have as to why you are still standing before me!"

Clieto turned to leave. "Do not take another step!" Poseidon's command was irrefutable.

She faced her husband, eyes glittering with resentment. "What can you possibly say that would alleviate my own torment?"

Poseidon was heartsick. All the confrontation this day had wrought was more than enough for anyone. He wanted this day to be done. He offered the only explanation he felt that she could live with. "I did what I had to do. At some point in the future, I reasoned that he would seek me out and ask for forgiveness, which I would willingly grant. Should that day arrive, I could allow him to resume his rightful position." He looked imploringly at his wife. "Clieto, if I banished him, I was afraid that I would never see our son again."

She huffed, temper still running high. "It would seem that all you have managed to do is tap into our son's vehemence, pride, and anger—the same feelings that run rampant through you! And now look where that brings us! Atlas will never come to either of us again!" Before she left, Clieto uttered her last words. Holding herself ramrod straight, she issued her command: "Do not attempt to come to our bedroom. You are not welcome. Tonight, we sleep apart."

Poseidon exploded. His voice shook the house, and windows cracked and broke. "There is no need to keep me out! I will find my comfort elsewhere!" He readied to leave, but bellowed one last salvo as Clieto ran from the room. "Do not look for my return! I am through with the lot of you!"

His roar was only silenced by the slamming of the entryway doors. The entire house shook so that doors trembled in their hinges, bolts flew out of walls, and loosened windows crashed to the ground, glass splintering everywhere. Clieto fled to the bedroom and fell to the floor. Lacking any more strength, she lay in that spot, wracked with grief. Though the night wore on, her cries did not cease. Clieto was inconsolable.

# CHAPTER
## 25

S INCONSOLABLE AS Clieto was, Poseidon, staggered by the explosiveness of his anger, plunged from his house in a mood to destroy. In a blind rage, he raced down the mountainside and was circumventing his temple when his gaze fell upon a lone woman leaving the temple and making her way down the steps. Holding her robes carefully so that she wouldn't stumble, she had yet to notice the seething presence of her god.

Snarling like a wild beast, Poseidon ran from beneath the darkening shadows and ploughed into the woman as she reached ground level. Barely cognizant of his actions, Poseidon ignored her harrowing shrieks as he lifted her off the ground like a pile of kindling. He clapped a hand over her mouth as she struggled to escape and fled the city.

Barely breaking a sweat, Poseidon carried his prize to an abandoned barn. Flinging the distraught woman onto a pile of old hay, he hurled himself on top of her body and began ripping at her robes.

The woman closed her eyes against the sight of such a wrath-filled face and ceased her struggles. She could no more resist the god's onslaught than she could stop the tides from flowing. Disappearing inside herself, she was reminded that she had known this would come to pass.

Accepting her fate, Kai-Dan eva Evenor, Most Sovereign Healer of Atlantis, reached for Poseidon. Deflecting his anger as best she could, she murmured gentle words in an attempt to soothe, and freeing him from his own garments, welcomed him into her. She did her best to keep her own thoughts from plummeting in despair; she prepared her heart to accept the resulting child with love and something akin to joy. Alone in her thoughts, Kai-Dan allowed herself the ghost of a smile. *Now, our future is truly assured.*

# CHAPTER

*26*

ATLAS'S TWENTY-FIRST BIRTHING day came and went without the slightest acknowledgement.

The chasm that had opened between father and son was a highly disturbing development to the people of Atlantis. They were unsure as to how they should relate to Poseidon's son. As of yet, no one knew the true extent of Atlas's powers. It was well known that he had surpassed all his father's expectations during his five years of study. As the time approached when he would assume the mantle of power, the young man had been relentless in his preparation.

However, since the explosive proclamation that Atlas would no longer inherit the position to which he had been born, Poseidon had not seen fit to designate anyone else "Bearer of the Heavens and the Earth," and the people of Atlantis were extremely uncomfortable with this particular outcome.

Atlas had refused to go back to the house for anything. He didn't want to see his mother. His heart was broken, and he only retained enough strength to take care of himself—he did not have the strength to comfort her.

He kept the small room he had shared with Alia and, as commanded, secured a laborer's job on the docks. Each morning, when the sun winked over the horizon, he rose quickly and made his way to the harbor. Back-breaking manual labor was the only way he could stop thinking about Alia. Rather than worry about her safety, he steeped himself in the hatred he held toward his father. With every heft of every sack and every step spent balancing gangplanks, the hate that simmered just under the surface drove him like a mad dog.

Secretly, he was pleased to be working near the sea. The lowly status of a dock worker suited his needs perfectly. Atlas was determined that if there was a way out of Atlantis, it would be as a stowaway onboard one of the many ships that sailed into harbor. He stayed alert and bided his time. He would be ready to take his chance when it was presented.

The devastation Poseidon had unleashed because of Atlas's betrayal was enough to terrify all of Atlantis. Every citizen down to the smallest child knew that Poseidon could easily have ripped their lands apart. Partially because of their god's furious display, and partially because of the chance that father and son could have another, deeper rift that would cause a worse cataclysm, people started meeting in small groups in order to explore alternatives.

Kai-Dan had even more reason for concern than the people of Atlantis. In her vast memories, she had never known a god to react in such a manner. It was evident that Poseidon had to make an example of his son. However, that his anger had severely impacted the whole of Atlantis made her fear that, should another confrontation occur between the two men, it would be for the last time, and no one would be safe from the tempest that their rampant feelings engendered.

Chosen as Atlantis's Most Sovereign Healer because of her gift of foresight, Kai-Dan had foreseen the future on many occasions and had guided her people with steady assurance through good times and bad.

At present, Kai-Dan wasn't too worried about Poseidon's sudden and unexpected return. It was public knowledge that their irascible god had ascended Mount Olympus, and rumors arrived daily, rife with tales of his drunken escapades. When a god was in a black mood, it was known that no maid within or without Olympus was safe. And Poseidon was on a terror; he was plowing seeds into every maiden within hailing distance and people feared that once he was done in Olympus, their daughters would be next. Kai-Dan kept her own experience to herself. She knew she was with child, but at the moment, she had other, more pressing concerns.

Atlanteans went about their lives cautiously, always keeping one eye toward Olympus in watchful anticipation and the other eye on their unmarried daughters. Not that anyone could have done anything to deter Poseidon's desires. Chaperones were in high demand, as they helped ensure peace of mind for the single females of Atlantis. Nevertheless, citizens were restive, on guard, and ready to hide their daughters should Poseidon be distracted from Olympus.

Because of the harsh sentence Poseidon had meted out to his son, Kai-Dan was fearful that once their god was through with his self-flagellation and returned to Atlantis, anything that could go wrong would go horribly wrong should he and Atlas meet again.

While Atlas kept his head down and continued to work hard, his lodgings, along with the work expected of him, made his life barely livable. Kai-Dan observed the long, hard hours the young man worked, and she was troubled that he never spoke to anyone.

Atlas had become a slow burning fire, and it was obvious to her that he was working toward a wild blow. If father and son became involved in another confrontation, no one would be safe anywhere. Kai-Dan concluded that she had to try and bring a measure of discipline back to her people. She needed to structure a plan that, should things once again get out of hand, would provide a contingency for her people. A contingency that, she hoped with all her heart, would not be needed.

Kai-Dan discussed her feelings with her twin sister, Kalli-Dan, and found that they were of like mind. It was not a matter of *would* Poseidon's passions erupt again … it was simply a question of *when*.

Kai-Dan sent a thought-form to all the healers throughout the land, calling for an urgent meeting to convene in two days' time. Because of the unusual nature of her request, healers immediately left their homes and traveled to Atlantis. Anxious to learn the reason they had been summoned so precipitously, the healers hurried to arrive at the appointed time.

When the two days had passed, Kai-Dan, sequestered inside the Temple of Poseidon, called the meeting to order. Women quickly took their seats and waited for their leader to speak.

Standing in their midst, Kai-Dan projected a radiant calm that she did not feel. Although she was of an incredibly advanced age, she held herself like a much younger woman and commanded great respect among all the healers. Even Zeus had heeded her counsel on occasion. In robes glistening white as the petals of a narcissus, she was a vision. Her long, white hair tumbled down her back in soft waves, and she moved with quiet dignity as she looked over the gathering and smiled at the upturned, expectant faces of her sisters.

"Thank you for coming at such short notice. Were it not of utmost importance, I would have spoken to you through our thoughts. However, I felt it necessary to address each of you in a meeting well hidden from prying eyes, to ensure that there are no misunderstandings regarding the critical nature of the subject I am broaching." She gazed at the healers and appreciated their rapt attention. "In essence, I am in need of your thoughts, your guidance, and your ideas." She paused for questions, but no one interrupted. All were waiting to hear the reason they had been called. Kalli-Dan motioned for her sister to continue.

"I know that we are mindful of the horrible ramifications visited upon Atlantis because of Poseidon's wrath toward his son. What you might not expect is that, should these men go for each other's throats again, all of Atlantis will be teetering on the brink of extinction." Kai-Dan heard sharp murmurs ripple through the crowd. The healers' unease was clear, and their fear spurred Kai-Dan to come to the point. "It is my thought that if their anger is once again unleashed, we need a plan in place that will give the most people the highest chance of survival." When no one said anything, Kai-Dan narrowed her eyes. "It is interesting that not one of you seems surprised at my last statement."

Esmer, a venerable healer from an outlying province stood, stepped forward, and bowed deeply, then addressed the Most Sovereign Healer. "Kai-Dan, my honored sister, I carry the distinction of being the oldest healer in our midst. My memories extend even further than do yours. It is by virtue of those memories that I am compelled to agree with your logic. To acknowledge that the anger of this particular god could cause catastrophic destruction to Atlantis is not emphasizing the danger enough. In my mind, we are hanging by a thread—a thread that could easily snap under the threat of Poseidon's wrath becoming ungovernable. The vagaries of Poseidon's mercurial moods imperils not only Atlas but the people and lands of Atlantis."

The gravity of Esmer's words served to underscore Kai-Dan's reason for meeting. No one stirred, anxious to hear what else she had to share. Esmer stepped next to Kai-Dan, seeking her support. Kai-Dan merely gestured for her to continue. Esmer licked her lips nervously and cleared her throat. "It is said that one picture conveys more than a host of words. I will share with you one of the memories I have retained." Esmer glanced at Kai-Dan. The healer nodded. Esmer eyed the women seated around the room. "You will witness the complete destruction of a civilization somewhere in another part of the world. I am not privy to the details of why the destruction occurred—suffice to say that it happened because of an issue that arose between a god and a human."

The healer then closed her eyes, an indication that everyone else should do the same. Esmer opened her mind, and the vicious scenes she had witnessed as a young woman unfolded in the minds of those in attendance.

Beneath the shadow of a sleeping volcano, an unnamed city thrived. Though not nearly as advanced a civilization as Atlantis, the city still bustled with life, and it was obvious the population was expansive, with many people living in close proximity.

The scene focused on a towering volcano that stirred, showing signs of life. A bit of gray smoke exited the top of the mountain. The smoke thickened, turning black as pitch, then lava started to spew into the air and drip down the steep mountainside.

The side of the mountain nearest the city and its unsuspecting inhabitants suddenly bulged outward, and in one massive explosion, the entire mountaintop blew into the stratosphere. A plume of rock and lava shot into the sky, climbing to such great heights that no bird could follow.

The healers felt the wrath of the god that had caused this catastrophe. Watching in alarm, a dark cloud engulfed what was left of the mountain then shifted to race down the sides of the vomiting volcano. The poisonous vapor descended with such rapidity that nothing living could get clear of its terrible path.

The cloud smothered the city in a thick blanket of gray and black, immediately snuffing the life out of everything. Wherever the huge cloud rolled, nothing moved in its wake. And still more was to come; lava gushed from the volcano's mouth with more force and more fury than anything the women had ever witnessed. The lava flow was so deep that the city was entirely engulfed. Nothing remained; there was no sign that anyone or anything had ever lived there. The people and their city had been utterly destroyed, and not a single trace of their lives remained to prove that they had once existed.

An audible sigh of sadness swept through the room as the horrific scenes ended. Once the healers' distress subsided and the terrible scenes had drifted back into their memories, everyone started talking at once. Some women broke out in tears, so great was their anguish.

Kai-Dan held up her arms, requesting quiet. When the women had once again settled, she stepped forward. "Not one of us has ever faced a time of danger like we have just witnessed. But know this: we are alive at the whim of the gods, and we are facing the high probability of a major catastrophe such as the one we just saw. I do not have any answers, nor do I have a clear idea of what we can do to avoid such a fate. Therefore, I open the discussion to you. Any suggestions, opinions, or ideas are welcome."

Kai-Dan fell silent and studied the women present. Most of the healers remained still, although others fidgeted in discomfort. But it was obvious that the healers were as perplexed as Kai-Dan as to what could be done. She was about to give up hope when her sister came forward.

Kalli-Dan timidly asked, "What about the possibility of digging into the heart of the mountain just outside of the city? If we could create an underground tunnel, just possibly, the granite would be strong enough to hold against the calamitous anger of a vengeful god."

Around the room, a look of dismay flitted over the concerned faces of the women, and from somewhere in the back, one of the healers ventured a question. "Who here knows about constructing such a thing? And really, what good would a tunnel be against the type of destruction Kai-Dan is suggesting?"

Someone else broke in, "Maybe we should leave Atlantis." Another thought was presented, "If we request an audience with Zeus, maybe he could talk some sense into Poseidon."

Other ideas and opinions were bandied about, but none of them made much sense. After giving everyone a chance to speak, Kai-Dan took charge again. "To answer some of your queries, it could take years to obtain an audience with Zeus. He is as mercurial, if not more so, than his brother. We would do ourselves and Atlantis a great disservice to hope that a single meeting with Zeus could solve a threat to our very existence." She glanced at her sister. "Kalli's tunnel idea holds merit, and it is certainly worth more consideration before we discount it entirely." Searching her mind for any deep tunneling that had been conducted within the bounds of Atlantis, Kai-Dan couldn't think of anything other than the small tunnels that had been built to supply water or eliminate waste. Those tunnels were pitifully small compared to what would be needed to house a frightened population.

Kai-Dan did not want anyone to feel complacent about the necessity of coming up with a workable idea, and soon. "By virtue of foresight, I tell you this! Poseidon and Atlas will have another clash. I do not know the exact hour when this will take place. I can only say that the next argument between them will be our undoing. It is imperative we start preparing immediately. A tunnel seems to be the only option we can think of, so let us find the person to help. It is our only chance of surviving the coming catastrophe."

Everyone jumped up and crowded around Kai-Dan. She held her arms up once again and waited for calm. "I caution you, as you make your way home, speak only to people you trust implicitly. We must find someone with the ability and the knowledge of tunnel excavation. We need a tunnel on a massive scale that will be able to house up to a thousand people." She looked over the sad faces awaiting her next words. Her admiration for each healer was immense. She knew they would not fail in their assigned task. "We need people who are willing to work night and day to make this happen. We have no time to lose."

She shook her head, sorrow pervading her soul. "Our only hope is that Poseidon remain in Olympus for as long as possible. Upon his return, the havoc we just witnessed will be nothing compared to what will be. So, I implore you to leave quietly. Do your research quickly and thoroughly. Time is of the essence; do not waste one precious moment."

In unison, the women bowed before Kai-Dan and signed a heartfelt goodbye. The meeting was adjourned.

# CHAPTER
## 27

THE HEALERS FLOWED out over the land like the tributaries of a massive river, their mission clear; it was crucial that they find someone who had a vast knowledge of tunnel construction and could create what was needed as soon as was humanly possible.

Each day that slipped by without locating this person of import kept the healers on edge and their search frantic. But it wasn't until a seemingly unlucky accident occurred at Ranol's tunnels that the pieces fell into place.

It came about during a practice dig when a large stone, unnoticed by either Heedrow or Ranol, fell, landing with a heavy thud on top of Heedrow. The stone caused a deep laceration to open, spilling copious amounts of blood over Ranol and the tunnel floor. Neither Ranol nor Mellor could staunch the bleeding, so they sent a thought-form to the nearest healer, who happened to be Kalli-Dan.

When Kalli-Dan received the frantic request, she was shocked to learn that Ranol, a master tunneler, practically lived under her nose. Accompanied by Kai-Dan, the sisters excitedly rushed to Ranol's home.

Kalli-Dan tended to Heedrow's wound while Kai-Dan questioned Ranol. The spry man humbly related his experience. "I have helped design and dredge every harbor in Atlantis. And though most of the tunnels now in use were devised by me, I reached a point in my life where it was no longer necessary to work." He gazed at Mellor and smiled. "By virtue of everything I have done, Mellor suggested I open a school." He laughed at the thought. "I believe she was worried that I would be bored with nothing to do every day and that I would become a bother."

Kai-Dan looked knowingly at Mellor and smiled. "How many students do you generally take on?"

Ranol pointed to Heedrow with great pride. "I have had many students pass through my doors; however, Heedrow has surpassed every expectation I could possibly have for anyone. Quite simply, this young man is without parallel; he is my prized pupil. I have never met anyone with more talent or more vision than Heedrow."

It was all Kai-Dan could do to keep from sobbing with relief. "How far along is Heedrow in his apprenticeship?"

Ranol scratched his beard, looking at Heedrow. "Well, his mother brought him to us after his sixteenth birthing day, and that was about five years ago." The master shook his head, frowning. "Come to think of it, his time is almost up."

"Just how are his skills?" Kalli-Dan had finished with her healing, and Heedrow's head was as good as it had ever been.

Blinking with awe, Ranol shook his head and offered a small whistle. "His skills are second to none. He surpassed my abilities so quickly that now it is all I can do to keep up with him!"

Kalli-Dan patted Heedrow and glanced at her sister. "May Kai-Dan and I have a word with you?"

The small man motioned for Heedrow. The lad jumped out of his seat and quickly went to his master's side. "Heedrow, continue what we were working on earlier, and once the ladies take their leave, I will rejoin you."

Heedrow nodded once, thanked Kalli-Dan for healing his wound, and then grabbed an apple from a huge bowl filled with fruit. Throwing the apple up and down, he happily headed back to a world he thought of as his playground.

Leading the healers into the sitting room, Ranol gestured for them to make themselves comfortable. "My wife is preparing refreshment. We cannot thank you enough for your visit. Heedrow has become like our own son."

Kai-Dan smiled. "I can understand the bond. He is an eager young man, and it is apparent that he thinks of you as a father." She leaned forward, all seriousness. "Ranol, the timing of our meeting is quite auspicious. You are a master tunnel maker and Atlantis is in dire need of your skills in ways heretofore unimagined."

She stopped as Mellor came in bearing a tray of tea and small cakes. Once Mellor had finished serving everyone, she took a seat next to her husband. "Please, continue. Ranol and I have no secrets, and I have a feeling that a visit by two of our most distinguished healers does not bode well."

"Mellor, my sister and I are sorry to meet you and Ranol under the present circumstances. However, you are perceptive. Our presence today brings bad tidings." She gazed helplessly at the master tunneler. "There is no one else that we can turn to." Then, Kai-Dan looked at her sister. "Kalli will share with you the reason for our visit."

Kalli-Dan looked terribly uncomfortable. She smoothed the rumples in her robe and took a sip of the hot tea in an effort to gather her thoughts. She didn't want to scare Ranol and Mellor, but she had to impress upon them the sense of impending doom she shared with Kai-Dan.

The healer told the couple everything up to and including the frantic search that had been undertaken in order to find a person of Ranol's caliber. At length, she set her cup back on the table and finished, "Kai-Dan and I envision an underground sanctuary. A place that will provide a strong enough shelter for the time when Poseidon and his son entertain another clash, for, make no mistake, they will precipitate the destruction of Atlantis."

Kai-Dan could see the questions forming in Ranol's mind. "Ranol, the only solution that seems feasible is the construction of a massive tunnel that could contain up to a thousand people. What we need to know is, is this idea even attainable?"

The man rubbed his bushy white eyebrows, grabbed an unlit pipe, and sucked on it thoughtfully. "This tunnel … how deep do you need it to be? And the completion date—how soon would we need to finish?"

Kalli broke in. "Depth is something that needs to be discussed. The date is set in stone. We must have the tunnel readied to house people, goods, and supplies before the sixth month mark. Master Ranol, there is no compromise in this regard."

Ranol considered the task they had placed before him. He rubbed his head, staring off into the distance as he absentmindedly sucked on his pipe. Once he had examined everything to his satisfaction, he took Mellor's hand. "I believe it could be done within the time constraints you have mentioned."

Kalli-Dan looked bemused, but before the healers could celebrate too quickly, Ranol cleared his throat. "The problem is men. How do we find enough diggers to work the hours necessary to complete your tunnel? Heedrow and I will share the helm, but I think we will need your help in securing workers." Before the women could speak, Ranol held up his hand. "With enough people, Heedrow and I can finish your tunnel in the required time, barring any difficulties."

An immense weight was lifted from the healers, and Kai-Dan flashed a thought-form to the others. *"Cease your search ... Kalli-Dan has found the men who can build our tunnel ... and we are assured it can be built in time!"*

"How soon can you and Heedrow start?" Kai-Dan knew she was pushing, but she had no choice.

Ranol peered at Kalli-Dan. "Well, I would say as soon as his healer says he is ready."

Kalli-Dan released a breath. "He will be ready tomorrow; he just needs to rest tonight."

Ranol nodded. "Do either of you know where this tunnel is to be started?"

At that question, both women knew they were completely out of their element. Kalli-Dan shrugged. "We lean on your expertise. We were hoping you might have an idea where the largest granite deposit is. When you determine that, then that is where the tunnel needs to be constructed. We will rely entirely upon the strength of the granite and hope that it will be enough for the tunnels to hold."

Ranol took Kalli's hand and patted it. "Do not worry. I already know where we will start. If you and Kai-Dan can send out a request, I will send a thought-form to the men I have used in the past. Together, we should be able to get enough workers for this project."

Kai-Dan and her sister rose and prepared to leave. Escorting them to the front entrance, Ranol addressed an obvious concern. "How am I to pay these men?"

Kai-Dan smiled. "The healers will take care of that problem. That is nothing you need worry yourself about."

Outside on the porch, the healers said their goodbyes to Ranol and Mellor. "We will be here at first light. Until tomorrow, then?"

Ranol's eyes twinkled with the excitement of the challenge. "Until tomorrow!"

# CHAPTER

## 22

URING A BRIEF lull in the chaos, Ni-Cio stood before one of the many Atlantean processors. He had been scouring different texts for the past two hours, and his eyes were protesting. Just as he was about to close everything down, he happened upon a small, critical piece of information that helped shed some light on what was happening to Evan. The article referenced "empathetic healing" and it stated unequivocally that the event was a rarity. Throughout recorded time, it was known to have taken place only once before, and then only because conditions were right for all parties concerned.

"Whatever that means," Ni-Cio muttered as he continued to scan the article. He blinked several times and sighed. Sending a thought-form to Kyla, he asked her to join him at her earliest chance.

*"I will finish this feeding and then I will come ..."*

Ni-Cio sighed and backed away from the 3-D image. "My friend, you are definitely empathetic towards your father and Daria or we would not be in this situation."

A tone sounded, and Kyla entered the research rooms. "Ni-Cio, what is it that you need? I have to be ready with Evan's next meal."

Ni-Cio grabbed her arm and led her to the article he had found. "Read this and tell me your thoughts."

Kyla took her time, then slowly looked at her brother. "This could explain everything. If it does, we are walking a metaphorical tightrope."

Ni-Cio was confused. "What do you mean?"

Kyla pointed at the piece she had just read. "If I am understanding correctly, the energy Evan is expending is tremendous … as we have witnessed. If what he is going through does not resolve itself soon, he will not be able to continue."

"That is not an option, Kyla." Ni-Cio swiped the hair back from his face. "We cannot hurry this process; we must let this play out in the only time frame allowed us, the time frame that is unfolding with Travlor's life. Unless Evan is able to continue until this situation resolves itself, you and I stand to lose everyone we love. So, whatever we can do, we must do."

"Ni-Cio, what are you proposing? I am already doing all I know to sustain a healer through a healing. If you have any suggestions, tell me. I am more afraid of losing Evan than anything. What more can I possibly do?"

Ni-Cio looked at his sister beseechingly. "It is up to us to find a way to make it easier for Evan. We must work together to try different things than have been tried before. Are there some different foods that will help enhance his abilities or his strength?"

Kyla looked forlorn. "If there are, I am not aware of them."

He took Kyla's hand. "Take heart, I will continue my research. If I was able to find this obscure article, there have to be others. I will do what I can to glean any information that could help us. In the meantime, if you and your helpers could try food variations, you might happen on something that could work."

She sighed, but nodded.

Ni-Cio rubbed his neck and paced the room. "It is odd that Evan is privy to a replay of Travlor's life. Odder still, I feel it is critical to allow the time Evan needs to reach a conclusion." He looked at Kyla. "There is a reason all this is happening now; we just have to find out what that reason is and be ready to give Evan the time to finish it."

# CHAPTER

*29*

THE NEXT DAY rose bright and beautiful and warm. A small breeze rustled the trees, and the sun looked down on a determined group of men. Ranol had just finished addressing the workers that counted about three hundred. Of varying sizes and strengths, they were eager to work and ready to follow direction.

Ranol and Heedrow stood side by side. While Heedrow towered over his small master, Ranol made it clear that Heedrow was their boss. "Understand, Heedrow's word is law, and if anyone doubts that, then they can find work elsewhere."

Between the two of them, they had found the perfect starting point. Situated far enough outside the city that the excavations wouldn't disturb the citizens, the site was positioned on a plateau on the side of an enormous granite mountain. Ranol had commissioned tents, including a huge mess tent, to be erected so that they could house all the workers. Kitchen staff was already preparing breakfast and would be on hand to provide the meals necessary for such a large crew. Ranol and Heedrow made the camp as comfortable as possible so that the men could stagger their work schedules. In this manner, the work would never cease, and the digging could proceed around the clock. Kai-Dan had been adamant regarding the paramount importance of speed. Her insistence that time was of the essence was all anyone needed. Everyone was there to work and work hard until the project was complete, or the unthinkable had come to pass.

Ranol had promised Kai-Dan that he wouldn't share the reason for the tunneling with anyone except the men he and Heedrow took into his charge. These, he swore to secrecy: "Not even your wives must know the reason you stay at the site. You signed on for the duration that it takes to finish the project. No breaks, no home visits, nothing. You are here to create an underground world in as little time as humanly possible. Unless someone is grievously hurt in an accident, there will be no leave until the job is finished to Heedrow's and my satisfaction." A few groans were heard among the throng. Ranol held up his hand. "I explained everything before you signed on. If any of you wishes to leave, do so now; otherwise, I do not expect to hear any more grumbling."

Most of the men suspected the reason they were there was because of the tensions between Poseidon and Atlas, however, once Ranol told them what he had learned from Kai-Dan, all of them were anxious to begin the project. Hardly anyone in Atlantis felt safe while blood continued to boil between the father and son. Armed with crystals and highly advanced earth moving equipment, they were shown where to start and how to start. Heedrow initiated the first cuts and positioned the teams where he needed them. Cautioning all of them, he stared at the ground and, counting his fingers, mumbled, "One: start slow, tunneling is fun. Two: speed up when you are ready. Three: no accidents … ask questions." He scrunched his brow and thought hard for a moment, then remembered. "Oh, four: when Master Ranol sounds the horn that means lunch." Heedrow finally looked up, blinking hard. "Master Ranol said, 'No breaks until I signal lunch.'" Shyly, he added, "But if you need to go" —he pointed at a small rise— "just behind that rise."

Heedrow searched his mind for anything else he was supposed to say, but he couldn't think of anything. He nodded at Ranol, who sounded a horn. As one, the men turned to face the mountain and began. The project was underway.

Once the entire area had taken on the look of a large hole in the ground, Ranol took a break. Lifting himself from the cave mouth, the older man stood and stretched his aching back. As he was about to turn around and join the others, he was surprised to see a long line of women climbing toward the campsite. All of them were bearing food or wine. Kai-Dan's thoughts reached out to Ranol as she moved to join him. *"I have sent thought-forms to women who are willing to work under cover in order to help provide sustenance for the workers ..."*

Ranol's appreciation was evident as he answered. *"You have thought of everything ... your underground home will proceed at pace ... barring unforeseen events, and maintaining tight schedules, we will finish on time ..."*

Kai-Dan moved from the shadows to stand next to the master. She allowed herself the ghost of a smile before she spoke. "Our time is critical; my sister and I will be close at hand for anything you might need. However, the healers will take turns staying in camp. Two healers will be stationed here at all times in case any accidents occur. Our men must be well taken care of, so Kalli-Dan and I have agreed that one of us will also be here throughout the duration."

Ranol's eyes misted over. He glanced at Kai-Dan and bowed his head, hands in prayer pose against his heart. "I am grateful for all that you, Kalli-Dan, and the other healers are doing. Your presence eternally buoys people's spirits, and these men are no exception." As Kalli-Dan crested the path to the excavation site with her sister healers, Ranol excused himself, a wide smile splitting his face. "Tunneling beckons." Kai-Dan nodded, then turned to await her sister.

When Kalli-Dan reached her side, they unconsciously reached for each other's hands as Kalli-Dan sent a thought-form to her sisters. *"The mess tent is there ... divest yourselves of your burdens, then meet us at the benches ..."*

The women did as requested while Kai-Dan and Kalli-Dan watched the initial steps towards the completion of their desperate plan. Kalli-Dan looked at her sister. "Do you really believe this will work?"

Kai-Dan shook her head, then hugged her sister as she whispered, "It has to work. A mass exodus of Atlantis is an impossibility. We are out of ideas and we are running out of time."

"Why are you trying to keep this secret?"

Kai-Dan kissed her sister's cheek, released her hold, and sighed. "Poseidon is in a highly volatile state, and I fear if he were to find out, he would destroy our efforts and then create such an impregnable wall around our city that no one would have a chance to escape Atlantis."

Kalli-Dan followed her sister to a gathering of benches that had been placed in shady spots further up the mountain. An unhindered view of Atlantis spread out below them, and together, the sisters sat under the pine branches, enjoying a quiet moment and basking in the view of their beloved city.

Kai-Dan finally broke the silence. "We have to find out who is willing to follow us into this underground mountain home."

She swallowed hard before she looked at Kalli-Dan. "I am afraid that a good many people will think we have lost our senses. This type of excavation has never been attempted, and many Atlanteans will laugh once they find out what we are doing." She looked out over the camp. "I want the men to get their bearings and work in peace before the word gets out. Once our secret is out, we shall see who believes us and who does not."

"But your gift of foreknowledge … it should be reason enough to sway people." Kalli-Dan halted suddenly, frowned, then continued, "I understand what you are saying, and truth be told, it is hard for even me to believe that you have seen the destruction of Atlantis." She took Kai-Dan's hand once more. "I promise to be very careful during my search. I will be diligent and I will select our families with great care." Then, cocking her head with a quizzical look, "Do you truly think if there is to be that much fallout from Poseidon's wrath"—she turned, pointing at the hole— "that this will work?"

Kai-Dan looked ineffably sad. She leaned forward, weary to her bones, resting her hands on her knees. Her white hair fell like a veil over her face, and her voice came low and soft as she intoned, "There are no other options. I know it will happen. I just hope we have the time in which to prepare. If we do not, and the conflict comes prior to that, then there is no reason to worry. We will just have to enjoy the time left to us."

She stood and pulled her sister next to her. Staring deeply into Kalli-Dan's shining blue eyes, Kai-Dan put the weight of certainty behind her last words. "As we are standing next to each other"—she glanced down, raising their clasped hands— "and your hand is wrapped in mine, the complete annihilation of Atlantis as we know it is at hand."

# CHAPTER

*30*

THE MEN HAD found their stride and digging ratcheted up to a breakneck pace, so it wasn't long before the winding tunnels and separate caves took on significant shapes and began resembling a home, albeit underground. Kai-Dan continually marveled at how deep and how spread out the tunnels were becoming. They wound through the mountain to its very heart, where, to the worker's unexpected delight, a much-needed water source was discovered. Although Heedrow and Ranol had hoped for such an outcome and had sent the drillers in the general direction they believed the water source to be, they were just as ecstatic to find a sparkling-clear, fresh water lake spanning the length of an enormous cavern.

To Kai-Dan's untrained eye, the separate rooms for families, rooms for eating, and rooms for gathering looked substantial. With each of her tours, the feeling of permanence became more pronounced, and she could feel the strength of the caves in their curved walls and domed ceilings. She was heartened to see that, through the intense efforts of everyone involved, and

Heedrow's extraordinary vision, the sanctuary was developing into a truly well supplied underground city.

Nevertheless, time slid by more rapidly than she anticipated. During her visits touring the tunnels and caves, she found it difficult to accept Heedrow's need to inject such beauty in the excavations. She could see that the young man was creating a city that almost rivaled Atlantis; she felt that his time was better spent on the project as a whole.

She had become frustrated by the minute attention to detail that Heedrow brought to his work. Kai-Dan wanted to tell the young maestro that he was wasting precious time with his carvings, his ideas for meandering streams, and his artistry. She knew the Atlanteans who agreed to go underground in an attempt to survive the onslaught were either going to live through the catastrophe or they wouldn't.

However, today, winding through the tunnels and trailing her hands over the creamy smoothness of the granite walls, watching the carvings come to life beneath the play of light and dark, a deep sense of peace descended over her. Carefully studying the intricate details present throughout the entire structure, she realized that the artistry Heedrow was creating would give the survivors a much-needed respite from their ordeal. The beauty gracing the new Atlantis would help take their minds off their perilous plight and provide a sense of joy and peace to help color their days.

Deep in thought, she approached Heedrow.

The boy-man started as he looked up from his work and stood quickly when he realized the Most Sovereign Healer waited to address him. He swiped at his clothing, trying to remove some of the dust and dirt, but all he managed to do was shower Kai-Dan with cave detritus. The healer held up a hand to forestall his apology. "Your work is exquisite. The survivors may have to live in this world for a very long time."

She took Heedrow's hand and, noticing that it was shaking, held it gently, letting the truth of her words fill with warmth. "I was not certain that so much artwork was necessary. However, I have come to realize that the beauty you are creating is just as important to their wellbeing as the air and water and food they need to sustain themselves."

Heedrow was at a loss. Uncomfortable with such high praise, he stuttered a tenuous thanks, then bowed his head as he felt the blood rise to his cheeks. "Most Sovereign Healer," was all he managed to utter.

Kai-Dan felt his timidity as well as his nervousness. She squeezed his hand, then let it drop. "I am honored to have known you and your work. I do not believe you will ever grasp the depth and breadth of your contribution."

Heedrow nodded dully, still avoiding her eyes. "Please, continue. I will not keep you any longer." Before she left, she imparted one last thought. "Atlantis will forever be in your debt."

Kai-Dan turned away and ascended from tunnels to attend other duties. As Most Sovereign Healer, her responsibilities did not bend toward healing—enough healers had volunteered to spend time at the campsite that she knew the workers were well tended to. No, her time leaned more toward leadership. She had to be sure that everything was functioning well, transcendences happened without problems, and that her healers, themselves, were kept in excellent health.

She oversaw the placement of highly powered crystal processors. To protect the delicate crystal tablets, she had the men secure them in the very heart of the mountain. She fervently hoped that the tablets would withstand the sinking. She knew that someday, their ability to adapt and learn would provide a way for her people to leave their underground habitat.

Under Kai-Dan's guidance, Kalli-Dan had located one thousand people courageous enough to enter the sanctuary city. Banding together, they had been bringing supplies and personal items to the site for several months. They placed everything in the massive storage rooms, and began to develop survivor mindsets. They no longer questioned the final outcome; they silenced their fears and followed their instincts. Handcarts, pushcarts, and wagons drawn by sturdy workhorses dragged furnishings, clothing, artwork, and supplies up the winding path. No one wanted to be without a reminder or some comfort of their lives before the impending devastation.

Kai-Dan stood, surveying the alternate groups bringing in more supplies, and she knew it was time. One last facet of her plan needed urgent attention. She issued a thought-form to Kalli-Dan. *"Meet me at our favorite spot ... there are things we must discuss ..."*

The reply was immediate. *"I will be there ..."*

Kai-Dan left the site and descended the mountain quickly. Making her way to the harbor, she saw Kalli-Dan waiting for her. She paused a moment. Kalli was alone, seated on a clear, crystal bench. Kai-Dan studied the sight of her lovely sister as a balmy sea-breeze ran playful fingers through her long, white tresses and stirred her silken robes. Her sister was beautiful, and Kai-Dan loved her more than anyone she had ever known. Tears threatened. The conversation she was about to have would not be easy. She dreaded it almost as much as she dreaded their looming future.

Kalli had spotted her, so Kai-Dan raised her hand and waved. She took a steadying breath and squared her shoulders. Pasting a smile on her face, she hurriedly approached her sister.

"You are late!" Kalli-Dan teased. "Or maybe you are just slowing down with your advanced age!"

Kai-Dan tried to laugh, but nothing would come. Kalli-Dan sensed her mood immediately. "Is something wrong? Why are you so serious?"

Kai-Dan sat down next to Kalli. "You must listen to what I am about to tell you without interruption. What I share with you has to stay between us. No one else must ever know. Do you understand?"

A look of profound puzzlement crossed Kalli-Dan's beguiling features. However, she didn't venture any questions. She nodded her acquiescence as she reached for her sister's hand. "I promise."

"It is as I thought: most of Atlantis does not believe Poseidon is capable of destroying the city that he created. The small band of people that are with us only number the one thousand that I had originally foreseen." She glanced sideways at her sister. "While that does not reassure me, it does bring another question to bear …" She wistfully scanned the thriving harbor, stalling for time before she announced her plan. Kalli-Dan waited quietly, building up her courage to hear what her sister had to share. At length, Kai-Dan continued. "Only one of us can go into the tunnel, and it will not be I."

Kalli-Dan gasped and dropped her sister's hand. Springing to her feet, she immediately broke her promise. "*What?* By all the gods that ever lived, what are you saying? What could possibly make you think I would go anywhere without you?"

Kai-Dan stood up and grabbed her sister by her shoulders. Frantically, she brought her into a desperate embrace and eased Kalli back onto the bench. She faced her sister, stroking her cheek in an attempt to soothe. Kalli pushed her hand away and started to rise again, but Kai-Dan pulled her down. "Listen to me! I do not know if the tunnels will hold. While the entire excavation seems strong enough to me, I have not been given any foreknowledge as to the aftermath. Because of my inability to discern the outcome, I am terrified that the tunnels will not hold and that no one will survive." She ran her gaze over the gentle waves that lapped at the harbor pilings. "I feel so strongly about this next statement that you have to know that it comes from a source other than myself." She took several deep breaths. "Kalli, sister of my heart, I have been guided to this decision."

Kalli-Dan was scared; instinctively, she knew she was not going to like what Kai was about to propose. "Poseidon's thunder, what is it that you are being led to do?"

"One of us must go out into the world." Her words blasted into Kalli's heart with the force of a tidal wave.

"No, we cannot be separated! We have to be together." Kalli-Dan looked about wildly, her mind searching for any alternative that would rescue her from this terrible news. She glimpsed the desperation in her sister's eyes and clenched her jaws to keep from screaming. Lips barely moving, she uttered, "I cannot be without you! We were to transcend together!"

Kai-Dan didn't know how to make the idea any more palatable ... to either of them. So, she pursed her lips, straightened her spine, and issued a well-used platitude as calmly as possible. "Kalli, you know as well as I do that we will always be together."

"But outside the borders of Atlantis, the chance of survival is minimal at best. Conditions are too harsh, and the people outside have not progressed. They are all—" She hesitated, trying to find the right words until she cried out, "They are all barbarians!"

Kai-Dan had recognized that Kalli would be anxious about this latest news, but she hadn't counted on her becoming frantic. Older by only a few minutes, Kai-Dan stiffened her resolve and hardened her face. "It is a chance we must take. I have no knowledge or sense as to whether the tunnels will hold, but hear me when I tell you that, one way or another, some remnant of Atlantis must survive. Kalli, we have to try. Can you understand that?"

Kalli-Dan nodded her head reluctantly. Her decision made, she presented her counter offer: "Very well—then *I* will be the one to leave Atlantis."

That very statement brought tears to Kai-Dan's eyes. She refused to wipe them away, instead letting them trail over her cheeks and fall from her chin like rain. She bowed her head, feeling the moisture build up in the folds of her gown. She whispered, "I knew you would say that." She sniffled and swiped at her nose, then looked up, smiling ruefully. "Your generosity and your warm heart are just two of the things I love about you. But it has to be me. It is the only thing that makes sense. We must split up in order to give our people a real chance. One of us must go into the tunnel and one of us must go into the world." Kalli-Dan raised a hand to object, but Kai-Dan rushed on. "Do not think that I have reached this decision lightly. I have thought about this long and hard. You will go into the tunnel pretending that you are me. Otherwise, I think the small following will lose faith and balk at going down into the caves at the last moment." She exhaled a long sorrowful sigh. Again, she questioned whether or not she had the strength to continue.

But she pressed on. "Our people will need the strength of 'Kai-Dan' and her leadership to help them through this tragedy."

The anguish on her sister's face said everything. "The reason I must go out into the world is to give our healing line an infinitesimal chance of continuing. I cannot tell you why I feel this is so important and so necessary, but it is." She slid her hand back into her sister's and, placing her other hand beneath Kalli-Dan's chin, lifted her face. Kai-Dan kissed each of her cheeks, then leaned into her, placing her forehead next to Kalli's. "You have to trust me once more."

Kalli-Dan's eyes filled with tears. It was too painful to speak, and she couldn't get a word past the lump filling her throat like a boulder.

Kai-Dan hugged Kalli-Dan with all her strength. Holding tight, she murmured, "Oh, my beloved sister, if I could think of any other way to avoid our separation, I would do it in a heartbeat. However, it has to be done this way. The healing line must continue, and our small band of survivors must be given their chance for continuance as well. Can you see this?"

Kalli-Dan swiped her eyes and nodded despairingly. She felt the weight of the world had just plummeted onto her shoulders. "If you say it must be so, then I offer no other argument." She took a shaky breath, and persisted, unable to keep the pleading tone from her voice, "I still do not understand why I have go into the tunnel rather than you. Your reasoning is thin."

Kai-Dan's tears coursed down her face, and her chin trembled. She finally reached for the hem of her garment and swiped her eyes. She coughed to clear her throat and, in a voice filled with agony, said, "Because you will not survive outside, and I know, without doubt, that I will."

Hearts breaking, they fell into each other's embrace. For them, the end of the world had arrived. Slowly rocking back and forth, they tried to comfort each other. However, every time the realization came that, they would never again see each other, touch each other, or hold each other in this lifetime, their sobs grew stronger, their shoulders shook harder, and their breathing came in trembling gulps.

They knew that, from this moment, there would never be any more comfort for either of them.

# CHAPTER

## 31

TLAS PUSHED HIMSELF harder than any of the other dock workers. His anger grew with every beat of his heart until a day came when he no longer felt he had a heart. It felt dead. He found no joy in anything or anyone. Up early and staying late, he put his back into loading and unloading the ships. He spoke to no one, and when orders were issued, he never questioned why; he put his head down and completed the job, no matter how menial or demeaning. The first to arrive and the last to leave, the solitary life he chose dwindled into a repetitious path of endless gray: home, work, seething anger, work, home.

Mentally, he acknowledged the loss of his beloved; however, his heart no longer ached for Alia's touch, the sound of her voice, or the merest sight of her beautiful face. Beneath the weight of his relentless anger, his heart marinated in a curdled soup of black silence. Every cell in his body, every thought waiting to be examined, every breath he drew, focused on one thing only: destroy the man who destroyed him.

With each passing day, the iniquities he suffered only served to worsen his fury, driving it deeper until it sickened his soul.

The more his strength increased, the more insidious his rage became until it seemed to exude from his pores. Men stood aside wherever he walked and people assiduously avoided him, especially when he was alone and in his cups.

He toyed with escape, but he had witnessed others trying to stow away. To him, it seemed that the secreted escapees were always hopeful of a voyage to adventure, but he found to his dismay that they were always discovered. Once that happened, the consequences were horrific. Sea captains didn't want any misunderstandings as to who held absolute authority over life and death aboard ship. More than once, the body of a keel-hauled stowaway, no matter the age, floated back to the docks—bloated, stripped of skin, with chunks of body parts missing, or worse, eaten. It made Atlas think twice about trying to escape, yet he never stopped looking for his opportunity. There had to be a way.

Drinking had never held any allure for him, as it had never been a pastime that he particularly enjoyed. Now, it was his only pastime. Unfortunately, the drinking exacerbated his slow, angry boil and, if possible, made him meaner. Surrounding patrons never knew from one moment to the next what would set him off. Imagined slights provoked him into lashing out, and even when heated disagreements had nothing to do with him, Atlas's hair-trigger temper provided the muscle to turn any drunken brawl into a free-for-all.

His welcome was worn out from one end of Atlantis to the other. Even the seediest bars closed their doors to him, the owners tired of having to mend broken furniture, broken bottles, and broken bodies. Even though Atlas always paid for any damage, it no longer mattered. No one wanted him in their establishments—least of all the patrons.

Nevertheless, one drunken night, he stumbled into Atlantis's oldest bar, situated in one of the loneliest spots on one of the oldest, most decrepit wharfs hugging the Atlantean seacoast.

For Atlas, drinking and fighting was his only release. He bedded no women, for he barely acknowledged their existence. He never even attempted to see his own mother. The only news he wanted was of Poseidon, and for that, he kept his ears attuned to any rumor no matter how vile. When he heard that the old man was drunk off his ass and running after all manner of women, men, goats, and donkeys, he felt a twisting in his guts like a smirk of vindication. His only ambition, and the only thing that interested him, lay in finding a way to hurt his sire as much as he had been hurt.

He slammed another empty beer glass on the table and looked over the derelicts who had drifted in for the night. Some of the usual customers warmed their usual seats, but there were also some new faces that he had never seen before. To his bleary eyes, they looked ripe for the picking, and as he swiped his mouth with the back of his hand, he decided he was ready for a fight. Somebody would challenge him in this group.

Atlas stood up, noisily shoving his chair back against the wall. The sudden crash of wood startled men from their ruminations. The noise level plunged as people looked up to see a huge man, muscles bulging, rabid and ready to fight. But nobody wanted any trouble. Suddenly, everyone's drinks became highly interesting. Avoiding eye contact, people stared into their glasses with intense interest.

Bleary-eyed, Atlas snarled, "No takers, you bunch of sheep?" Staggering outside, he stared down the people gathered on the porch. No one moved, and most of them held their breath, hoping he would just leave. "Buncha sheep," he muttered before he stepped off the porch and into the gathering night. Atlas rubbed his face and decided he needed to be a whole lot drunker.

He lurched away and found his feet taking him to the main harbor. A cool breeze rose off the water and dried the sweat on his brow. As beautiful and serene as the night was, Atlas took no notice of the alluring beauty surrounding him. His anger had started to wane a bit when a younger man, clearly drunk, pushed away from the railing and ran into him.

Atlas shoved the man out of his way and growled, "Watch where you are going!"

The youth, secure in his own physical prowess, decided Atlas was worth a round or two. At once, to Atlas's surprise, he was suddenly staring up at the young man from a splayed, seated position. When he realized that he had been pushed, he bellowed like an enraged bull. Springing to his feet, he lowered his head and charged. His plan involved something akin to wrapping his arms around the bare torso with enough momentum to crash through the railing, taking both of them into the water below. However, the youth had other ideas. Faster than Atlas could react, the young man easily sidestepped his onslaught, and as Atlas passed by, the youth brought both fists down on the back of his neck.

Surprised, but not close to being cowed, Atlas spun about and charged again. His arms were spread wide, and he pushed his legs like a stampeding stallion. Again, he never came close to touching the youth. The younger man executed a quick, one-footed pivot and planted his other foot into his opponent's face. Atlas staggered back to a seated position. Rubbing his jaw, mouth open, he blinked hard and focused on the challenger. "What moves do you make?"

A lopsided grin played over the youth's face, and he offered a hand to help Atlas up. "It is a miniscule glimpse into the *Cabala of Ares*."

Atlas rolled his eyes and rubbed his neck. "Ares, eh? The god of war? Who taught you this technique?" The fight had gone out of Atlas, but his curiosity was peaked.

Once the young man decided that he no longer needed to prove himself, his demeanor changed at once. He sidled up to Atlas and shared his secret. "I was taught by Ares himself."

Atlas couldn't believe what he had just heard. No one had seen the god of war in ages. It had even been rumored that he had passed into other realms. Although the rumor had never been confirmed, it certainly was never refuted by his appearance in Atlantis.

Atlas shook himself and crossed over to the still intact railing. He hoisted himself to the top bar and gazed at the youth. "Where did Ares teach you this?"

Joining Atlas, the young man leaned against the railing and, as casually as if he were ordering another beer, announced, "He taught me at my home."

Atlas was tired of the evasiveness, and he didn't like that the youth seemed to enjoy the question game a bit too much. "Alright, I am prepared to hear your story … however, I am not prepared to ask a lot of questions to get there. Are you going to tell me or not?"

The boy looked at him and smiled. "With an offer of some type of payment … like a drink … I could be persuaded."

Atlas laughed—he had forgotten how good it felt. "Fine, I will buy you that drink, but you must tell me the full story. Deal?" He held his hand out.

The youth grabbed it and shook heartily. "Deal."

Leaving the harbor, Atlas led him back to the bar he had just deserted. Seating themselves on the porch, away from the other patrons, they made themselves comfortable. Once their order had been placed, the young man leaned into Atlas conspiratorially. "My name is Tereus. I am a son of Ares."

Atlas sat back and snorted. "You are joking, yes? Everyone knows that Ares never took a lifemate."

Tereus crossed his arms and sat back as the tired bartender delivered their beers. "Do you think the man was celibate?"

Atlas laughed at the absurdity of that thought. "So, who was your mother, one of the goddesses?"

Tereus laughed and shook his head. "No. I am like you; my mother worked for a living. She was the eldest daughter of an unimportant king who ruled somewhere outside of Athens."

"Why have I never heard of you?"

The youth swigged his beer and sighed with contentment. "Ah, that goes down easily." He looked at Atlas and quirked an eyebrow. "I have been away for a very long time."

"And what brings you back now?" Atlas couldn't help himself; he was intrigued.

Tereus shrugged. "I have traveled far from Atlantis, and I have met some interesting people, learned some incredible things, but I find that I am road weary. I think it might be time to find a woman to take as a lifemate and have some quarreling offspring."

Atlas was jealous of Tereus's unfurling future. He drained his beer in one swallow, slammed the glass on the table, and bellowed for another round. As he waited for their order, he studied the young man. "You do not know how lucky you are. Have you spent much time with your father?"

With a quick shake of his head, Tereus looked disgusted. "No. I wanted to, but you know how fickle the gods are. I seemed always an afterthought. In retrospect, I am happy he took the time to teach me to fight. Otherwise, I probably would not have survived my travels. The world is populated by some very unevolved types, making it difficult to even relate to them as people. I meted out some of the more extreme techniques I learned."

"This … technique, is it something you could teach to others?"

The young man thought for a moment. Searching his mind, he saw no reason he couldn't share what he had learned. "I believe so. Why, do you want me to teach you?"

Atlas nodded slowly. "My father never taught anything like that. It was assumed I would inherit the position he had mandated for me, so it was not necessary to learn how to fight." He furrowed his brow. "I will say I learned a lot of divine skills, and while I suppose I could use those talents in a fight, I would rather not have to."

Their second round of drinks arrived.

"Finally! Here is our order." Atlas sent a scathing look toward the bartender making the man leave quickly and quietly. Atlas glanced back at Tereus. "If you teach me what you know, I will pay you well."

The young man raised his face to the sky and smiled. "It is always nice to be employed." He held out his hand and Atlas took it with gusto. "You have a deal, but I warn you, it will not be easy."

"I think we have much to teach each other." Atlas and Tereus clinked mugs and drank deeply. Another round was ordered and the deal was sealed. Atlas smirked inwardly and thought, *This night holds promise. Beware, Father.*

# CHAPTER
## 32

OGERT SILENTLY ENTERED Ni-Cio's quarters and carefully studied his friends. The only sounds stirring the tepid air were the soft healing tones falling from Evan's lips. Enshrouded in gloom, Ni-Cio sat next to the bed, holding Daria's hand while Evan continued his healing efforts.

From what Rogert observed, their leader looked drained. He knew that he had hardly left Daria's side, and though Kyla prepared food almost every hour on the hour for Evan's and her brother's nourishment, he was shocked by Ni-Cio's appearance. It looked as if he hadn't eaten in days. His eyes were ringed by deep circles and spoke of his exhaustion, and, most shocking, his physical stature seemed shrunken, somehow … diminished.

He was deeply concerned for Ni-Cio's health. Rogert realized the news he carried would do nothing to alleviate the stress weighing upon their leader's fatigued shoulders.

He started to back out of the room when Ni-Cio listlessly raised his eyes and impaled him with a dark look. Their leader's eyes burned deep purple, as though he raged with fever. He acknowledged his stalwart friend and quietly encouraged him. "What is it Rogert?" Rogert cleared his throat nervously, hesitating. Ni-Cio urged, "You would not have come unless it was serious. Tell me."

Rogert crossed to Ni-Cio's side. Pulling a chair with him, he sat next to the weary leader. He glanced at Evan; the comparisons were starkly evident. Evan looked fairly rested. Though his eyes were closed, Rogert could see that his breathing was regular, and he still held Travlor's and Daria's hands clasped tightly in his. His voice, soft though it was, was strong and unwavering in its tonality.

Rogert shifted uncomfortably in his seat and plucked at his bioskin. Finally, he barged ahead: "The world situation is strikingly grave."

"Go on." Ni-Cio placed Daria's hand back by her side and leaned forward to hear the rest.

"The lack of news of the 'Savior's' plight is causing anarchy to break out. The media, world governments, and the general population are losing patience for want of an announcement regarding the health of their religious leader." Rogert shook his head. Even with his taciturn nature, it was hard for him to believe the world teetered yet again on the brink of disaster. Their respite had not lasted nearly long enough. "I fear that if we do not release some kind of reassurance, the powers that be will again edge toward a nuclear solution, simply because people are frantic and getting out of control."

Ni-Cio pushed his hair back from his face and straightened up, stretching his aching back. "Then that is what we must give them." Glancing at Evan, Ni-Cio continued, "When Kyla returns, I will inform Evan of these recent developments so that he can give us an idea of what we need to say."

Rogert sighed. "Can he not awaken Daria so that she can supplement his healing?"

Ni-Cio closed his sore eyes and yawned. Standing up, he signaled Rogert to accompany him out into the hallway. He led his friend from the room and waited as the door materialized behind them, then turned back to Rogert. "Daria, our baby, Travlor, and Evan are all tied together somehow. There is nothing anyone can do until Evan either completes his healing or …" Ni-Cio refused to give voice to the alternative. "Their fates are intertwined, so the only thing Evan can do is keep them in stasis until Travlor is through reviewing or reliving his life. Once that is done, we do not know what will happen."

Nodding thoughtfully, Rogert considered their predicament. He furrowed his brow and cocked his head to one side as the spark of an idea fueled a startling thought. "I probably do not know whereof I speak, but has it occurred to you that even in stasis, the energy from Daria and your baby might be assisting Evan in some manner?"

A light dawned in Ni-Cio's violet eyes and a small smile strayed over his lips. "I had not even considered that possibility." Looking up with something akin to excitement, he pressed, "Rogert! That might be exactly what is taking place." He slapped his friend on one muscled shoulder. "By the gods, that is an intriguing thought. Why, I even find my appetite stimulated. Come, we will examine your suggestion further, but while we do, I need some food. Let us accost the kitchens and throw ourselves on their mercy."

The energy surge from Ni-Cio was heartening to witness. Rogert readily accepted the invitation. "Come, my friend, it is past time for you to renew your resources."

Together, they hurried to catch Kyla before she brought the next tray to Evan. "Rogert, you have given me pause for hope. It is possible that my beloved's condition is not as dire as I anticipated."

# CHAPTER
## 33

THE FIFTH MONTH of excavations appeared ominously on Ranol's calendar, but the work was proceeding better than either Heedrow or Ranol had expected. The crew, now well versed in their duties, suffered few accidents after the first cave-in two months back.

It had been due to a judgement in error, in technique, and in patience; a worker, hollowing out one of the tunnel branches, had had his mind focused on lunch rather than the job at hand. He'd wanted to get to the mess tent rather than allow the crystal laser to proceed at the designated pace. Carelessly, he'd rushed the task, and the laser light had glanced off a rock wall that was not part of the outline he was supposed to follow. The cave-in happened so suddenly that he had not been able to get away.

The resounding crash of soil and rocks falling to earth brought men running from every direction. Digging frantically to clear the rubble, Kalli-Dan was immediately summoned.

When the men finally dragged their co-worker from beneath the granite, he was a mess. Torn and bleeding profusely, he was unconscious, but his heartbeat was slow and steady. On their way to the healing tent, Kalli-Dan and her sister healer, Lanias, met the men as they emerged from the opening. Following on either side of the carrier, they initiated the healing rites immediately.

Although the injured worker healed properly and suffered no residual effects, the poor man had determined that he was suddenly very claustrophobic. He never wanted to go back under the earth again, and consequently, he'd left the site as soon as he was able. Another Atlantean had quickly volunteered to replace him, and the digging continued unabated. Since that time, there had been few, if any, mishaps.

Heedrow was deeply moved by Kai-Dan's appreciation of the home that was evolving; he drove himself even harder. The self-contained habitat that he and Ranol were creating became the embodiment of all of Heedrow's dreams. Kai-Dan's sincere appreciation of his efforts emboldened him to broaden the spectrum of his initial vision.

Without consulting Ranol, Heedrow took it upon himself to search out local artists willing to enter the tunnels and create immense murals, statuary, and tile work that stretched throughout the project. The smoother walls became canvases, granite boulders became works of art, and tiled rooms of surpassing beauty emerged from the hollowed-out earth. Heedrow encouraged all of his artisans to follow their hearts. The artwork that materialized exceeded even Heedrow's expectations. He was so thrilled by the outcome that he enlisted the aid of Atlantis's most renowned water workers.

Specialized aquatic engineers, working closely with Heedrow, introduced plans for a water system that utilized water from the underground lake. Heedrow insisted their designs provide a deep sense of normalcy and peace. He wanted to give the survivors a place to rest and relax in an environment that resembled home as much as humanly possible. Because of Heedrow's ingenuity and his own dogged persistence, the engineers worked long, hard hours to reproduce his vision. Once Heedrow approved their final plans, workers set about bringing to life the amazing water features that eventually wound throughout every part of the cave system.

It wasn't long before trickling rivulets, rain pools, quiet ponds, and babbling streams appeared. Water flowed gently over life-like waterfalls and wound lazily through almost every part of the new Atlantis.

To Heedrow's unending delight, his designs mimicked nature so remarkably and so well that he knew, one day soon, the survivors would forget that everything was man-made.

When the waterways were complete, Heedrow ordered every type of plant flourishing throughout Atlantis to be brought in. The new Atlantis became its own lush and flowering paradise.

With Heedrow's unstinting supervision, the evolution of his sanctuary moved forward rapidly. Even the workers, stepping back to study their work, gazed in unending awe at the beauty Heedrow had brought to bear. The underground mazes reflected topside life so well that, at times, the men were hard pressed to remember it was their work that had brought Heedrow's dreams into reality. It seemed that the new Atlantis had always been there, just like the old Atlantis. With the design concepts that Heedrow continued to introduce, many of the workers became so comfortable underground that they never wanted to go topside again.

By degrees, everyone, including Ranol, started coming to Heedrow for advice. It seemed that the young man entertained an endless supply of patience. He never rushed an explanation, always taking time to ensure that his suggestions were completely understood before allowing any digging to continue. It didn't take long before Heedrow had complete control of every aspect of the project.

Ranol was so proud of his student that, even though it was redundant to recognize his incredible achievements, he and Mellor invited all the workers to attend a short ceremony one starry night, honoring Heedrow as Master of Design and Excavation.

Shyly acknowledging the resounding applause and admiration the workers showered on him, Heedrow tried to stay for the beer and the company, but he was extremely uncomfortable in social settings. Never having developed a feel for small talk or gatherings of any kind, he finally slipped away from the party and gratefully descended into his deserted underground sanctuary. For the first time since the digging commenced, he let himself wander at will, lost in the grandeur of his creation.

So it was, on the eve of the fifth month, the search for people intrepid enough or adventurous enough or willing enough to follow Kai-Dan into the tunnels ended. Some families accepting Kalli-Dan's offer came from among the workers already employed at the dig site. No longer wary of Kai-Dan's reasons for creating such a place, and comfortable in the underground environs, they didn't hesitate to volunteer as possible survivors. Although some of their families followed reluctantly—whether because they didn't believe that Atlantis would ever be destroyed or whether they were somewhat claustrophobic—no one questioned their reasons as long as they came. So, people were chosen from every walk of life, chosen for their requisite skills. It was the only way Kalli-Dan could elevate their chances of survival. But, while everyone was made welcome, the healers made certain that each person understood that if they became uncomfortable for any reason or developed a stronger sense of claustrophobia, their departure would not be questioned, and no one would prevent them from leaving.

After the initial phase was complete, families poured into the new Atlantis. Bringing food, supplies, personal belongings, clothes, and memories, some even opted to stay on site. As individual living quarters were completed, many of the families were encouraged to create their own sense of personal space. Kai-Dan and her sister agreed that their survivors needed to feel as comfortable and safe as possible.

Heedrow and Ranol required the survivors to learn, in concentrated depth, how to run the systems keeping the new Atlantis viable. It was Heedrow's thought that until more advanced technology could be discovered, the use of crystals for light and energy would suffice. However, as he walked along the tunnels one night, Heedrow experienced an epiphany. There was a possibility of capturing the energy from an Atlantean's transcendence and converting it into sustainable energy for the underground habitat. Although Poseidon had introduced that particular gift ages ago, when he'd initially created Atlantis, Heedrow was completely baffled how to go about copying his model. But the thought of a perpetual energy supply was such an exciting challenge that he could hardly wait to pursue his idea further.

So, along with everything else he was doing, Heedrow kept copious notes, recounting in great detail all the ideas and suggestions that could possibly help run future technology and elevate the living standards of his beloved city.

Heedrow considered the new Atlantis his own home and treated it as such. He was well aware of the reason for the initial excavation. So, as hard as it was for him, one dark night, as he sat under a secluded copse of trees gazing at the stars, he came to the conclusion that he did not want to live in his under-earth city.

Fueled by a deep desire to keep his mother safe, he determined that when the time came, he would make his way home and take his mom as far away from Atlantis as possible. He had no doubt that something terrible was going to come to pass. Every day, he felt the approaching cataclysm in his heart and in his bones, and every problem that arose reminded him that the time he had allotted to get his mother out of Atlantis was dwindling. However, his loyalty and determination were such that the thought of abandoning his post and fleeing to help his mother never occurred to him. Until the work was completed to his satisfaction, he never even considered that he had any other place to go.

Once he'd made his decision, he greeted each day with joy and new dreams and ideas for bettering his design. He never tired; he never ceased his writing. He appropriated a little used room. It was his thought to supplement the interior to withstand the very worst he could imagine. To that end, he oversaw the construction, and when it was complete, he moved his copious notes and journals into the space.

When he finished moving all his writings and plans to the room he considered his "library," he led Kai-Dan down through the tunnels until they could proceed no further. Standing before the fortified door, he said, "This is a special room." Then he opened the door and they stepped inside. He pointed to the shelves bearing his plans, journals, diaries, and hurriedly scribbled ideas. Nervously clearing his throat, he tried and failed to meet Kai-Dan's gaze. Finally, addressing the ground, he mumbled, "This place is not meant for others." He pulled a journal from one of the stacks and showed Kai-Dan. "For you."

Carefully taking the book from Heedrow's grasp, she flipped through the pages, gasping at the breadth of the young man's vision. "Heedrow!"

Immediately, Heedrow felt the blood rush to his face, and his hands trembled. Afraid that she had misunderstood, he tried to explain, but Kai-Dan held up one hand as she continued to peruse the compilation. Finally, she replaced the book on the shelf from where Heedrow had retrieved it and looked at the veritable child standing next to her.

"Heedrow, the repository of ideas you have gathered in this one room is almost impossible to fathom." She ran her hands over the other tomes. "You have made it possible for the survivors to continue to learn and grow, and the sense of continuity you are providing is nothing less than miraculous!"

Heedrow quit shaking so hard and glanced at the healer from beneath thick eyebrows. He grinned unabashedly and nodded, then resumed his watchful fascination with the floor. Kai-Dan hadn't expected much of a response from the shy young man, but when nothing else was forthcoming, she realized that Heedrow had reached the limit of his capacity to address her. Quietly, they made their way back to the surface.

It had come to Heedrow's attention that more and more people were beginning to venture out to the excavation site. Some Atlanteans watched in silent wonder, while others jeered at the workers and at the people bringing supplies.

As he and Kai-Dan greeted the sun, Heedrow watched a man approach the healer.

The man exuded a particular air of distain and disbelief. He blocked their passage and issued a challenge. "Why are you encouraging this? People are scared because of you! All you need to consider is that Poseidon is our supreme god and he would never destroy Atlantis—why, it is the pinnacle of his creation! You are wrong, healer, and you should put a stop to this madness!"

Heedrow couldn't believe his ears. He tried to insert himself between the man and Kai-Dan, but she stopped him with a gentle hand on his arm. Gazing at the interloper with wise eyes and a heart full of understanding, Kai-Dan tried to reassure him. "You are Cosimo, yes?" The man huffed and nodded. Kai-Dan continued, "I know your family, and I have healed some of them. I am very fond of your delightful daughter, Nia."

Cosimo frowned, because he had no idea where this was going. "Yes, I appreciate your efforts on their behalf. However, that does nothing to erase the fear you have brought into the community. You need to stop."

Kai-Dan shook her head. "Cosimo, you have yet to see the wonders beneath this earth. Would you join me in a tour?"

The man scowled and shook his head. "I refuse to go anywhere near that cave."

"Then it is my suggestion that you let everyone continue their task, and cease causing disruption. You are free to ignore my warning. However, you must let others come to their own conclusions. Cosimo, this is entirely out of your hands. It is my heartfelt desire that you reach a different, choice." Stepping around the man, she and Heedrow continued on.

"Most Sovereign Healer," Heedrow ventured, "why are people not taking this more seriously?"

Looking steadily at Heedrow, she took both his hands in hers. "Heedrow, do not concern yourself with the doubters; they have their own paths to follow. But I must share something with you that can go no further than the two of us."

Kai-Dan considered the bashful young man, who was patiently waiting to hear her words. She considered him Atlantis's preeminent protector. However, as self-effacing as he was, she knew that he didn't view himself in that light. He remained blissfully unaware of the monumental effect his efforts had on the future of Atlantis. Searching for a way to repay his efforts, when the approaching date had been made known to her, she had been presented a solution. That had been the moment she had known what she must do.

Baffled, Heedrow bided his time. At last, Kai-Dan spoke.

"I know the day of the coming event." She studied the young man, but he remained silent. "Heedrow, look at me." The young master raised his gaze with difficulty. "My warning is for you and only you. Do you understand?"

Heedrow nodded solemnly, then Kai-Dan continued. "I share my knowledge with you because it is my gift to you." She hesitated for a heartbeat. "You must have the new Atlantis finished, and you must be prepared to leave in four weeks' time." She heard the anxious intake of his breath, so she hurried on, "Before you leave, I must caution you that the new Atlantis will sink, and it will sink further than I had previously thought. I have seen water everywhere. Therefore, it is imperative that you construct more than one interior barrier. You must do everything in your power to strengthen the initial barricade, but also to add more barriers and make certain they are airtight as well as watertight."

Heedrow didn't move a muscle, but his thoughts ran rampant. Quickly calculating the time needed to erect the barricades the Most Sovereign Healer needed, he determined that it could be done. He anxiously looked up and said simply, "I will."

Kai-Dan couldn't help herself; she grinned. As kindly as she could, she broached her other concern. "Heedrow, while I appreciate the artistry you have brought to the new Atlantis, it is time to cease those efforts. Time grows too short for anything other than your best efforts for survival."

The young lad looked at her with his soulful eyes and mumbled, "Beauty can help remind people what they have to live for."

Kai-Dan stared in wonder at the young man. "It would seem that you are wise beyond your years, and you are quite right. I will say no more. Do as you will, and may the gods watch over you and speed your efforts."

She took a moment to appreciate the serenity surrounding them. Spread out below, the splendor of Atlantis shone like an array of fine jewels, glorious in its majesty. Kai-Dan's heart squeezed. She refused to contemplate a life without Kalli-Dan, but she couldn't help acknowledging how much she was going to miss her life in Atlantis.

Drawing her robes around her swelling belly, she forced herself to finish what she had come to say. "Heedrow, you are to go to your mother as soon as possible and leave Atlantis." A plaintive tone crept into her voice when she saw the fear rise in Heedrow's eyes. "You must promise me that you will leave no later than four weeks from this day."

She could barely hear Heedrow's reply, but his face reflected immense sorrow as he nodded his agreement. "I hear, Most Sovereign Healer." He stuttered a bit, then managed, "Thank you for your gift. I will be ready in" —he held up four digits— "four weeks. I will help Mama leave."

"Heedrow, hear me. If you have a chance to leave well before that time, you must take it. You and your mother have to get as far away from Atlantis as possible."

Heedrow nodded once more, then dropped his hands. She could tell that he needed to get back to his work. Satisfied that she had done all she could, she gathered her robes. Before she left, another thought occurred to her. "Heedrow."

Startled that the healer had more to say, he halted.

"When you are ready, you will take me with you."

The new Master of Design and Excavation studied the sky for a brief time, then looked directly at Kai-Dan. Summoning all his courage, he took both of her hands again and gently squeezed before he let them drop. "I understand, Most Sovereign Healer. I will be ready sooner than four weeks, because the new Atlantis will be ready and you will come with me and Mama."

Leaving Kai-Dan, Heedrow gave thanks for a good day of building and quickly reentered the caves. He briskly walked the same path he had unveiled to the healer until he came to his library. A heavy sigh swirled up from Heedrow's chest; he felt as though he might cry. He didn't want Atlantis to be destroyed, but he didn't doubt what the healer had told him.

A fevered determination washed over him, and he pushed all thoughts that dealt with anything other than work aside. Extracting his most current journal, he took a seat at the desk. He scribbled as fast as his thoughts emerged; he annotated in great length how Atlanteans could take advantage of a never-ending supply of energy. He entitled his thoughts: *Transcendence Can Supply Energy for New Atlantis.*

Kai-Dan watched as the young man disappeared back into the caves, marveling that she and Kalli had found such a person. Rousing herself, she quickly departed to look after more problems. She couldn't believe how much needed to be finished before …

She chided herself. *Quit wasting time. Worrying helps nothing.* Making her way off the mountain, she considered her future traveling companion and spoke to the child growing inside her. *Combining efforts will either increase our chances of survival or it will ensure our demise. Stay with me, little one; we have far to go.*

# CHAPTER
## 34

# Σαντορινι Τοδαψ

EU NEWS ASSOCIATION
SANTORINI, GREECE

## SAVIOR ALIVE TEETERS BETWEEN LIFE AND DEATH!!!

SURROUNDED IN SECRECY AND SECLUSION, THIS REPORTER HAS LEARNED THAT THE NEW SAVIOR HAS BEEN HOSPITALIZED IN A PRIVATE COMPOUND ON THE ISLAND OF SANTORINI, GREECE. ONE OF THE MEN RESPONSIBLE FOR HIS CARE, DECLINING TO BE IDENTIFIED, STATED, "WE ARE DOING EVERYTHING WE CAN. TEAMS OF PEOPLE ARE WITH HIM AROUND THE CLOCK AND WHILE THE WORST OF THE TRAUMA HAS BEEN STABILIZED, HIS PROGNOSIS REMAINS GUARDED."

WHILE THE SAVIOR STRUGGLES TO RETURN FROM THE BRINK OF DEATH, THE WORLD WAITS, HOLDING ITS COLLECTIVE BREATH. PRAYER VIGILS ARE BEING CONDUCTED AROUND THE WORLD AND FOLLOWERS ARE REFUSING TO EAT UNTIL THEIR SAVIOR RETURNS. HIS FOLLOWERS REMAIN STEADFAST IN THEIR BELIEF THAT A MIRACLE WILL OCCUR AND THEIR SAVIOR WILL RETURN HEALED AND IN FULL HEALTH.

# The Washington Crier

Associated Press Bureau, Washington

*FLASH...FLASH...FLASH*

## Tempers Flare Between Believers and Non-believers!

As the world waits for news of the Savior's condition, tempers ignite around the globe. In nearly every country around the world fighting rages between followers and non-believers. Referred to by the Savior's church as 'Heretics,' world governments struggle to control the anarchy sweeping through towns, villages and major cities.

Cities in crisis are demanding the government step in to help quell the violence. To date, the total number of deaths related to the spreading violence numbers in the hundreds of thousands. Hospitals and emergency services are taxed beyond capacity.

The President of the United States has placed the entire country in a state of emergency and has called on the National Guard in towns across the states to mobilize.

China's war machine has been met with deadly force as determined resistance continues to rise throughout the country.

The European Union and NATO are doing everything possible to contain the violence overtaking Europe. There is speculation that unless the anarchy can be contained, governments will once again activate the nuclear option, only this time the target will be its own citizens!

# CHAPTER
## 35

POSEIDON, STANDING NAKED before a full-length mirror, studied himself. Overweight, knots of hair matted to one cheek, and eyes the color of blood … he yawned, scratched himself, and mumbled, "By Zeus, I disgust even myself!" He swiped at a trail of drool trickling down the side of his mouth. "Maybe it is time to end this crazed debauchery."

Bleary-eyed, he glanced at the immense bed. Covers and pillows were ripped and strewn everywhere, but that wasn't what startled him. No, he was shocked at how low he had actually stooped. He rubbed his aching eyes to make certain that what he was seeing was actually there and alive.

Staring back at him through slitted eyes, the thing defied description. Part animal, part human, part reptile … Poseidon decided he didn't want to dwell on last night's events. Never one for introspection or regrets, he bellowed a command. His man servant appeared almost instantaneously. "Get that thing out of here and make ready the baths! I want the water next to boiling, and bring a flacon of watered wine. It is time to clean up."

The servant, utilizing a supreme effort of will, hid his deep revulsion for his god's choice of bed partner and manhandled the beast towards the door. However, before he could depart, Poseidon fell back onto the bed, demanding, "And bring plenty of food. I am starving."

The servant bowed hastily and, dragging the beast behind him, left to fulfill his god's commands.

Poseidon pushed himself up and dragged a heavy golden bowl from the side table. It was filled with cold, clear water, and gardenia petals floated on the surface, permeating the air with their enticing scent. Splashing the liquid on his face, Poseidon let the droplets run over his hair and beard, washing away the worst of the night's choices.

"By the beard of my own brother, what was I thinking?" He chuckled as he continued to douse himself with the refreshing liquid. He couldn't imagine what had gone through his mind, but he could care less. His thinking was fuzzy, but he seemed to remember seeking comfort from all kinds, in all sorts of ways. But the reality was that no matter what he tried, or how much drink he washed down his gullet, he had been sadly disappointed at every turn. Nothing had worked. His heart hurt, and although he didn't even want to admit it to himself, he felt a twinge of guilt.

He was still reeling from the fact that his human wife had had the temerity to kick him out of her bedroom. No one—god or human—had ever treated him that way before.

He reached for the linen he knew was on the table, but when he couldn't find it, he gave up and used a portion of the sheets to dry his face and hair. He sat hunched over, head pounding, and relived the terrible scene between Clieto and him. "Ah, woman, if you only knew how close I came!"

Poseidon may not have cared to examine his motives, but he knew himself well. He had left Clieto's presence before his anger had driven him to do something that he would regret forever. He had come so close to smiting her that he had frightened himself. "Wife, you were much safer with my absence than you will ever know."

It was no secret where he had gone. Olympus was the playground of the gods; it was where they retired when they grew weary of toying with their humans. Overtired of Clieto's and Atlas's stubborn ways and their ridiculous weaknesses, Poseidon had been glad to be rid of the lot of them. Once he had ascended to his luxurious realm in the clouds, he'd drowned his anger in an ocean of liquor and gratefully sank his seed into one woman after another. At last, growing tired of everyone, he had dismissed them all.

He ran his hands through his hair and rubbed his pounding temples. Remorse coursed through him when he realized that he had sunk lower than he ever had in his long lifetime. He wasn't proud of his actions, but he certainly didn't feel the need to apologize to anyone … most of all Clieto.

Dimly, he blinked at the sun and determined that he had been away from Clieto for long enough. A sufficient amount of time had passed, and she should be thankful upon his return. He searched his memory and calculated that he had been gone from her side for the better part of five and a half months. "Too long." Muttering to himself, he stood and went to the window, thrusting the coverings aside. "Damn you, woman, I miss you. I miss everything about you."

He sighed deeply and looked up as his servant entered, signaling that his bath was readied. He followed the diminutive figure through the connecting rooms and into a room billowing with warm steam. Lowering himself into the scalding water he lay against the tiled edge and let his mind drift.

Eventually, his thoughts circled back to his son. "I can only imagine what you are doing." He thought about their last meeting and his ire started to crest again. "I must stop this train of thought." Shutting his mind to the existence of Atlas, he picked up the bottle left by his man and took a long swig. The garnet liquid washed down his throat. When he felt the warmth slide down to his belly, he lay back, enjoying the slight glow. It would take a while to rid himself of the stench of his depravity, but he would be prepared to rejoin his wife very soon.

It was then that the rumblings started. Barely noticeable, people went about their daily lives blissfully unaware of the miniscule tremors. In Atlantis, rumors immediately swirled through the citizenry.

"Poseidon awakes."

"Beware! Our god returns soon."

"Where is Atlas? He should be told."

Although relieved to know their god was ending his self-imposed exile, the citizens were still uneasy and unsure of the state of his mind upon his return.

Heedrow and Ranol, always existing in a state of heightened awareness, stared at each other as the first tremor snaked beneath their feet. They had been discussing the need for one more airlock—they ceased their discussion and waited for the vibration to subside. Ranol spoke first. "It seems we have reached our time limit, my friend."

Heedrow nodded sadly. "No more doors."

Ranol agreed. "No more doors." He glanced at the plans and pointed. "The doors we have will be sufficient." He looked at the young man. "They will hold."

Heedrow was confident that they had done the best they could, but he was still scared. He did not want his creation to fail. He knew in his heart that he would feel responsible if anything happened to the people willing to take their chances in the underground habitat. And even with the reassurances of Kai-Dan and Ranol, he could not accept the thought that people might die trapped in a design of his own making. He shuddered. "I will pack."

Atlas had heard the rumors preceding his father's impending return, and though he had thought that he never wanted to lay eyes on the Olympian deity again, he had since changed his mind. Tereus had taught him so many new fighting techniques that Atlas decided he was ready to face his father once more.

He had managed to reign in his anger as he studied under Tereus, but when the rumors began, he decided that he was spoiling to even the score. He was ready to test the methods from the *Cabala of Ares* in the only way he knew how.

While Atlas was aware of the deep tunnel construction and he admired the tenacity with which the diggings continued, he never considered joining the small band of people who had chosen to live in the underground caverns. He couldn't imagine what would prompt him to adopt their survivor mentality.

Ironically, during one of his workout sessions, he had admitted to Tereus, "I imagine that the first time my father and I traded words encouraged the dig. But Tereus, this time will be different." He pivoted and blocked the blow he had known was coming. "He will not see me coming until he is on the ground looking up at me."

Tereus aimed a well-timed kick and caught Atlas broadside. "Do not let your ego take hold." He finished with a sweep to Alta's knees, dropping him to the ground. "No one gets the better of a god. You would do well to let it rest." He held out a hand to help Atlas back to his feet.

Atlas didn't respond, but his soul clamored to avenge the banishment of his beloved Alia. Though he had been hoping for some word as to her plight, he had been thwarted at every turn. It was as if his father had placed him back inside a solitary cell. No one offered any news of her whereabouts; consequently, he never knew whether she had survived her pregnancy to live and raise their son or had succumbed somewhere, alone, abandoned, and afraid.

And so, his heart, his soul, and his mind raged on. Bounding up without Tereus's help, Atlas executed the twenty-fifth form perfectly and took Tereus to the ground. Then he stood and offered a hand to his companion.

Tereus brushed himself off and slapped Atlas on his shoulder. "Excellent! There is little more that I can teach you; you have come farther than I thought possible."

Atlas beamed, but before he could comment, Tereus hurried on. Shading his eyes from the bright sun, Tereus squinted at his friend. "However, unless you learn to control your anger, you will have missed the most important lesson Ares teaches us."

Atlas stared at Tereus, but the young man's wise words never registered. The sole obsession lodged in his heart and his mind grew like a cancer that pervaded both his waking and sleeping hours.

As he took his leave of Tereus and walked toward the docks for another day of work, he repeated the words that had become his mantra. *I will teach my father a lesson or I will die trying.*

KAI-DAN STOOD BEFORE her sister while Hee-drow waited quietly in the background. The twins had run out of words, and neither knew what to say or do in this last moment of their shared lives.

Kai-Dan refused to cry; they had done all they could and were out of time. With no other recourse open to them, and the survival of her sister and the Atlanteans being of tantamount importance, any other concerns faded into silence.

She held her arms out and Kalli-Dan, still weeping, fell into them with a terrible sob. "How can I live without you? I am losing half of myself."

Kai-Dan felt exactly the same. "We will stay conjoined in thought until the event. Should the outcome favor you, and I find out that you have survived the cataclysm, we will cease all communication." Holding Kalli at arm's length, she peered into her eyes. "Be strong, my much-loved sister. We cannot afford weakness at this juncture. We must adhere to our plans and never look back." Kai-Dan wiped the tears from her sister's cheeks and whispered, "Remember, only the one designated

Most Sovereign Healer can know about our ruse; the people must never know."

Kalli-Dan's sobs echoed under the trees. "I do not understand why you refuse to let me know whether you have made it away from Atlantis and have found someplace safe. At least I could live with that knowledge."

Kai-Dan frowned. "Please, we have been through this. Know in your heart that I have made it and that I am living in safety and peace. Hold to that thought and let that be your light. It is better to imagine the best rather than have to live with the knowledge that I did not survive."

An objection rose in her sister's blue eyes, but before she could give it voice, Kai-Dan hugged her with all her might. "Our people will need all your single-minded devotion, guidance, and strength to get through this." She sighed heavily. "If you know of a certainty that I have not survived my journey, it will kill your spirit at a time when our people need you the most." She placed a hand on Kalli's heart and one over hers. "Know in your heart that I will make it. Trust that over everything."

Kalli-Dan barely managed a sorrowful nod. She knew the argument; she didn't like it and she didn't totally agree, but she had promised to abide by Kai's request, so she repeated, "I cannot afford to be distracted, as the first year of survival will be the most crucial and will make the difference." The words made her cringe, but she looked at Kai-Dan, her heart shining out of sad eyes. "I will not let you down, my beloved sister." She hugged Kai-Dan as hard as she could, memorizing the feel of her sister's spirit next to hers. They had rarely been apart. From the moment of their birth, when Kalli had followed Kai through the birth canal without letting go of her hand, they had thought to live their lives together until the time came for them to transcend.

Kalli-Dan uselessly swiped at her eyes and backed away from Kai-Dan. Gazing at her sister, she uttered her last words. "Go, find safety and find a good life. I pray that our line continues through you. You are and always will be my example and my heart. I swear that I will lead the one thousand bravely and fearlessly, and they shall never learn our secret."

Kai-Dan nodded. She didn't trust herself to speak. A lump the size of a stone had lodged itself in her throat, and she couldn't have uttered a word even if she'd wanted to. She hugged her sister one last time before turning and walking away. Taking Heedrow's hand and placing her other hand on her stomach, she said, "Are you ready for our next adventure?" Even Kai-Dan wasn't sure if she was addressing Heedrow or her baby.

Heedrow smiled and held the healer's hand tightly. He could hardly wait to see his mama, and somehow, he just knew they would all be fine.

# CHAPTER

*37*

ALLI-DAN WAS THE last to enter the tunnel. She watched Kai-Dan and Heedrow as long as she could.

When they finally disappeared from sight, she shook herself from her stupor. She busied herself making certain that everyone that had chosen to go into the tunnel had arrived. Standing on the rim of the cave leading to the underground shelter, she waited as long as she dared for anyone else that might show up.

She and Kai had decided to allow anyone brave enough to heed their warning a chance to come at the last moment and enter the habitat. And so, she waited and watched. However, no one came—not even a breeze ascended the mountain. Far below, Kalli watched as people went about their business in blissful ignorance.

At last, she entered the cave mouth and stepped through the first seal. She closed the door behind her and secured it as Heedrow had taught her. Issuing a prayer to Zeus, she murmured, "Keep us safe, and please let the doors hold."

Heedrow had told her that the first door would most likely give way. However, the young master had built not just the requisite three barriers—unsettled with the idea of any of the survivors dying from a breach in his seals, he and his men had installed ten more watertight barriers. As she closed each door to the outside and sealed the locks the way Heedrow had taught her, she closed her mind to any other thoughts of the outside world. Once she had finished sealing all of the doors, she joined her people in the room Heedrow had called the Great Hall.

She remembered that Heedrow had wanted to honor Poseidon by naming the Great Hall after him, but the people seeking asylum in the vast underground sanctuary had resisted using their god's name. It would be a long time before the survivors would feel comfortable enough to abide by Heedrow's request.

She entered the last chamber and her ears continued to clear as she wound down into the very heart of the granite mountain. She didn't know how far down Heedrow had insisted they dig. She knew that he had created their home with the thought that it would be their only habitat for a very long time. She refused to let herself think about the intervening years—if she did, she thought she might lose her mind. She stiffened her spine as she acquired the lowest level.

She eyed the structure critically, not that she knew anything about construction or the strength needed for their home to withstand the coming cataclysm. She just hoped with all her heart that Heedrow was the genius they all thought him to be. He had reassured her throughout construction that the inner chambers would keep them safe and secure. She gritted her teeth. They would endure what was coming; they had to.

Kalli-Dan experienced a brief sense of panic rising in her chest. It made her heart skip several beats before pounding against her ribcage so hard that she could *hear* the staccato rhythm. For a moment, she was gripped by the crazy idea of throwing wide the doors, denouncing the destiny that Kai-Dan had foreseen, and running to join her sister. She closed her eyes and reminded herself to breathe. How was she supposed to do this on her own?

Before reaching to close the last seal, she attempted to settle herself. She imagined Kai-Dan urging her on with a stern reminder to seal the door tightly. In her mind's eye, she saw her sister send a kiss, and Kalli-Dan released her breath. She opened the door and walked in with her head high and her back straight. Behind her, two men waited to lock the seal for her.

Shadowed by the two men who had waited for her, she followed the path down to the Great Hall. The lighting was very low, making it difficult to pick out her friends. It was all part of Heedrow's grand design. They had been advised to save as much energy as possible in case of emergency. Kalli almost laughed. If this didn't constitute an emergency, she didn't know what did. She made her rounds through the great cavern. Huddled in family groups and holding each other securely, people waited, their heavy silence lending an oppressive feel to their gloom. Their fear was palpable. Kalli-Dan walked into their midst and lifted her arms. She blessed the assembly and then announced, "This day will end as it is meant to. Your fortitude and bravery are an inspiration to me. Breathe easy; all will be well."

When a rush of love and pride suffused her being, she knew that Kai-Dan still watched over her.

# CHAPTER
*38*

OSEIDON ENTERED HIS home like the god he was. Even though he felt a bit sheepish, he had made up his mind that he would be damned if he let Clieto know. He fully expected her to look upon him and realize how much she had missed him. Seeing his magnificence, he wanted her to fall in love with him all over again. "Clieto! Come and attend me, love!" And he would be munificent in his reception of her admiration. He was becoming more and more excited to see Clieto, and his voice boomed through the house. "Where are you my wife?"

However, nothing but a sullen silence greeted his ears. There was no sign of movement anywhere in his house. The kitchens seemed unusually still. Puzzling over why no servants had arrived to attend him, he wondered if the entire household had decided to step outside. If Clieto had asked for help in tending the garden, the servants would have gladly pitched in. He smiled to himself. Those gardens were his wife's pride and joy, and at this time of year, they were lush and ripe with fruit.

Still looking forward to his warm reunion, Poseidon hurried to the veranda, threw open the doors, and stepped outside. He took a deep breath and surveyed the view. There was not a bit of movement or sound anywhere.

"Clieto?" Nothing. Poseidon was confused. He scratched his head and moved back into the house. He went to the kitchens. Nothing was being prepared, and it looked as though the pots and pans had been unused for a while. Moving through the house, still wondering where everyone had gone, he finally stood before their bedroom. He opened the door and was stunned to see that the room was empty.

Not one piece of furniture had been left, and there was not one item of clothing in evidence. The room was swept completely clean, as if his wife had never existed. Poseidon stepped inside and, to his dread, saw a length of abandoned papyrus. At his approach, the paper rustled, as though demanding his attention. It looked to Poseidon as if the paper had been left on the floor almost as an anxious afterthought.

A terrible feeling of foreboding gripped his heart as he bent to pick up the scroll. Turning it to the light, he recognized Clieto's writing. He didn't want to read the words, but he couldn't help himself. His gaze trailed over the words, but it took several readings before Poseidon grasped the full import of the message.

*Husband –*

*I am leaving you. Do not look for me, do not send your men after me. I am leaving Atlantis and all that I have known because of your actions. I can no longer look upon your face with anything but contempt. You have torn our family apart, and I will no longer be*

*party to your absurd whims backed by your uncontrol-
lable temper. I am sorry it has come to this. I did love
you so.*

*Clieto*

Poseidon's outrage knew no bounds. His scream of defiance
was so loud and so long, he felt as if his head would explode.
The paper he clutched in one fist burst into flames as his eyes
bulged and his mind blanked. Dropping the burning scroll,
Poseidon screeched, "Clieto! I will hunt you down and I will
kill you with my own hands! No one leaves me!"

Poseidon vaulted from the room. The stones underneath his
feet erupted in flames and the house shook as though a lightning
storm had been loosed inside. Windows blew out at his approach,
and beneath his fiery gaze, furniture ignited into massive bonfires.

Beyond words, Poseidon blindly raced from the house. He
had barely cleared the front gates when the entire structure
detonated. Lifted from its very foundations, the house Poseidon
had built with such care exploded into nothingness. Where
a house once filled with love and laughter had stood, not one
stone, not one tile, not one tiny plant remained. In Poseidon's
wake, all that remained was a swirling tornado of powdery
white dust.

# CHAPTER

## 39

THE EXPLOSION WAS like nothing anyone had ever experienced. Rocking the air, it sounded as if ten thousand lightning strikes hit the ground at the same moment. Screams from panicked animals and terrified citizens echoed through the city. All over, Kai-Dan's warnings fell from frightened lips. Petrified families gathered and discussed climbing the mountain and begging entrance into "Heedrow's Tombs," a derisive term adopted by the majority of the city's most cynical inhabitants.

Businesses closed hurriedly, signs still swinging in windows, as owners fled to their own homes. Afraid to venture out, people waited in dread for the arrival of their god. That he was on a rampage never before witnessed by any living member of the community was evident. What precipitated his outburst caused speculation to run wild.

However, no one came close to guessing the real reason for Poseidon's hellish tantrum. Unbeknownst to any Atlantean, Clieto had left, along with all her servants, in the dead of night. She had not wanted anyone to know. She had not even informed her servants until the night she had packed and given them the choice of staying behind or accompanying her on a very long and arduous journey. If there was an outside chance of alerting her husband to her intentions or her whereabouts, Clieto did everything in her power to prevent that from occurring. Her secret preparations prevailed. No one, much less her husband, knew she had left Atlantis.

Poseidon was beside himself. Still recovering from his massive bout of debauchery, he hurt everywhere, which only served to intensify his anger. The fact that his wife had left him struck him like a thunderbolt, and again, his maddened roar split the air. "First Atlas defies me and now you!"

The earth heaved under the weight of Poseidon's tread. At his passing, trees were uprooted, fences were obliterated, animals were immolated where they stood, and houses were vaporized.

Some of the smarter people living on the outskirts of Atlantis fled the city with just the clothes on their backs. Others crouched in their homes, praying that Poseidon's temper would abate and that he would depart again for the comforts of Olympus. Still, no one truly believed their god would destroy his most favored and most beloved city.

Atlas had secreted himself inside Poseidon's temple. Anticipating his father's arrival, he waited in the dark for his chance. His anger rose in relation to the sounds of destruction visited upon Atlantis by his father. Each detonation that pummeled his heart released a new blast of hatred into his soul. He was primed and he was ready. Over and over, as the sounds of his father's wrath circled closer, Atlas repeated his mantra: *I will teach my father a lesson or I will die trying ... I will teach my father a lesson or I will die trying ...*

As his father drew nearer, the threats roaring from his mouth chilled Atlas to the bone. The savage epithets Poseidon hurled at he and his mother were monstrous. Any resemblance to a human being had disappeared; the sounds that presaged Poseidon's arrival were horrendous, unlike anything he had ever heard before. It was as if his father had opened the very gates of hell and was leading the pack.

Shakily, Atlas crept from his hiding place and took up the fighting stance that Tereus had taught him. *I will teach my father a lesson or I will die trying ... I will ...* The words lost all their meaning, and Atlas couldn't even remember why he had come to the temple in the first place.

It was then that Atlas remembered Tereus had chosen to enter the tunnels, taking his new wife with him. He had tried to talk Atlas into coming, but Atlas had flatly refused. With his pride in his new fighting skills secure, he had no doubt that he could catch his father unaware and extract his revenge. Wishing Tereus well, he had told him the truth. "I have to do this; it is the only way I can retain my sanity. It is not in me to forgive him."

Tereus had said something that he had soon forgotten. However, he was fairly certain that it was his usual admonition of not letting his anger get the better of him.

Peering through the gloom that had descended upon the temple, Atlas finally caught a glimpse of his father. The rage that colored his countenance made him unrecognizable. He looked like a snarling, savage, feral beast. Atlas had no idea what had caused Poseidon to react in such a manner, but he knew better than to challenge his father now.

Darting behind the throne, Atlas held his breath as Poseidon bounded up the stairs and burst into the temple. The noises his father made were sub-human. It was then that Atlas realized that Kai-Dan had spoken true. Havoc was about to reign down on Atlantis.

As quietly and as quickly as he could, Atlas crept from the temple and bolted for the hills. His thoughts found Tereus. *"I am coming ... will you be able to open a path for me?"*

An anxious answer pounded back. *"I will wait topside for you ... the doors will be open ... but hurry, the ground is already shaking us!"*

Atlas put all the power of his lineage into his legs. Running faster than he ever thought possible, he ascended the mountain as though he had sprouted wings. Nevertheless, when he reached the entry point, he was relieved to see Tereus waiting for him. Barely out of breath, he motioned Tereus to begin the closing sequence. As he joined his friend, he shouted, "It is happening! Go, go, go!"

Securing the first door, Atlas ran after his friend. Their feet thudded against the tunnel floor, and Tereus led him down the dim caverns as the ground began to shake even harder. At each lock, they frantically took turns sealing the doors.

They passed into the final tunnel and ran up to the last water-tight lock as the floors and walls began to writhe. Out of time.

Atlas and Tereus slammed the door and secured the closing sequence. They sped into the Great Hall, and no sooner had they taken their seats and anchored themselves as best they could than the world they had known as home blew apart.

# CHAPTER

*40*

THE COMMOTION WAS beyond imagination. Deep inside the heart of their mountain, sealed inside the Great Hall, it sounded to the terrified survivors like the mountain was screaming in pain. Tearing and rending was heard from all sides. At times, during the worst of the bucking and shaking, most people thought that they were taking their last breath.

Some Atlanteans cried, others screamed; some crept into corners like frightened animals, covering their ears and closing their eyes and curling into fetal positions. Others passed out from sheer fright. No one could move or do anything to help anyone else. People held to anything they could, trying with all their might to keep from being thrown about the Great Hall like marbles. In what turned out to be the longest night of everyone's life, the fearful quaking built to a frenzied crescendo. As people prayed to their gods for deliverance, the mountain heaved and shrieked.

Just when it seemed that all was lost, a searing silence penetrated their awareness, causing some people to think that the worst was over. In that precipitous instant the mountain suddenly canted crazily to one side, sending people sliding over the granite floor.

Scrambling to grab onto anything substantial enough to stay their slide, the survivors waited to die. With another ear-splitting scream, the mountain, screeching its fate to the heavens, sank with sickening velocity down into the earth.

The noise was mind-numbingly horrific, and to the few Atlanteans still cognizant of their surroundings, the slide seemed to last forever. Every moment that passed felt like a doorway to their last moment on earth. Oblivion would have been better than the hell they were in.

After what seemed like an eternity of sustained fear, the mountain emitted a last gasp and shuddered to a stop. In the aftermath, the silence was deafening. People eventually began to stir. Rising from their prone positions, no one could quite believe they had lived through the actual event. That the caves were still intact was due to Heedrow's genius. The young man had somehow created a sanctuary able to withstand the worst that an enraged god could throw at it. The new Atlantis was, in truth, a miracle.

Kalli-Dan came to her senses almost immediately. She reached into her mind for any support from her sister, but none was forthcoming. Silence, just as Kai-Dan had said. Blinking her eyes in wonder, she closed her mind to any thoughts of her sister and sat up, checking herself for injuries. Finding nothing noteworthy, she rose. She brushed the dust from her robes and began making her way through the groups of frightened, displaced survivors.

After designating sister healers to take charge of bodily injuries, Kalli-Dan assumed her role as Most Sovereign Healer and went about repairing the most emotionally traumatized Atlanteans. Other survivors, following their healer's lead, began their checks of the cave systems. People recovered slowly, and as they did, the search for loved ones began. Standing in the midst of her people, Kalli-Dan addressed them. "Once we have seen to everyone and made certain our home stands strong, let us come back to this Great Hall. We are all grieving. We have all suffered extreme loss today, whether it be family members, loved ones, or the homes and homeland we inhabited for so long. Our hearts must heal, and while it will take time, we will start our healing today. Let us come together to sing our tribute to all that we have lost this day." She signaled a few couples. "Once we are finished with the tribute, open the kitchens. We need sustenance and rest. We will not stint on this night. When we are done, go to your quarters and take what rest you can find. Tomorrow will bring with it new challenges."

Food was brought out in abundance and the wine flowed freely. It was not a night for abstinence. That would come later, as the days passed and the survivors, living under sustained and severe rationing, fought to live.

This day would become a day of celebration and remembrance. A day that would live in their memories forever.

Atlas stayed in the shadows. The last one to make it to the caves, he wasn't sure how his presence would be received, so he kept to himself. As others busied themselves with different duties, Atlas reviewed the destruction wrought by his father. He let his mind reach beyond his current confines and realized, before anyone else, that the destruction of Atlantis had been merciless and complete.

Beneath waves towering hundreds of feet into the air, not one remnant of Atlantis remained. It was as if the entire continent had just disappeared. As far as his mind could travel, Atlas saw nothing but a vast expanse of ocean where a thriving nation had once lived.

He shut his mind down. He couldn't bring himself to look any further. Assailed by a terrible feeling of vertigo, Atlas grabbed the rock next to him to keep from falling back to the ground. He had not wanted to believe that his father was capable of destroying everything he had ever loved. But the evidence was irrefutable.

Sliding to the floor, Atlas despondently buried his face in his hands. "Could you not have at least saved her?" Not knowing that his mother had escaped Atlantis's fate, he hoped that her death had been fast. He didn't want to think of her suffering at all.

With his head still in his hands, Atlas cried. He cried for the loss of his mother, for the loss of his father, and for the loss of Alia; but most of all, he cried for the loss of his innocence.

# CHAPTER
*41*

FOLLOWERS THE WORLD over were screaming for more news of their Messiah. People, governments, and nations were demanding to know where he was and how he was. No one had seen or heard anything after the first press releases—now, his followers were demanding proof of life.

After the tragic massacre at the complex and the ensuing investigation, no one could say with any amount of certainty whether the Messiah still lived or if he had finally succumbed to his terrible injuries.

The world's superpowers, fearful of Travlor's ever-growing army of believers, raised their nuclear alert level back to DEFCON One. Amid the terrible outcry, it seemed the entire world had lost its collective mind. But, until news of Travlor's status was forthcoming, the heightened tension continued to drag the world to the breaking point.

As the Armies of the New Messiah grew more aggressive, conspiracy theories ran rampant. The latest rumor maintained that their Messiah was being held against his will. So, when believers were encouraged by their leaders to depose any powers that thwarted them in their righteous path, the burgeoning armies staged bloody but successful coups all over the world. Where Travlor's armies moved, reason and the rule of law fell before mob mentality and mob rule. When the first bombs were dropped by the Armies of the New Messiah, no one was surprised by the ultimatum that followed: "Find our Messiah and return him to us or we will unleash a never-ending war!"

America moved its National Guard throughout the states, blocking both borders and firing on any dissenters. Russia mobilized its own troops in Eastern Europe and announced a "take no prisoners" policy as it tried to quell the violence. China quit talking to anyone; firing at will into massive crowds of demonstrators, the Chinese troops took down anyone in their path. Missiles were again turning in their silos. Talk was over.

# CHAPTER
## 42

RAPPED IN THE comfort of family and friends, warm food and good wine, the long night stretched before the survivors with a bit more promise. People, recovering from the harrowing experience they had just lived through, began finding reasons to push on. Although it was a dark time, and it was a fearful time, it was still a beginning. One by one, survivors began to hope that they could make it. That it was possible to actually create a life deep beneath an ocean that had not been there before.

The mountain had sunk beneath the wild waves of a hellacious storm, but no one knew how deep they had been driven. Facing a monumental effort to learn how to adapt and survive in their underwater sanctuary, families and friends were glad for the reprieve of a simple yet filling meal. Loaves of fresh bread, still warm from the kitchens, huge wheels of thick, crusty cheese, and piping hot oyster stew helped bring about a sense of home, of continuity and continuance.

Stinting on nothing, Kalli-Dan signaled for a barrel of the finest wine to be opened and passed around. The honeyed elixir, which had been the pride of Atlantis, helped almost more than anything. Giving the survivors a chance to relive and discuss the miracle of their ordeal, the heady wine not only helped numb the pain of losing loved ones—it eased the agony of losing their beloved home.

Atlas had wanted to be alone. Avoiding the others, he slipped into the shadows of some of the fallen boulders. Gratefully, he sank his teeth into his loaf of bread and chewed thoughtfully. He couldn't help marveling at the extent of his father's wrath. His vengeance had been so merciless and so absolute, so stunningly final, that Atlas had trouble accepting the fact that Poseidon was his father. He admitted that he was as quick to anger as the next man, and yet the thunderous fury of the man's bestial roars still rang in his ears. "To think you were capable of such annihilation! What kind of person are you? You killed everyone!"

Atlas didn't realize he had spoken out loud until he felt the nearby stares. Startled by the animosity with which his gaze was met, he knew it wouldn't be long before stares of hostility turned into something more violent. Atlas felt the weight of their hatred when a few of them muttered loud enough for him to hear, "Why is he here? He is the cause of this!"

One female, liquid courage surging through her veins, faced him, eyes full of blame. "How is it that you survive and so many of our loved ones did not?" She tried to hold Atlas's gaze, but her face crumpled with grief.

Atlas wanted to comfort her. He needed to explain that what his father had done wasn't his fault. But the words wouldn't come; wracked by his own sense of guilt and sorrow, he didn't know what he should do.

He tossed his food aside and stood. He started to leave the room, but Kalli-Dan had witnessed the exchange. She rose quickly and walked into their midst. She held her arms up for quiet and waited for the noise to subside. Looking over the assembled group, she knew exactly what to do. She held her hand out for Atlas. Confused as to what she wanted from him, he stood apart from the others. "Atlas, come to me."

Worried that the healer should draw so much attention to him, he hesitated. Kalli-Dan felt his distress, so the healer crossed the distance and took his hand. Holding tightly to Atlas, she faced the others. "There is no one—and I cannot emphasize this strongly enough—*no one* who is with us who does not belong!"

People harboring doubts about Atlas's presence shrank into themselves under the weight of their healer's stare. Kalli-Dan did not waver. Her gaze raked over each and every one of her frightened survivors. At length, she spoke again. "Do not succumb to turbulent emotions. Every one of us" —again she cast her gaze over each person in the room— "has survived a mass extinction that no one should ever have to experience." She paused to let her words register. "We will get through this. We have no other choice. However, we will only get through this if we depend upon and trust each other without reservation. If you truly believe that we have been given a remarkable chance to rebuild our lives, then it is now—this very moment—that we put the past behind us."

Murmurs of assent passed through the crowd, making Atlas feel a bit easier. Nevertheless, he still felt animosity emanating from some of the more stubborn inhabitants. He knew the healer could feel it, too, when she continued. "It is imperative that we come together so that we can make it through the next few days. What we do now is crucial for our overall survival."

People stirred, and Tereus, the one person Atlas considered a friend, stood to address their Most Sovereign Healer. "We are

with you, Kai-Dan, and we are ready to do what is necessary."
He glanced at Atlas and straightened his shoulders. "I think I
speak for the majority of us when I tell you that, even though it
was your father who brought about this monumental disaster,
we are all with you."

The heat rose in Atlas's face. Lowering his head, he brought
his hands to his heart in prayer pose. Humbled by the man's
willingness to forgive, he mumbled, "Thank you. I shall try to
be worthy of your forgiveness. It is a lesson I need to take into
my own heart."

The healer eyed Atlas and issued a thought. "*See me in my
chambers after we eat … you and I are not quite through …*"
When the young man did not respond, Kalli-Dan followed
up quickly, "*This is not a request …*"

Atlas lifted a brow and quirked the side of his mouth. "After
dinner."

Atlas found the healer's quarters, but before he could close the
door, Kalli-Dan turned on him. "Do not bring your remorse
into this group! I need everyone working and living together
in as much harmony as possible. There will be no time for drama
from anyone." She stepped back and studied the man towering
over her. "I do not know how you got here; you never indicated
that you wanted to be part of this group. So even I am surprised
that you came."

When Atlas started to explain, she held up a hand. "Let me
finish, because it is important that you hear and comprehend
what I say." She pulled herself up to her full height and let the

power of her position inject her words with steel. "Whatever transpired between you and your father must be put behind you. We are facing the fight of our lives. When we look back upon this initial devastation, it will look like nothing compared to the struggle that lies ahead of us." She took both Atlas's hands and squeezed hard. "I need your full support and attention."

Atlas didn't move. He regarded the healer from beneath pitch-black brows, then decided what it was he needed to say. "Kai-Dan, I am not here to burden you." He let her hands go and gestured toward the couches. "Will you sit with me?"

Kalli-Dan lifted her robes and did as Atlas had requested. Once she was comfortable, Atlas sat next to her. Solemnly taking her hand, he held it easily. "Before all of this came to pass, I accepted an obligation from Poseidon. While I may not be able to fulfill that particular obligation, I can still help sustain us."

Kalli-Dan, heartened by his words, encouraged him. "Share your thoughts with me."

Atlas blinked slowly as he gathered his thoughts. "Poseidon gave me the duty of being a pillar between the earth and the sky—I was to hold them apart so that life could find its place."

Kalli-Dan cocked her head. "I am listening."

"I have not thought this out entirely … however, we are trapped in this environment until we devise a method that enables us to leave." He stopped and looked questioningly at the healer.

She shrugged, gesturing for him to go on. Atlas furrowed his brow and blew out a deep breath. "It is possible that I can be the pillar between the ocean and topside."

Atlas could see the questions running through Kalli-Dan's mind. However, excited by the possibilities he had just raised, he continued on: "I am not like most humans. Being half god, I do not have the same requirements that other humans do."

He could still see the questions circulating through the healer. "Do you understand what I am saying?"

Kalli-Dan shook her head. "I must admit that I am not sure what you are offering."

Atlas's imagination caught fire. Impatient to make the woman understand, he laughed. "Think about it! I can swim through the oceans without aid. It is one of the gifts of my birthright!"

Kalli-Dan's face lit up. "You can do that?"

Atlas nodded so hard that his neck hurt. "This cave does not have to become a prison. By moving between this home and new lands, we can discover new things—our technology will continue to progress. At some point, we will either have the means to live comfortably in our underwater home, or we will have the technology to leave. I have the ability to change the course of our lives!"

The healer shifted in her seat and moved closer to Atlas. "So you truly believe that, with the powers you possess, you can help us thrive in this environment?"

"That is exactly what I am saying! I can be a messenger between both worlds. Eventually, we will all have the choice of staying here or leaving to live topside."

At last, realizing Atlas's vision of the future was possible, Kalli-Dan felt better than she had in months. Remarkable as it seemed, the thought that the young man who had brought about the destruction of Atlantis could possibly turn out to be their savior was overwhelming. She felt intoxicated, excited, and relieved. She did something she had never thought to be able to do again. She laughed aloud. "I never thought to say this, but Atlas, thank the gods you are here!"

# CHAPTER
## 43

LL IN ALL, people recognized the truth of their healer's advice and readily accepted Atlas as an integral part of the whole. By banding together, the surviving Atlanteans were able to help each other through the worst of the disaster. Heedrow's genius continued to amaze and delight the small band of Atlanteans, and when it was discovered that their new home had suffered minimal, if any, damage, a celebration in his honor was enjoyed by one and all.

Still, a few survivors were finding it difficult, if not impossible, to adjust to their new reality. It was only due to the efforts of Kalli-Dan—disguised as her twin sister—and her sister healers that those people were able to hold onto their sanity and their purpose. Without the healers, no one would have made it through the dark times.

Eventually, a routine involving everyone in the care and maintenance of their new home was established. Kalli-Dan knew that everyone in her small community needed to feel useful and cared for.

Survival became the norm in the Atlantean's everyday life. People were immediately assigned the tasks of clearing and repairing blocked waterways, removing debris, and righting quarters. Stiff rules of rationing were put into effect, but, at the close of each day, people could see the results of their hard work.

Initially, only small changes were noticed. Nevertheless, those small changes started to add up, and as their home became more comfortable and less alien, people's flagging spirits began to lighten. Because of their heightened morale, survival became less of an issue; a feeling of home and permanence and comfort rose to buoy the small community.

Bigger changes appeared. Healthy gardens sprang from the rich Atlantean soil. Kitchen crews, challenged with the paucity of rationing, were constantly coming up with interesting dishes. Life began to reassert itself and, by and large, people began to find happiness again.

However, as the survivor's burdens eased, a shift of attitude took place. As absurd as it was, people began to imagine that their topside world had somehow survived the holocaust. That irrational hope proliferated until some people were absolutely certain that their original home had been spared.

In a general meeting, when it had been determined that there were no new problems to address, it was decided that the time had come for new tunnels to be created. For Atlas to follow up on his promise, he needed a way out to the open ocean.

A good many Atlanteans volunteered to help dig the exit tunnels. Although no one dared give voice to the idea that the old Atlantis had survived, no one wanted to refute the foolishness of that hope. So, the tunneling became the sole focus of their survival. Atlas thought it was insane to believe they would find the old Atlantis just the way they left it, but he also knew it was useless to try and dissuade anyone from such folly. *Hope is hard to stamp out, no matter how ridiculous it may be.*

Once the first exit tunnel had been constructed, a huge send-off was prepared. Kalli-Dan knew Atlas needed all of his divine strength and energy to make it to the surface. Even so, she wasn't at all sure it was going to be as easy as he believed. The healers warned him to eat as much as possible, so when people passed on their own rations so that Atlas might partake of their portions, he accepted their generosity in the spirit it was given. Everyone was anxious for news of home and, though he knew differently, Atlas refused to douse the fire of their hopes.

On the morning of Atlas's first foray outside of Atlantis, survivors crowded into the exit cave until the small room was filled to capacity. Anybody arriving late had to be content with their tunnel view.

Well wishes had been exchanged the night before. So, Atlas did what he could to look as confident as possible. Before he dove into the pool which would lead him out, he looked around at the people crowded around him. In their anxious faces, he could see expressions of hope mixed with fear. He tried to come up with something profound to say, but instead, he just raised an arm in salute, then turned and plummeted into the freezing, black ocean water.

Those watching held their collective breath as Atlas disappeared into the dark pool. Upon the noisy exhalation of someone's breath, everyone realized what they were doing. A ripple of laughter ran through the crowd, helping ease the tension. Kalli-Dan addressed her family: "Come, it will do no good to stand and wait. He will be back when he can. The time will pass more quickly if we stay busy."

A few grumbles could be heard circulating the exit chamber, but no one argued. Everyone but Tereus shuffled back to their assigned tasks. Drawing the Most Sovereign Healer aside, he whispered, "I told Atlas I would wait for him."

Kalli-Dan looked at his determined face and knew it was no use arguing. Nodding her assent, she said, "I am sure he will feel your presence on his journey. I just hope it helps."

Tereus allowed a small smile. "That is my hope as well. If he needs help, I will be here for him."

Kalli-Dan squeezed his shoulder before she departed. "You are a good friend to him. Atlas needs friends."

Atlas was helped from the pool by Tereus. His body was depleted, and Tereus was ready with warm food. As the two men sat on the side of the pool, feet dangling in the water, Atlas wolfed the meal down. Between hurried bites, he noticed the big question in Tereus's eyes. Shaking his head, Atlas managed a garbled, "Nothin'."

Tereus had been under no illusions as to the fate of their beautiful city, but hearing the finality of his words was greatly disheartening. He had clung to his own secret hope that something, anything remaining of Atlantis could be found.

Atlas ate his fill, then when he was reenergized, Tereus escorted him to the Great Hall. Everyone was assembled. Looking at their grim faces and sad eyes, Atlas wished he had better news to share. He didn't want to make his report. Seeing his hesitation, Kalli-Dan took the lead. "Atlas, please … as difficult as we know it is for you, tell us what you saw."

Setting his jaw, Atlas rested his gaze on the healer as if she were the only person in the room. Gaining strength from the set of her head and the steel in her spine, he quit stalling. "There is no sign of any land as far as I can see. There is not so much as a twig left from our old world. There are no survivors. We are all that is left. We have only ourselves to rely on."

There was little talk as the somber group quietly disassembled. News of their absolute isolation was almost more than some of them could bear. For those who had clung fervently to the secret hope that some portion of their old lives could be restored, it was as if they lost their home all over again. It would be a long time before the old feelings of joy could be rekindled.

The years slipped by, and Atlas continued to be a life-sustaining pillar to his underwater community. He never ceased his wanderings, and as he became more acclimated to his underwater habitat, he gained in strength. At ease in his ocean, Atlas lengthened his explorations. He swam in ever-widening circles, knowing that one day, he would find land.

With each report, people became more resigned to the fact that they were alone in their underwater realm. However, stories of Atlas's unceasing diligence began to circulate. And in the way of stories, his exploits took on superhuman proportions. There was no one alive in the new Atlantis that didn't admire and appreciate his boundless efforts. Soon enough, a nickname evolved. Started by Tereus, and adopted readily enough by Atlas, the new moniker served to give him a sense of belonging and acceptance. By combining two words—traveler and lore—into one, Atlas was longer referred to by his given name. "Travlor" emerged as an important and well-regarded figure in the community.

Meanwhile, Atlanteans never ceased their efforts to create the perfect underwater home. The men of science who had survived the sinking worked endlessly to develop a means whereby anyone could leave their home in relative comfort. Their axiom was, "We need access to the ocean, and we need a way to traverse it both body and craft."

With the intense focus that these learned men brought to bear, no more than two generations passed before the idea of a bioskin came into being.

Using living cells, they replicated human skin. By genetically engineering the tissue, they figured out how to sustain life outside of Atlantis. The bioskins, created to emulate human skin, evolved slowly. It was only after numerous failures that scientists found a technique that would provide the heating and cooling needed for the wearers.

Along with knowledge of how to implement the heating and cooling systems into the 'skins, the scientist discovered a method to convert energy exerted by a wearer into an endless supply of air. The last piece of the puzzle fell into place when the means to increase the tensile strength of the 'skins came about. No longer subject to the crushing pressures at such depths, the bioskins enabled anybody access to the open ocean at any time.

As people began to explore the ocean depths on their own, it became necessary to create a council. It was at that time that the Council of Ten came into being. Members of the council were given the authority to oversee the welfare of the small community and ensure that the Canons were upheld.

In an early meeting, it was determined that another set of rules or "edicts" were needed to address their current environs. While Poseidon's Canons were sufficient for most of the needs of the new Atlantis, the edicts served to expand upon Poseidon's original eight Canons.

Realizing that it was only a matter of time before Travlor happened upon other lands and peoples, an exclusive edict was voted into effect. Adhering to the original Canons, the council decided it was necessary to expound upon Poseidon's most important Canon: no mixing of cultures or races. Accepted by the entire Atlantean society, the new edict made separateness and anonymity law. No Atlantean would ever be allowed to mix with topsiders. Anyone in breach of that particular Canon would suffer severe repercussions.

Technologically, the next leap was made when biospheres, the direct descendants of bioskins, were completed. Refined to an incredibly high degree, biospheres made it possible to "fly" through the oceans without bioskins. Now, the world beckoned to be discovered.

Travlor was finally able to quit swimming and utilize the biospheres to continue his explorations of the topside world. With the new ease of mobility, Travlor became even more fascinated with topside life.

He watched and reported as cultures matured, learned, thrived, and died. He stayed apart from the peoples of the world and never felt confined by Atlantean law. He not only refused to mix with anyone, Travlor disguised himself on his expeditions so that his Atlantean self was never detected. He blended so well into the societies he visited that often he was mistaken for a local.

It was during one of his topside excursions that he discovered his masking abilities. Using those abilities to his advantage, he found it was to his liking to keep himself hidden from topside societies. He felt that he had more than learned his lesson.

With the passing of each generation, the friends Travlor made aged into transcendence. With each transcendence, Travlor was left behind feeling more bereft and more alone than ever. When Tereus, his oldest and dearest friend, finally transcended, Travlor's feelings of isolation were complete, and he simply withdrew from community life.

He kept to himself, but he never wavered in his duties. He continued to go between water and land and back again, and never questioned the task he had set himself. However, life seemed to leech away from him with every passing day. Eventually, his skin started to gray.

Until …

Evan looked up with a start, not recognizing his surroundings. He blinked to clear his mind and vision, and when a figure swam into view, his heart skipped a beat. Kyla was with him. *"Beloved, I am losing track of reality …"*

He gratefully accepted the food Kyla spooned into his mouth. *"I am with you, always … I am here to keep you anchored to this reality …"*

When he could no longer hold himself up, she held him against her. He must have fallen asleep, because when he roused himself, he saw that Ni-Cio and Rogert had come into his room. Shocked at the change in Evan's health and appearance,

Ni-Cio knew he had expended energy well beyond anything anyone they had ever witnessed.

As Evan rested and waited for more food, Ni-Cio dared pose a question. "My friend, how much longer can you continue to sustain yourself, much less Daria and Travlor?"

Not wanting to waste the effort it took to talk, Evan swallowed and sent a thought-form. *"I can't be sure, but I feel the baby is somehow transferring strength to me ..."*

Ni-Cio didn't dare use anymore of Evan's energy with useless questioning, but his mind swam. *How is that possible?*

He got up from his chair and crossed the room to take the tray from Kyla. He thought his sister looked almost as tired as Evan. However, when he had risked her ire by *mentioning* it, she had been adamant in her refusal of a break. She had walked away from him and huffed, "I am never long from his side. I have introduced other foods into his diet, but no luck so far. Ni-Cio, you know I am the only one allowed entry to his rooms. So do not bring this up again."

He remembered shouting, "Kyla! Why are we waiting? It has been two days since we entered Atlantis and nothing has changed!"

Kyla whipped around to face him. Her face was white with strain, but the colors writhing over her countenance demonstrated her strength and resolve. "Whatever Evan can do, we *will* continue to sustain him. No one knows how long this will take, but as long as we have breath in our bodies, Daria and Travlor and your daughter will breathe with us."

Ni-Cio's head dropped, and he nodded slightly. "But the world had gone mad seeking Travlor ..."

"Ni-Cio, stop it right now! We can only do what we can do. Anything that takes place outside of this moment and outside of this room is beyond us. Remember your own advice: one foot in front of the other."

Ni-Cio remained silent, head bowed. Kyla had watched him for a moment, then slipped away. Squaring her shoulders, she sent a wave of love to Evan and hurried to the kitchens. "*As long as we have each other, I do not care how long it takes ... I will be back soon, my love ... we will get through this ...*"

# CHAPTER

## 44

IN EVAN'S VISION, Travlor's biosphere coursed through the waters with such ease that it almost flew.

The explorer had determined his mission for this day, and he was looking forward to learning more. He had explored a very different continent referred to as "America," and he was fascinated. Infatuated with the boundless energy and the spirit of the people, the entire society seemed incredibly hopeful.

As Evan watched Travlor's life play out, time as he knew it ceased to exist. Had it not been for Kyla's loving presence, it would have become impossible for him to discern reality from memories—in his mind, past, present, and future merged. Evan realized that while he sustained Travlor's life, his father's memories progressed through his mind at the pace of a normal life, whereas in reality, the memories were revealing themselves in the blink of an eye.

Learning more about his sire than he had ever known, Evan was transfixed by the man who had destroyed Atlantis. Mind-bending as it was, Evan had accepted the fact that Travlor was as he said he was: half god, half man. That he was a direct descendant of Poseidon only served to inflame Evan's curiosity. If he hadn't required so much food to recoup his energy, he would have been happy to stay locked in those memories until he had learned everything he had ever wanted to know.

He was missing a vital piece of information. For Evan, it was necessary to discover the reason Travlor had existed in such a bitter state for so long. Having only met the man in his early thirties, it was hard for Evan to understand why Travlor had never shared anything about his life. The man had been shrouded in mystery and secrets from the start.

Evan was particularly curious as to why Travlor had never revealed himself to him when he was growing up. Content to remain an enigmatic voice in his head, the only thing Travlor had ever told him was that he had an agenda that could not be revealed until he was older. So, Evan had done as Travlor requested, and followed the path his father had set for him.

Evan took sustenance when it was offered and accepted the ministrations of Kyla as she washed and cared for his body. It was hard to fathom that only three days had passed since they had been carried into Atlantis.

He was still unsure why his father had needed to come back to Atlantis. It seemed to Evan that it would have been easier to care for everyone topside. Alone in the room, he shifted so he could study the man lying beside him. He detected Travlor's rapid eye movement and realized that the man was continuing to relive his very long life. *Travlor, I will stay tied to you as long as I can, but I need to know why your vengeance got so out of hand. I want to know why you decided to kill every last Atlantean.*

Willingly letting himself be pulled back into Travlor's vast review, he sank into his father's mind. He watched his father stop the biosphere and study the people bustling about the harbor. Travlor's thoughts came as easily to Evan as his own. *Ahh, it is good to have been sired by a god, but it is clear my powers have limits. Nevertheless, it is good to be alive to see all of this!*

Evan watched, through Travlor's eyes, as horse drawn carriages avoided the newest spectacle: cars. Pedestrians laughed and pointed at the newfangled machines, but Travlor was thrilled by the possibilities presented with such a mode of transportation. It would make his forays into the country much easier and faster. *This culture has come far—they deserve a more in-depth study.*

The Atlantean processors were almost sentient in their own right. Housed deep in the heart of their mountain prior to the sinking, vast stores of knowledge—the knowledge of the gods—had been stored within the memory systems. As the decades passed, the processors became a welcome and necessary part of Atlantean life. With more leisure time, the crystal processors brought the topside world to life for the Atlanteans. Studying the world's cultures made Travlor's reports even more relevant and necessary. One of the most surprising discoveries came when Atlanteans realized that their lifespans extended far beyond the lives of topsiders.

Time continued its forward march through Evan's mind until another dismal fact of Travlor's dreary existence came to light. Having lost everyone he had ever cared about, the man quit trying to make friends. Travlor was alone so much of the time that his history was becoming lost to Atlantean memories. Because of that, a strange dichotomy came about; as integral a part of the fabric of life as Travlor had become, no one knew him any longer. He was a complete mystery—a mystery that no one cared to solve. Consequently, Travlor became more and more reclusive.

He instituted extreme measures to avoid any and all contact with topsiders. When he was in residence, he retired to his quarters, refusing overtures from his Atlantean family. By his own actions, he retreated into a dark prison that kept him alone and apart from any human contact.

However, deep in his quarters, when all was quiet and sleep refused to spend time with him, he would remember the girl. It was then that his soul cried out in anger and grief for the life he had missed. Alia … a name, a time, a remembered song, a light extinguished too soon …

The more guarded Travlor became, the more his depression deepened. At length, the bitterness of his life once more found a target in Poseidon. Alone, with only his thoughts for company, bile rose in Travlor's throat when he relived the destruction his father had visited upon his faithful children. *And to think you caused that destruction because a beloved wife and child dared defy you!*

His anger grew until it hardened into bitterness. When bitterness morphed into hatred, the thought of avenging himself against his father was the sole motivation that kept him going.

And the years passed.

Travlor started using his powers solely to help himself. He stayed camouflaged and moved topside through the world's communities at will. He gave reports when requested, but more often than not, the Atlanteans simply left him alone.

With the passage of time, the Atlanteans adapted well to ocean life. Their underwater home reflected the Atlantean attributes of harmony, beauty, joy, and love. And as subsequent generations came and went, their skin began to reflect the colors of their ocean environment.

Initially, most of the children maintained the more muted skin tones; however, in a very small cross section, vivid colorations started to appear. Through the years, more Atlanteans began to display the same marvelous skin tones, until everyone but Travlor exhibited the trait. The varied skin colorations served to keep them well hidden as they swam through ocean waters.

As the Atlantean skin tones took on more depth, Travlor's skin faded. The regret and hatred flowing through his veins leeched any trace of color from him. The ghastly gray color of death permeated his skin, but he gained the ability to mask it. By letting all the color drain from him, he could take on the colors of his surroundings. In that manner, Travlor blended seamlessly into anything, animate or inanimate.

During the experimentation of his different coloration capabilities, he found that he could also slow his metabolism. By decelerating his heartbeat, blood flow, and nervous system, he was able to descend into a somewhat suspended state. Travlor was invisible, and no one could detect when he was near.

Yet still, he traversed the world. During his wanderings, there were times he would catch glimpses of some dark haired girl bearing a slight resemblance to Alia. When that happened, his loneliness and isolation suffocated him like a wet cloak, bearing down on him until he could hardly draw a breath. At those times, the weight of the world clung to his shoulders like a demon. Still, he never shirked the duty he had assigned himself.

He carried on. He traveled the world, reported his findings, ate just enough food to maintain his strength, slept, woke, and started again.

Of all the countries he explored, he was drawn to America more than any other. He appreciated their differences as a society. As a young country finding its way, they had broken from a strong dictatorial rule. Even though two horrific wars had been fought on their continent, the resiliency of the American people never ceased to impress him. Watching Americans take hold of their future and bend it to their will was a trait to which Travlor could relate.

Evan took a deep breath as he finished the last bite of food. Resting his head on a mountain of fluffy pillows, he watched Kyla bend over him. He kissed her beautiful lips and whispered, "I think I'm ready to begin again." When an objection rose in Kyla's eyes, he shook his head weakly. "Our lives could depend on what I learn." He paused to catch his breath and realized that talking was taxing his energy too much. He reverted to thought as he sent Kyla a question. *"What is the state of Travlor's military? Have you heard anything?"*

Kyla cleared her throat and placed a tender kiss on Evan's cheek. *"Love, that is not your concern … do what you have to do, and the rest will take care of itself …"* She glanced around the room and shrugged in resignation. *"Right now, we have no other choice …"* She massaged his neck and shoulders. Sending a wave of love to Evan's heart, she admonished, *"Be strong, my love … we will get through this …"*

Evan closed his eyes and took a deep breath. When he opened his mind, he saw that Travlor was living in a different time, a time in history that felt closer to Evan's own reality. He closely observed Travlor wandering the streets of a city with which he was quite familiar. Boston. He couldn't imagine why his father was in that particular city.

Sinking deeper into the visions, he watched his father wading in and out of a busy noontime crowd of people. Bostonians were out hunting lunch, friends, or a quiet place with alcohol to help wash away the day. Travlor, tired of avoiding pedestrians, decided one of the local pubs looked like a good place to sit for a while and observe.

He entered the dimly lit space to find that it was stuffed with people. The noise level was deafening. Cigarette smoke swirled through the air like fog as he took a seat at the bar. He ordered a local beer and savored the smoky taste of it as he peered about the room. His attention was suddenly caught by one person. A woman.

The hair was different. Unlike the dark tresses she used to have, the blond highlights gleamed like gold under the low lighting. Her figure, an exact replica of the one woman he had let into his heart, mesmerized him so that he couldn't move. Caught in the thrall of his memories, Travlor could hardly breathe.

She turned toward him, tray in hand, and her gaze caught and held his. Staring into eyes bearing the same startling shade of emerald green he had known so long ago, Travlor's heart nearly leapt from his chest. It was her. His Alia.

# CHAPTER

## 45

IS TEMPERATURE SOARED, causing his forehead to break out in a feverish sweat and his heart to pound. His mouth was so dry that he couldn't have talked if his life had depended on it. He frantically tried to will some color into his skin so that he didn't look quite so leprous, but it had been too long. He knew he didn't resemble anyone close to normal. Feeling as though he was sixteen again, he slipped off the stool and waded through the restaurant, never taking his eyes from hers.

Studying his approach, the woman looked at him, a quizzical expression on her exquisite features. When he stopped in front of her, she queried the stranger. "Have we met? You seem familiar, but …" She laughed. "People come and go in this pub all the time, and I usually forget them as soon as they're out the front door." She cocked her head to one side. "But you—why would I feel that I know you?"

Travlor's tongue was stuck to the roof of his mouth. He took a quick swig of his beer to help loosen it, but when he still couldn't address her question, he signaled her to follow him.

He needed a secluded corner where they could hear each other over the noise.

She followed without hesitation; nevertheless, Travlor could see the questions swirling in her head. As he held a chair out for her, Travlor noticed that she had left her tray somewhere. Before he knew it, she was leaning into him; she closed the last little distance left between their bodies. When she brushed his hand with hers, they were both jolted by the same shock of recognition. Travlor thought he was going to explode. They fell into each other arms.

They explored each other's mouths, kissing deeply—and as they did, the gulf of time separating them dissolved. Travlor couldn't believe that he had lived long enough to find her again.

He finally broke away from their kiss and looked deep into green eyes blazing with passion. He had to try to explain. He motioned her to sit, and as he took his chair, he signaled for another beer. But when he couldn't catch anyone's eye, he swallowed hard and forged ahead. "What I am going to tell you will seem like a lie, a tall tale, something people only read in novels or watch in movies. At the very least, I ask that you try to keep an open mind and wait to hear what I have to say."

The woman didn't respond—she just reached across the small table and took one of Travlor's hands. He cast about anxiously for the right words. He was terrified that he would frighten her away. Nervously clearing his throat, he licked his lips. "I have been on this earth longer than I care to admit. I will not tell you how long because I do not want to scare you into running out the door." Taking both her hands in his, he gazed into those wondrous eyes and continued. "We were sep- arated from each other a long time ago, in another lifetime." Travlor coughed to staunch the tears that threatened to fall.

"By the gods, I have looked for you the world over, but I never thought to find you again."

Sitting back slightly, the woman again cocked her head in that way Travlor remembered so well. She paused before she spoke, but Travlor could see the wonder of their meeting lighting her eyes. "It's hard to doubt what you say. I feel as though I know everything about you. The way you hold me"—she glanced at his mouth—"the feel of your body next to mine, the shape of your mouth, the way you hold yourself—these things are all so familiar." She ran her hands through her hair, bewilderment clouding her face, "I don't know how something like that is even possible." She reached for him again. "But as sure as I'm touching your hand, I believe you. So, now what?"

Travlor shook her hand. "I am Travlor."

The woman smiled and gave his hand a soft return shake. "I'm Ali."

"Ah … in another life, I knew you as Alia." He never wanted to let go of her, so he reached to stroke her smooth cheek. "Mere words could never do justice to your beauty, but a man once wrote that 'a rose by any other name would smell as sweet.' Truer words have never been written. They must have been about you."

Ali was about to reply when she heard her boss clamoring for attention: "Ali! What'er you doin'? Customers are waiting!"

Cringing at his tone, Ali peeked over her shoulder. "I need to get back to work." She stood up and straightened her apron. "Will we see each other again? I feel like there's so much we need to talk about."

Travlor smiled for the first time in … ever. He couldn't remember the last time that had happened. It had been so long since he had felt anything other than gloom that he almost felt like his face was going to crack. "When do you get off work?"

Studying the exquisite lines of her face, Travlor waited as Ali grimaced and glanced at her watch. "I can meet you around three o'clock, but I have to be back early to set up for the dinner crowd."

Travlor took her hand again. "I will be at the old clock tower at the designated hour. If I could only see you for the span of one heartbeat, I would gladly wait there forever. Time becomes my only enemy today."

Ali didn't want to leave. Torn between the incredible man she had just met and a job she needed badly, she hesitated. Kissing Travlor one more time, she said, "I will come for you."

# CHAPTER

## 46

EVAN GASPED. HIS *mother*. He had just met his mother! It took all of his willpower to stay tied to Daria and Travlor, when all he really wanted to do was leap from the bed and jump for joy. Because his mother had died during his birth, he had never known anything about her. His father had never shared even the smallest crumb of information with him. So, as much of an enigma as his father had been during his life, his mother had hovered just out of sight, a tantalizing mystery waiting to be solved.

Evan grinned to find out that she was even kinder and more beautiful than he had ever imagined. He stole a quick glance at Travlor. *My god, the man's hanging by a thread.* Another startling thought hit: *He's holding on for me!*

He sent a hurried request to Kyla: *"I need you, love …"* Waiting for Kyla to arrive, Evan continued to follow the path of his previous thoughts, musing, *He stays tied to life so that I can learn what drove him to the maniacal schemes he manufactured.*

Kyla entered the room, worry coloring her face with concern. "What is it that you need, my heart?"

Evan looked up and smiled. "I think Travlor is taking me on a review of his life for several reasons. Kyla, I just saw how he and my mother met! I've had so many questions about her. I have to know what happened."

"Oh, my darling, I am thrilled to know that you have glimpsed your mother." Relieved that Evan was doing better than she expected, she still transferred to her thoughts so as not to deplete his energy further. *"You have lived with such a huge hole in your heart ... why is he showing you now? Why not before all this tragedy?"*

*"This review is not just for me ... I think it's as much for him, too ..."* Evan waited for Kyla to adjust his pillows. He went on, *"Maybe he needs to relive everything in order to move on ... once we reach the present, maybe he will awaken from this terrible state ..."* He sighed and, feeling depleted all of the sudden, sank into the comforting support of the downy pillows. *"I'm grasping at straws ... all I really know is that I'm glad to see his history, as it concerns me."*

Kyla rubbed his neck and shoulders again. She was dismayed to feel how tight his neck muscles had become ... she could only imagine the tremendous strain Evan felt. Evan's body trembled as she worked to help loosen his shoulders. His whisper barely reached her ears. "If you could, please bring something to eat sooner than we had planned. The energy drain is wearing me down, and I'm going to need all my strength for what is to come."

Merely nodding, Kyla slipped quietly from the room as Evan prepared to sink back into the life that had been his father's.

Ni-Cio hardly left Daria's side but, because of the tragic events surrounding Aris's death, he was needed topside—whether he wanted to be there or not. His people were still grieving. When he finally entered the compound, he was astounded to realize that he had selfishly left Mer-An alone during her own bereavement.

When he found that she had been comforting everyone else, he was humiliated by his actions. Certainly not the mark of a true leader. He wasn't sure if he was going to be able to forgive himself for not considering the time Mer-An needed to grieve the loss of her beloved lifemate.

Barring her delight over her burgeoning pregnancy, Mer-An kept her feelings regarding Aris buried. Her stoic manner reflected nothing of her old devil-may-care attitude. The only time she experienced anything close to contentment was when she felt the child growing within her. That Aris had known about the baby gave her a small measure of peace; nevertheless, she refused to let herself dwell on his absence from their lives.

Ni-Cio needed to locate Mer-An. Eventually, he found her in the garden and approached cautiously. He didn't want to startle her, but he should have known she was aware of his company. She stood and brushed the dirt from her pants. "Ni-Cio, it is good to see you. What brings you from Daria's side?"

Ni-Cio gently pried the rake from her work-hardened fingers. "Mer-An, I am here for you, and I am concerned."

The young woman tried to shrug off his kindness, but Ni-Cio would have none of it. He took both her shoulders and looked deep into her sorrowful eyes. "Mer-An, I owe you my deepest apologies. I have not taken care of you the way Aris would have wanted." He shifted uneasily, but refused to take his gaze from hers. "While you have been comforting everyone else—including me—you have not taken the time you need to grieve your beloved, not even after we consigned his body to the chosen cairn." Still holding her shoulders, he took a small step back and studied her. "I am worried about your health, as well as the health of your baby."

Blinking against the bright yellow sun, Mer-An tried to focus on her council leader. She knew Ni-Cio was right, but there didn't seem to be anything she could do about it. A knot had formed inside her heart the moment she had felt Aris leave the earth, and she didn't know how to unknot it. The child kept her going, but the joy she had known had seeped from her like the blood that had seeped from Aris's body.

She shook her head and took the rake back. Without a word, she started moving the garden dirt into ordered rows. Ni-Cio didn't know what else to do, so he turned away and started to make his way to the kitchens. A soft breeze touched his cheek, bringing with it words softer than thought. "I do not know how to live without him, Ni-Cio. I have loved him since I can remember—how do I go on? How did you go on without Daria? And even now, how do you cling to any kind of faith that things will turn out?"

Ni-Cio turned around and ran back to Mer-An. Dropping the rake, she let him take her in his arms. Holding her as though he could be her lifeline, he realized that he didn't want to let her go. Smelling her scent of sunshine and sweet grass, a mournful thought flitted through Ni-Cio: *Aris would have loved that smell.*

When he finally felt her shoulders start to shake, he prayed that the knot around her heart would gradually start to unwind. *At least it is a start.* Holding tight to the wife of his best friend, Ni-Cio cried, too.

In a meeting with Ni-Cio, Rogert was worried. He could hardly bear the thought that their council leader was succumbing to the pressures that he carried. Rogert looked around the table and could see the same concerns on the faces of their friends. Ni-Cio had been through too much. He needed rest.

Rogert rose and placed a big hand on his friend's shoulder. "You need someone to relieve you of your duties. You need to be in Atlantis with Daria and Evan."

Ni-Cio's objections started before Rogert could finish stating his offer. Uncharacteristically of the stalwart Atlantean, he interrupted Ni-Cio. "If you want me to step in, I am prepared to take care of everything until such time you feel you can come back."

Ni-Cio loved Rogert. Even being incredibly strong physically, Rogert's physical aspect paled in comparison to the strength of his spirit. He had always been a quiet rock upon which anyone could rest.

A small grin crossed Ni-Cio's lips, and before he could stop it, a bone-weary sigh escaped. He looked down and nodded. "You might be right. It is difficult to leave Daria, and when I am here, I feel torn. I am not sure that I am serving anyone's needs well."

Peltor and Mer-An nodded their agreement, and murmurs of assent could be heard ringing the table. Ni-Cio, lost in thought, could see no other choice, and finally decided his friends were right. "Rogert, you are respected and well loved. I even remember when Marik suggested you for council leader should I not survive Travlor's assault.

"I am relieved." Ni-Cio stood up and hugged his friend. He slapped him on the back several times and nodded. "Thank you. I feel the burden already lifting from my shoulders. I will never be able to thank you enough."

Rogert's bronze coloring became tinged with a subtle shade of pink, and it made everyone around the table laugh. It was a well-known fact that the man embarrassed easily under effusive praise or the slightest show of emotion. Ni-Cio couldn't help but think that the laughter was a much needed and welcome sound, even if it was at Rogert's expense.

Ni-Cio would have liked to say more, but he found that he was already thinking about his trek back to Atlantis. "I will fill the bags I have brought with more food and I will be back when I can. In the meantime, if you could assign someone else that duty?"

"Already done." Peltor stood. "I offered to take over that duty earlier, when Rogert approached me. I will be down soon with more supplies. Is there anything else you might need me to bring?"

"No ... obviously, I am leaving everything in very capable hands." He turned to make his way to the kitchens and sent a thought-form to Evan and Kyla. *"I will be down soon, Rogert has taken over my duties as council leader ..."*

Evan's thought returned quickly: *"That's good, Ni-Cio. I may need you when the time comes to let go ..."*

Ni-Cio didn't have time to ponder Evan's statement—he just stuffed the bags with as much food as possible, said his good-byes, and made his way toward the cliffs. *"Hold to me, my love, you are not going to die—our daughter is not going to die—if it takes every last breath in my body to keep you tied to life*

..." He shrugged the pack over his shoulders and descended the windswept trail.

Wars were raging all over the globe. Whether by a stroke of sheer luck or by sheer terror of the consequences, nuclear warheads had not yet been released, but every person on the planet knew that just because it hadn't happened yet didn't mean it wouldn't. Fingers were poised over buttons and codes were checked and double checked.

The Armies of the New Messiah flooded the airways and print media with demands for their savior's body. No longer believing Travlor still lived, their demands for a body had escalated into outright war. The unfortunate soldier who had accidentally shot the Messiah had been tried in a kangaroo court and found guilty. He had been drawn and quartered shortly after the verdict was announced, and his head was impaled on a spike outside the Bogota capital building.

Pandemonium raged throughout South America, Central America, the Latin countries, and Eastern Europe. The U.S. was holding on by a thread, but North Korea was taking advantage of the situation and was launching more of its arsenal in a show of aggression and strength.

Civil war spread like wildfire, and it seemed that nothing could stop the revolt. Even the U.S. was powerless to stop the erupting chaos hurtling through the fifty states. Unless a body was produced, followers everywhere made it perfectly clear that they were willing to burn down everything and everybody.

# CHAPTER
## 47

RAVLOR WAS BESIDE himself—he hadn't felt like this in so long. He had forgotten how it felt to be in love, to feel … giddy! He laughed out loud, startling some passersby. He couldn't help it; he felt like a youth again. "The whole world lies before you like the most succulent oyster, just waiting to be savored!" He chided himself, *my god, you would think I had never experienced women before; I am on pins and needles.* That thought made him laugh again. *The Atlanteans will never believe this! My exploits are widely known, and they are aware that I have never hesitated sampling Terran life—the food or the women. And I have certainly entertained them with a story or two, but they will never believe this!*

His mood shifted a bit when he realized how long it had been since he had enjoyed anything, Terran or Atlantean. He had stopped sharing stories of his wanderings a long time ago. *It was my own fault. I was the one becoming more reclusive and more secretive. I seem to remember someone saying that getting information from me was like trying to squeeze water out of a rock.*

Another boisterous laugh. *If they only knew what has happened ... it is truly a miracle.*

Deep into his father's life, Evan watched the sun sink behind the Boston skyscrapers. The buildings looked as if they were being outlined in gold. He was elated to experience his father's excitement. Watching him try to breathe evenly and calm himself before Ali arrived was almost life changing for Evan. The man had real feelings!

When Ali finally appeared around a corner, Travlor's heart leapt, and the butterflies in his stomach took flight. He jumped from his seat at the fountain and stood, entranced. She moved like poetry, every line perfect, every movement adding to the whole. She was everything, and his eyes feasted.

He would have known her anywhere. There had never been anyone like her. Every line, every curve, every hidden aspect of her body had been seared into his soul and embedded in his heart.

Upon her approach, Travlor watched with unbridled admiration. She held herself like a dancer: head high, shoulders back, weightless, effortless. To Travlor, it appeared as though she floated while other, lesser humans trod the cement jungle like heavy beasts of burden.

Ali ran to his arms and, without hesitating, planted kisses over his face and neck; her breath tickled his ear as she whispered, "I thought the time would never pass."

A dire thought suddenly raced through Travlor's mind. *We will never have enough time. It is my penance to live forever, while you—my breath, my heart, my life—are mortal.* His heart lurched and his stomach turned. *I am headed for more heartache than I have ever known.*

Squelching the negative thoughts pummeling his brain, he lost himself to the alluring feel of her. He kissed her deeply, savoring her taste, her smell, the feel of her body clinging to his. "Ah, my love, how I have missed you." Travlor traced her lips with a finger and whispered, "My soul has never felt complete without you."

Ali looked up, eyes shining. "I don't understand what's happening, but I've never felt this way about anyone. It's like I've waited for you my whole life and now my life has finally begun."

"I was unsure what you would feel comfortable doing. I have booked a room, but if you are not ready, there are other options."

"I would say that there *are* no other options." She took his outstretched hand, feeling the thrill of his touch spark from her fingers. Electricity raced through her body until her entire being was filled by him; her body trembled.

Wending their way through the throngs of people, Ali grinned as her heart did flips. She couldn't believe the surge of feelings flowing through her. Gazing at the strength of Travlor's shoulders, and the set of his spine, she knew without a single doubt that he was everything she had ever wanted or ever dreamed about. She knew with every fiber of her being that there would never be another man for her.

They entered one of the pricier, downtown hotels. But Ali didn't notice. Wrapped in the thrall of Travlor, she realized that she needed him as day needs night, as the earth needs sunshine and rain. The rampant desire to feel him enveloping her body and soul caused the rest of the world to disappear.

The top suite, held for visiting dignitaries, celebrities, or heads of state, was immense. Tumbling through the front entrance, the lovers didn't even attempt to make it to the bedroom. Clothes presented an unfortunate impediment, and without thinking, they attacked their garments as if they had been set on fire. Tearing, ripping, and shredding, they finally fell, naked, to the floor.

Aware of nothing except the feel of lips grazing skin, hands exploring bodies, and the unimaginable feeling of finally coming into each other, they embraced. The endless years of loneliness dropped away as if they had never been. Unlike anything either of them had ever experienced, their lovemaking sent them soaring into the realms of the gods.

At the same moment, their release came swift, immediate, and violent. Arching into each other, their bodies spasmed, clenching and releasing as their ecstasy elevated them to the heavens. Gasping for breath, hearts beating wildly, the wetness of their bodies mingled, and they became one. Lying on the floor, wrapped in each other's arms, the life-affirming scent of musk and spice wafted over them as they drowsed. They had found home in the circle of each other's arms. The night came, and Ali started awake. "What time is it?"

Travlor chuckled softly. "Why do you care? Have I so suddenly lost your interest?"

She squirmed out of his arms and started scrambling for her clothes. "My job—I was supposed to be back"—she looked at her watch and grimaced— "hours ago."

Dropping back into Travlor's strong arms, she looked at him and scrunched her face. "Too late now. It's a fair bet that I'm not employed anymore."

With his lips, Travlor lightly traced her eyebrows, moved slowly to her eyelids and took his time savoring the salty taste of her. Slowing even more, he teased her cheeks until he made his way down to her luscious mouth, murmuring, "My love, we are here in this moment; there is nothing you need worry about."

Before she received his questing kiss, she had to respond before she lost herself in his touch again. She pushed away and looked Travlor up and down. "I really needed that job. In all honesty, the clothes you wear are not expensive, and I'm not sure how we're going to afford this place." She ran her hands down the length of his muscled torso—she would have gone lower, but she stopped short, looking chagrinned. "Do you have some miraculous plan that will keep me from having to hold down a forty-hour-a-week job?"

Travlor pulled her to his chest and lovingly stroked her back. "There is much for you to learn about me and the past. When I tell you that you have no need to worry about money, you must believe me."

Laughing at the seriousness lingering on Travlor's face, she playfully bit his neck. "If you say so. Just who the hell are you, anyway?"

"There is more than enough time to talk about our pasts and our future. Right now, let us focus on the present." He kissed her mouth again. "If it is at all possible, I request your presence in the bedroom. This floor is much harder, now, than it was before." He stood and offered his hand, helping her to her feet. "I hear their beds are the best money can buy. Shall we test that theory?"

Ali closed her eyes and surrendered to the magnetic man standing next to her. "To tell you the truth, I never much liked that job anyway."

The night was far from over.

Evan squirmed. The memory of Travlor's hands stroking his mother's body made him extremely uncomfortable. However, he hadn't been able to close the memories Travlor chose to share. Still, his curiosity burned—the only way to find out what he needed to know was to let Travlor's life unfold as his father remembered it. He had to find out what had happened that had caused his father to leave his mother's side as she went into labor. What had happened in Atlantis? The door dematerialized, and Kyla and Ni-Cio entered with a massive amount of food and drink. Not wanting to tax Evan any more than he already was, they stayed quiet.

To Ni-Cio's trained eye, it looked as if Evan's strength was regenerating too slowly. He feared that his friend was losing more ground than he was gaining. However, when he asked Kyla about it, she reiterated that the stasis Evan held everyone in was the only way they were still alive. To halt the stasis would mean death for everyone involved, including Evan. "Ni-Cio, if they can hold on long enough, and we can keep Evan strong enough, a solution will present itself." Taking her brother's hand, she could see the depth of his fear. "Trust me in this."

He accepted that she was right … nevertheless, it was still unsettling to see how depleted Evan had become. He bent to spoon some food into Evan's mouth, and when he did, all he could think was, *Something needs to happen soon.*

The first nuclear bomb was launched. From North Korea, the warhead detonated so close to the western seaboard of the

United States that the American government, primed and ready, unleashed their nukes in retaliation.

Watching the missile exchange between the U.S. and North Korea, China launched their own intercept missiles in an attempt to thwart all-out war. When their computers suddenly went rogue and the warheads diverted from the assigned trajectory, all the Chinese government could do was stand by and watch helplessly as their rockets screamed towards Russia.

# CHAPTER
## 48

VAN WATCHED AS Travlor's and his mother's life flicked by. He found to his immense joy that their love never wavered. If anything, their feelings for each other grew stronger with each passing day.

Because of his need to stay close to Atlantis, Travlor moved Ali to Santorini, and together, they moved into a lovely little house overlooking the Aegean. It suited their needs perfectly.

His mother loved Santorini. The colors lifted her heart and thrilled her eyes. The deep sapphire blues, rust-reds, volcanic blacks, and stark whites never ceased to inspire her. Evan wished with all his heart that things had turned out differently. He wished he had been allowed the time to live with them in the small, white-washed cottage. He could only imagine how happy the three of them would have been.

Travlor and Ali took frequent trips all over the world. Travlor wanted to introduce Ali to all of the things she had never known before. However, as much as she loved their explorations, Evan knew that she was happiest and most content when they were ensconced in their house below the white-washed town of Oia.

Ali had learned much about her lifemate during the time she and Travlor shared their lives. She wanted to believe that he had told her everything about himself and his past so that they had no secrets from each other. Still, she sensed that he kept a small part of himself hidden. Finished with straightening their bed, she stared out the window, enjoying the newness of the day as she rinsed the morning dishes. Wiping the counter, she admitted to herself that Travlor's air of mystery was one of the things she loved about him. She grinned when she remembered what he had told her: "We met as Native Americans."

His story of their life back then didn't feel quite right, but since she experienced only a deep "sense" memory of him, she had no way to determine the veracity of his recollection. In her soul, it felt to her as if their history extended further back in history. However, she didn't dwell on their past. It was the here and now that mattered, and she was ecstatic to have found the one man her soul clamored for. To have Travlor next to her was almost more important than drawing her next breath. She felt empty when he wasn't around.

While he was away on another business trip, Ali contented herself with days of gardening, basking under the bright Greek sun, and swimming in the blue Aegean. The times she climbed to town, she was surprised at how well her Greek lessons were progressing. She had gotten to know her neighbors, and many of the local business men and women were treating her as one of their own.

Life had slowed to a leisurely pace, and while she enjoyed her continued discovery of Santorini, at times she had trouble filling her days when Travlor was away.

This time, she could hardly wait for him to get home. She had just confirmed what she thought to be true, and as she absent-mindedly replaced the receiver in its cradle, she hugged herself and twirled through the kitchen, out onto the veranda. They were pregnant! *A baby! I can hardly believe it. I've wanted a baby since I can remember!*

She sat back on one of the recliners and put her feet up. Shading her eyes from the glare of the sun, she tried to imagine Travlor's reaction. *I'll call him right now. He'll be thrilled.* She reached for her cell and hesitated. *Maybe I should wait until he's back. Maybe I can think of a fun way to break the news.*

With him due back any day, Ali looked forward to his return with heady anticipation. The attraction she felt for him never dimmed, never wavered, never changed. They were truly one and the same. She loved him with the entirety of her being. There was nothing she wouldn't do for him.

On the day she heard his deep baritone ring through the house, she was euphoric. "Ali, love! Where are you? I have a surprise!"

She surreptitiously checked herself in the mirror. She had been lying down and wanted to look fresh for him even though she felt incredibly exhausted. Fluffing her hair and straightening her clothes, she smiled a secret smile and caressed her flat stomach. *It's because of you—couldn't you at least share some of your energy with me?*

Laughing because it was the first time she had actually addressed their baby, she pinched her cheeks for some color, then opened the door. Running into Travlor's outstretched arms, she reveled in the feel of his embrace. "Oh, my God! I've missed you!" Hugging him as hard as she could, she exclaimed, "I didn't think you would ever get back!"

Travlor inhaled deeply. Her scent was intoxicating. He caressed her hair and ran his hands down the length of her back. All he wanted to do was lose himself in her. It was then that he remembered his surprise. Holding her at arm's length, he gazed into dancing green eyes. "By the gods, you are even more beautiful than I remembered, and, if you have not realized it by now, my memory is prodigious!"

She joined his laughter. "So? What's the surprise?"

Travlor retrieved a soft-sided bag, about the size of a gym bag that he had left at the door. Carefully lowering it to the tiled floor, he pulled the zipper open and reached inside.

Wondering what the man could have possibly brought, she shouted in delight when she saw what he held in his hands. Carefully cradling the tiny bundle, Travlor presented her with the whitest, softest puppy she had ever seen. She flew to his outstretched hands and gently took the puppy into her arms. "Boy or girl?"

Travlor smiled. "Why, a little boy. I thought you were partial."

Ali's heart was overflowing, and tears stung her eyes as she snuggled the little soft ruff. "Where did you get him?"

His voice adopted a cartoonish cadence, and in the manner of all heinous villains, he rolled the ends of an imaginary mustache and cackled. "I haf my vays."

She rolled her eyes and shook her head.

"Sometimes surprises are best left as a mystery." He reached to pet the little dog. "Suffice to say that while I am away on business, you need to have some company. I happened by this little fellow, and he told me that he was looking for the best mom in the world." Travlor sat on the floor and enjoyed the dilemma of whom to caress. Giving up and using both hands, he glanced at Ali. "Call me crazy, but I thought of you."

"I'm going to be very busy indeed." Her eyes sparked like green fire.

Travlor suddenly had a feeling that something other than the puppy was stoking that green blaze. He studied her carefully. "What else do you have to tell me? Those eyes of yours have taken on quite a mischievous glint."

She couldn't contain herself any longer. Shifting the puppy from her lap, she placed him next to her and went to Travlor's arms. As she nuzzled his neck, she whispered, "I don't think one baby in this household is going to be enough." When Travlor straightened to look at her, she laughed and exclaimed, "We're pregnant!"

Stunned, Travlor sat immobilized. *A baby? I had no idea I was still capable of producing offspring. I thought that was finished long ago.* Words stuck in his throat, and he couldn't think of what to say.

Ali mistook his silence, experiencing her first moment of uncertainty. "Are you not happy? I thought children were what every family wanted."

When Travlor lifted his gaze to hers, there was no mistaking his feelings. Before she could move, he threw his head back and let out such a loud Atlantean yell that the puppy, startled at first, joined the fun: closing his eyes, he lifted his furry head and howled wholeheartedly. The small household was filled with the noisy sounds of love and laughter.

Evan smiled. *What a happy time. At least my father wanted me at that point.*

Kyla heard him stir and was ready with a soothing cloth. She didn't have to look at his eyes to know how tired he was. Her beloved was in dire need of sleep, but his dogged determination to hold Travlor and Daria to life was a fanatical devotion that she would not try to sway. *If anyone can hold them to life, it would be you, my love.* She gingerly washed his face and the backs of his hands, then let her hands run down the length of his tired body. She kneaded aching muscles and warmed other areas to encourage circulation. She didn't waste Evan's energy in talking. She refused to even send a thought-form. *The less said, the better for his departing energy.*

She sat on the ground and massaged Evan's feet one at a time. *So far, it seems that things are going as well as anyone could hope.*

Her loving touch brought a small amount of relief, but Evan knew if something didn't happen soon, he was going to lose this heart-wrenching battle. He allowed himself a deep breath and remembered Ni-Cio's admonition: *One day at a time, and if necessary, one minute at a time.*

# CHAPTER
*49*

IT WAS HARD to believe that only three days had passed since the debacle at Travlor's Columbian headquarters.

To Evan, it felt like he had been tied to his father, Daria, and the baby his entire life. Even with all the incredible dishes Kyla fed him, and all the massages and care he received, he knew he was starting to fade. *I feel like I'm slipping away.*

It had been a while since he had benefited from the energy sent by the baby. It was as if she, too, had fallen into her own deep stasis. All Evan could do was keep up the healing tones and cling to their hands and hope. With a sigh, he thought, *My hope is starting to run thin. All of us are nearing the end of our strength.*

Suddenly, things changed. Travlor's memories surged forward in a rush, and his hand cramped. As difficult as it was, Evan twisted his head so that he could see what had just happened. *Oh, my God! He's gripping my hand!*

Shocked, Evan wasn't sure what he should do. He tried to separate himself from the memories in order to call Kyla, but he couldn't seem to pull himself away anymore. He was being drawn down into Travlor's memories against his will. The blackness opening before him frightened him more than anything he had ever experienced. He didn't want to know what lay on the other side. He decided he had learned all he needed. Struggling to stop the inexorable slide, Evan felt the intense energy drain on his body. *If I keep fighting this, I'm going to lose, and so will they.* Left with no other choice, he surrendered to the pull. He fell deeper into the abyss, exhausted.

The scene opening before Evan was of a Spartan hospital room. A woman lay on a bed in a pool of sweat that poured from her body in waves. Steeling himself for what he knew would come, Evan watched his mother writhe in pain on sheets soaked with her own blood. Travlor hovered near as doctors and nurses rushed in and out doing what they could.

It was near her time to deliver, but Evan knew it was still too early. Ali and the baby were in extremis, and for the first time since Evan had known his father, it was obvious that Travlor didn't know what to do. He was on the edge of panic; he didn't want Ali to know how grim the situation was.

In hard labor for two days, Ali's screams had lessened only because she was becoming hoarse. Travlor rubbed her back and kept muttering ridiculous phrases in an attempt to calm both their fears. "You are doing fine—everything is going to be okay."

Gasping for breath and trying to rest between pains, Ali clenched her teeth and cried, "Love, this pregnancy has been so hard. I don't know how we're going to get through it." Her sobs escalated.

Sending a thought-form filled with love, Travlor initiated a healing tone to calm her. It seemed to help. Ali dozed for the first time in two days. One of the doctors came in to check her progress. Removing his gloves, he faced Travlor. "It could be hours, it could be days. If you need to take a break, now is the time. We are considering the possibility of inducing."

Watching her rest, Travlor knew what he needed to do. He looked up at the doctor. "I do need to finish something. I will not be long. Just promise that you will not do anything to induce until I get back."

The doctor stood at the door. "We'll wait as long as possible but, she's not dilating as she should. Inducing could help."

"I understand. Do not do anything until I get back." Travlor waited for the next contraction to hit. When it passed, he gathered Ali gently into his arms. "Beloved, I need to leave for a very short time. There is something I must do, but I promise, l will be back before you have the baby."

Ali grabbed his hands and shook her head frantically. Droplets of sweat flew from the ends of her hair. "No, you can't leave. Not now! The baby could come anytime. I can't do this without you. Please!

Travlor did what he could to send her calming thoughts—he also introduced the slightest touch of sedative into her system. Although the sedative was too mild to affect the baby, he felt it would ease Ali's fears and help her relax between contractions. Ali's eyes drifted closed, and Travlor kissed her lips. Whispering so that only she could hear, he swore, "I will be right back; it will not be long, I promise. I love you, Ali. You are my heart."

Racing from the room, Travlor headed for his Jeep. He decided that he was through. He had had enough. *To hell with duty! To hell with Atlantis! I will be released or they will suffer the consequences. Once I inform the council, they have to release me. I refuse to be obligated any longer!* He thought of Poseidon. *All these eons, I have held to a desperate hope that you would somehow find it in your heart to forgive me. But nothing—not a word, not a thought, not even a slight twinge since the day of the sinking. To hell with you, too!* Looking at the storm ridden sky, Travlor hopped into his Jeep and floored it. A cloud of dust surrounded him as the vehicle slid to a stop next to the pier. Camouflaging himself so that he was invisible to the naked eye, he slipped quickly into the water and swam to his biosphere. He charted a course, then shot through the clear blue waters of the Aegean and descended with mind-numbing speed straight for Atlantis.

Evan's breathing escalated with Travlor's swift departure. He needed to warn his father. "Stay with her! Don't go back!" But it was useless; his father couldn't hear. The memories were Travlor's, and the events of his life were playing out as they had happened. Evan was helpless to change anything. His heart was flooded with sorrow. Even though he knew the outcome, he had to witness the unfolding events whether he wanted to or not. Disconsolate, he waited in silence.

Travlor stood alone before Marik, Na-Kai, and the rest of the Council of Ten. His pleas were falling on deaf ears. Marik stood up and straightened to his impressive height. "So, you are demanding to be released from your duty so that you can live the rest of your days topside?"

Travlor stood his ground. "I have done more than was ever asked of me. I bequeathed this duty to myself in order to try to make amends for the destruction of the old Atlantis. I have fulfilled that duty! My wife and son died in childbirth which excludes me from Canon Law. I am no longer responsible for Atlantis. I want no more of you or this place!"

The council leader shook his head in bewilderment. "So, just because you have decided to inform us that you have fallen in love with a topsider … an outsider … you think you should be released from Atlantis because they died in childbirth?"

Marik's voice boomed through the hall and echoed off the walls. "How do you not recognize that you have yet again transgressed Canon Law?"

Reigning in his temper the best he could, Travlor tried logic. "Members of the Council—Marik, Na-Kai, I did not have to come back for your permission. I could have just as easily disappeared, and you never would have known where to find me."

Na-Kai rose from her place on the dais and, joining Marik, looked forlornly at Travlor. "We offer our sincere condolences on the deaths of your wife and child. You have suffered a great deal of loss in your life. However, had you adhered to Canon Law, their deaths could have been prevented!"

Marik turned four different shades of red, colors slithering over his face like serpents. "Hear me and hear me now! Atlantis was destroyed because of you! You are mistaken if you think we are prepared to condone yet another flagrant abuse of our sacred laws!"

"Know that we have not entered into this decision lightly." Na-Kai stared into Travlor's piercing black eyes and uttered the council's final pronouncement. "Atlas, son of Poseidon, you are from this moment forward bound to Atlantis forever. Unless you find release in your own physical death, you will never leave Atlantis again."

Instantaneously imprisoned in an overpowering thought-form, Travlor was unable to move. The healer had summoned an ancient energy unfamiliar to him. No matter how hard he fought, Na-Kai's thought-form was too powerful to break.

Travlor's rage erupted in a primal scream that exploded through the halls of Atlantis. There was not one soul who didn't hear the excruciating sound of his pain echoing through the hallways.

Na-Kai sent a thought to the men waiting in the next room. Hurrying in to the Great Hall, they approached Travlor as the deadly adversary they knew him to be. Though he struggled with every last ounce of his energy, the men easily hoisted him onto their shoulders and carried him through the tunnels and down to his rooms.

# CHAPTER
*50*

VAN WATCHED IN horror as his mother spent her remaining breath crying for Travlor. The doctors waited as long as they could, but as Ali weakened, they gave her a shot to induce labor in a last attempt to save her life. She was gripped by a massive contraction. The doctors waited anxiously for the contraction to ease, and thirty minutes passed before they accepted the fact that they were out of options.

They made the hard decision. They slipped an oxygen mask over Ali's face. The morphine they gave her helped ease her pain and gave them the time they needed to save the child.

During the emergency Caesarean section, the baby was pulled, screaming, from his mother's womb. The doctors hustled the newborn from the room while Evan watched the last of his mother's breath leave her lifeless body.

Shuddering from the strength of his sobs, Evan lost all hope. They had reached the end, and he prepared himself to release Daria and Travlor from his grip. He had started to loosen his hands when the scene in his mind went completely dark. Instinctively, Evan's hands tightened again as a quiet voice soughed into his mind. Infused with strength and kindness and infinite sadness, he recognized his father's voice. *"Do you now understand why I became the man I did?"*

Evan roused himself. Clinging to his charges with the little strength left in his body, he waited for his father to continue.

*"I make no excuses for my actions ... and as much as I wish I could change events, I cannot go back ..."*

He couldn't help himself; Evan had to know. *"How is it that you talk to me? You're in stasis ..."*

*"I am near death, but I need your help ... I cannot do what has to be done on my own ... that is the reason I have opened my life to you ..."*

Evan couldn't imagine how he could help his father, but Travlor didn't give him a chance to ask. *"There are two things I must do ... I must face my father ..."*

That statement took Evan entirely by surprise. It wasn't what he would have expected in a million years.

*"It is past time to seek his forgiveness ..."* Travlor paused to gather what little strength remained. A few breathless moments slid by as Evan waited to hear the rest. *"The other task is to beg your forgiveness ..."*

"Why now, Travlor? Why not earlier?"

*"We have gone through all this so that you could understand my actions ... however, I have also had to relive my life again in order to gain a better understanding of myself and the hand I played ..."*

Another lengthy pause.

*"Pride caused my fall from grace ... as much as I loved your mother, I knew the cost of my actions ... I was careless with her life and with her love ...*

*"I need forgiveness so that I can find release and peace in whatever form it takes ..."*

"Travlor, it's not my forgiveness you need; you need to forgive yourself ..."

"My son, our time grows short ... please, listen to me ... the child Daria carries is special ... if you and I can combine the last of our strength with the baby's energy, we can open a new dimension ..."

Travlor paused to rest. More precious moments were exhausted, then, pushing himself to continue, he tried to explain. "That is where I will meet my father ... in order to keep the dimension open, it will drive all of us to the very edge of our endurance ..."

There was not a sound of life inside Atlantis. No one stirred, and even the air had taken on a somber quality. "I will not require this of you, should you have any hesitation ..."

Evan was perplexed; this was a side of his father he had never seen. He was astonished to hear such remorse and sadness from the man who had commanded the attention of everyone on the face of the earth. He considered their predicament. Travlor wanted—no, needed—the chance to make amends. It was past time for him to make peace. If I can't forgive my father, nothing we've been through makes sense.

Evan inhaled deeply and exhaled slowly. His thoughts slipped into his father's mind. "I am so sorry for what you have endured ... I open my heart so that you can feel my forgiveness ... it was always there; I was just waiting for your acceptance ... I will help you any way I can ... I love you ..."

"Follow my lead, hold to life and to love, and know that all will be well ... I love you ..."

With another determined inhalation, Evan followed Travlor as he slipped into the deepest recesses of his mind. Suddenly, the baby appeared, smiling at both men. Travlor and Evan felt a renewed rush of vigor. It was evident that the child's spirit was pure and strong and new.

Down and down into the void, the three of them plunged. There was nothing to see, nothing to feel. It was even becoming difficult to sense each other's presence. At length, their fall halted. They had arrived. Evan waited in a place where time did not exist. Finally, a voice interrupted the darkness.

*"Why are you here?"*

An endless black hole opened before them, drawing all energy to itself. Evan wanted to turn and flee. His soul cried out to leave this unnatural space, but Travlor's calm words settled him.

*"We are almost there. Remain strong, remain vigilant ..."*

The darkness gathered strength, swallowing the Universe. It seemed that there had never been anything else. A light flared, drawing them closer. And as they came closer, the light flashed abruptly and grew until it had completely engulfed the darkness, as though even the thought of darkness had never existed. Where the darkness had been, now there had never been anything but the light.

A fathomless voice broke the silence surrounding them. The commanding sound, painfully loud, made Evan want to cover his ears. However, just as that thought occurred, he realized that he felt no pain.

Again, the booming voice. *"Once again, I would ask, why are you here?"*

A hazy figure began to appear.

In a sight he never thought to witness, Evan watched Travlor fall to his knees, eyes downcast. His father lifted his arms in supplication, and when he finally lifted his face to look upon the godly countenance, tears were streaming down his cheeks. His voice, weak at first, grew stronger as he stood reverently to approach the immense figure.

*"I am here, Father … it is your son, Atlas …"*

*"What is it you request?"*

*"I am at the end of my life … I am here to beseech your forgiveness … by my actions, I have imprisoned myself in my own private hell, but I have also inflicted that same hell upon the people of this beautiful planet …"*

Silence. Travlor continued. *"Although I wish to feel your love and favor again … if it is not in you to forgive me, then I come only to ask that you save the earth and her people … it is not their fault …"*

The moment dragged until Evan feared that the misty figure would depart. The child turned restlessly, and Travlor trembled. It was as if they awaited judgement day. At the moment of their greatest doubt, the outline of a man came into focus.

The visitors watched as Poseidon, in all of his majesty, revealed himself. He came toward them, formidable in his godhood, his might clinging to him like a second skin. Quaking in fear, Evan and Travlor waited for Poseidon to speak. When his gaze came to rest on the child, the baby moved. The light inside her blazed forth, matching the power of the god standing before them.

Poseidon stepped toward his son and looked down upon Atlas. His voice was kind and filled with wonder. *"My son, I never thought to see you again … I have waited a long time to hear your words …"*

Travlor prostrated himself. *"The choices I have made have caused immeasurable damage … please forgive the hurt I have caused you and the world … let me go, and let the world return to peace … let our ties to each other be done …"*

Poseidon hesitated. *"Before I give you my blessing, you need to understand that your mother was always safe … in your life*

*review, you saw that she left Atlantis before the destruction ...
I never would have hurt her, no matter how angry, but I never
saw her again ... I, too, have lost everyone and everything I have
ever loved ..."*

The baby smiled and looked upon Poseidon. When she
spoke, her voice was so ethereal that it reminded Evan of the
voice of an angel. *"There is no transgression that cannot be forgiven
... love is all ... if we do not learn to forgive, then we have lost all
hope ... because all love is lost ..."*

The sun shone from Poseidon's countenance. *"I have sworn
never to visit such wrath upon a people's again ... as you can see,
I, too, have suffered at my own hand ..."* He looked upon his
son. *"The child speaks the truth ... love is all, yet I, too, have done
my share of hurt ... it is time for it to end ... Atlas, come to me ..."*

Evan watched his father walk on trembling legs, tears still
coursing down his face. Crossing to the god, the man became
a boy the moment he fell into his father's fierce embrace.
Their embrace was everything. All-encompassing, it spoke
to both their souls of love, of forgiveness, of compassion and
understanding.

In the midst of their tearful reunion, two other figures
gradually came into being. Everyone recognized Daria and
Na-Kai. In a voice soft as down, Na-Kai spoke to Daria. *"Do
you see now, my beloved? It is as I told you, change is never easy ...
in order to construct, one must first de-construct..."* Na-Kai gazed
at Travlor. *"While you were part of an ultimate plan ... neither
you nor Daria are aware of the closeness of your connection ..."*
Travlor and Daria looked uncomprehendingly at each other,
and then back at Na-Kai. *"Poseidon's actions ensured the healing
line survived through Kai-Dan ..."* Na-Kai's loving gaze flowed

from the daughter of her heart back to Travlor. *"Daria—as is your brother, Travlor, so, too, are you ..."*

Travlor and Daria were stunned, unable to move or speak. Poseidon stepped in as Na-Kai's voice trailed away. Enfolding both of them into his powerful embrace, Poseidon's joy was boundless. His thunderous laughter resounded through infinity. *"My son, my daughter—had our actions not played out as they did, the mixing of Atlanteans and topsiders could never have taken place ..."*

Baffled, Travlor still couldn't believe what he had just been told. Blinking to clear his mind, he looked questioningly at his father. *"But why was so much hurt and destruction and loss of life necessary?"*

*"My son, do you not understand even now? Atlanteans and topsiders need each other ... a new world must come into being for the betterment of all ... by your actions, you and Daria have brought that about ..."*

At last, everything fell into place. Travlor turned to his own son and held his arms out. *"Evan, come, my son ..."*

Travlor's essence began to glow from within. Evan went to his father and stood before the man who had nearly destroyed the entire world. As they embraced each other, Travlor's words came to him in love and devotion and hope.

*"We will undo the hurt ..."*

Evan looked from father to grandfather, and then looked at the child. *"How is that possible? How are we to fix the world?"*

*"Through our combined strength, watch what enough love can do ..."*

As they joined thoughts, the exalted combination of the father, son, and child was terrifying to behold. In the blink of an eye, a green flash as bright and powerful as a thousand suns ripped through the void and covered the world.

In the space of one heartbeat, Travlor transcended, and Evan heard his voice for the last time: *"It is finished ..."*

Upon Travlor's transcendence, Poseidon and Na-Kai disappeared. Evan, Daria, and the baby were back in Atlantis. The sheer force of Travlor's transcendence was such that the energy to Atlantis was restored, and Daria immediately awakened, suddenly in the throes of childbirth. Evan yelled for Ni-Cio.

People of the world thought the horrific green flash signified the end of all life on earth—that nuclear winter had been unleashed, and soon, all life would be extinguished. Rising from the dust, they stood in wonder. It was as if time had suddenly been reset. To their vast amazement, there were no more falling bombs; there was no nuclear fallout, buildings no longer resembled hollowed out shells, and everything was as it had been before the bombs exploded.

Where chaos had run rampant, calm reigned. Through the might of Travlor's transcendence, the world had been wiped clean. Not one person remembered a messiah—thoughts of war were forgotten, and no longer were governments trying to annihilate each other. With the help of his son, grandson, and granddaughter, the world had been reset by one of the most powerful gods ever known.

Life resumed a normal pace; it was as though all the war and misery and unbridled greed had never taken place.

Back in Atlantis, the miracle of birth rocked the underwater world. Ni-Cio held one of Daria's hands and stroked her golden hair with his free hand. He was overjoyed that Daria and their child were fine, but he grimaced as Daria experienced another contraction. Smiling through clenched teeth, she said, "Our baby, Ni-Cio—she is almost here."

Ni-Cio nodded. "Let her come, my love—we are ready."

"Where will we raise her?"

Ni-Cio's violet eyes darkened to purple. "Why, here, my love … in Atlantis."

Daria dared to look around and was astounded to see that the energy had been restored. "But the power—how?"

Ni-Cio threw his head back and laughed, long and loud and hard. "It is good to know the grandson of a god!"

## THE END

# EPILOGUE

THE MOST BEAUTIFUL baby girl arrived, healthy, happy, and delighted to be with her parents. While her memories were still upon her, she blinked up at her mother and father and smiled in recognition. Ni-Cio and Daria lovingly gazed at their remarkable daughter, shocked to see that her eyes flashed from the deepest aquamarine to darkest violet. Ni-Cio kissed Daria tenderly and whispered, "She is the embodiment of the best of both worlds." Falling soundly asleep, the baby's memories slowly drifted out of her thoughts.

Daria sighed gently. "Have you thought of names?"

Marveling at the baby's perfect little toes and fingers, Ni-Cio shook his head as he watched their daughter sleep. "I have not, love. Have you any ideas?"

Closing her eyes, too, Daria decided to join her daughter in sleep, but not before she murmured, "Maybe we should talk to Mer-An. I was thinking that we could name her after Aris somehow ..." Daria's voice trailed away.

Ni-Cio sat up, a wistful smile on his face. "What a brilliant idea, my beloved." He leaned over Daria and softly ran his fingers over his daughter's sparse chestnut-gold hair. He kissed the top of her head, then slid back to place a kiss on Daria's forehead, too.

Glancing at Evan and Kyla, Ni-Cio's smile widened. "I guess we can share the news with everyone at the compound."

Kyla beamed. "You are a bit late in that regard, dear brother. As soon as your baby was delivered, I made sure everyone knew."

With a deep sigh, Ni-Cio closed his eyes and leaned back into the pillows. He didn't want to admit how exhausted he was, but he decided to rest while he could. He knew the celebrations would start soon enough.

At the compound, the party had already begun. With no reason to wait, Rogert had thrown open the wine vault, and Mer-An and the other kitchen staff turned out an incredible array of food. Boisterous Greek music sailed into the evening air, and festive lights twinkled from every available surface. Kyla's thoughts soared into her friend's mind. *"Mer-An, you need to come see this beautiful child ..."*

Mer-An's head cocked as she sampled the smoked clams. Stroking a hand lovingly over her own belly, she replied, *"I am leaving now ..."*

Mer-An let everyone know that she would be back to the party, but Rogert joined her before she started down the cliffside trail. "Do you mind company? I would like to see the child, too." Mer-An nodded, and they quickly made their way to the biospheres.

Jetting through the dark waters, Rogert unerringly steered the 'sphere toward Atlantis while Mer-An's thoughts wandered. She couldn't help but remember the last time she and Aris had swum through the deep together. She could still hear the bright sound of his laughter. She chuckled to herself. Aris had always been enchanted with the ocean, and he never tired of exploring the watery environment. She glanced at Rogert and said, "Aris believed the oceans were the place to search for the meaning of our existence, because everything is always in a state of eternal flux." She shook her head. "No one knew Aris had a deeper side to his nature. He was amazing."

"He was an exceptional friend. I remember him telling me one time—and this was before you were together—that he thought the ocean was the perfect place to confront his loneliness." He looked at Mer-An. "You know that you filled that loneliness for him." Before Mer-An could reply, Rogert announced, "We are here." Hauling the 'sphere onto the dock, the pair hurried through the corridors, arriving in front of Ni-Cio's quarters slightly out of breath. A tone sounded, and the door dematerialized.

Entering the main room, Evan greeted them. "They're all sleeping."

Rogert nodded. "All of us need rest." He settled himself on one of the couches. "However, since we have nothing pressing, we will wait as long as it takes for them to awaken."

Ni-Cio must have heard their entrance; his thoughts found them. *"Come back ... we are awake ..."*

Everyone gathered next to the bed, standing in reverent silence as they admired the newborn. The baby, still sleeping, was gorgeous. Daria carefully passed her to Ni-Cio as Ni-Cio whispered to Mer-An, "Come meet our baby daughter, Aria." Ni-Cio looked up into Mer-An's glistening eyes. "She is Aris's namesake."

Tears gathered in Mer-An's eyes as a slow smile lit her face. "Her name is as beautiful as she is. Aris would have loved her." Blinking in wonder, she looked at Daria, "When you chose her name, did you know the meaning?" Daria and Ni-Cio both shook their heads. Mer-An came forward and took the baby from her father. Holding her high for everyone to see, she said, "In Hebrew, her name means 'lioness of God.' In Persian, her name is interpreted as 'noble.'" She paused and kissed the top of Aria's soft head. Inhaling deeply, she savored the sweet scent of the new baby. She looked up, her radiant smile lighting the room. "And in Greek, her name is taken from Ariana, meaning 'very holy.'" She gently placed the sleeping child back into her father's outstretched arms. "A propitious child, carrying an important name, who will have a very special role in the new world."

The world had been reborn during the advent of Aria's birth. Presaging the dawn of a new age, Aria would eventually bring Atlanteans and topsiders together in loving harmony.

It was just as her father had said. Aria was the embodiment of the best of both worlds.

# TOPICS to CONSIDER

- *Is the Atlantis story more than legend? Is there any basis in fact?*
- *What evidence is there for Atlantis to have been in Greece?*
- *Do you have a "vision" of what Atlantis was?*
- *Can people of different cultures ever truly understand one another?*
- *Was Traveler unjustly held in Atlantis?*
- *Was Traveler a product of his time and place, or was he "contaminated" by contact with other cultures?*
- *Is the desire for power, such as Traveler has, a result of his contamination?*
- *What kind of inner struggles do you think the original Atlanteans had with the quest for power?*
- *Should alien cultures, such as the Atlanteans, be revered by topsiders or feared?*
- *What can topsiders and Atlanteans teach each other?*
- *Do you believe Ni-Cio's "love at first sight" experience?*
- *Where does love come from?*
- *If you were given the opportunity to decide the most important rules under which a society should live, what would they be? Poseidon gave Atlantis only eight canons, is there any significance to that number? Can you think of any other canons could the Atlanteans have used?*
- *Do you see any similarities to today's world?*

# ABOUT *the* ATHOR

USAN MACIVER GREW up in Roswell, New Mexico. She has stated, emphatically, that she knows nothing about *The UFO Crash*. However, since she claims that she never wanted to be a writer, it is curious as to where she got the idea for *The Atlantis Chronicles* Trilogy.

She attended The University of Texas in Austin, where she enrolled in dance and acting. Her acting career was brought to a screeching halt when, at her first student audition, she was informed that she had quite a strong accent. She claims her accent was a by-product of southeastern NM, but it sounds suspiciously Texan.

Intervening years occurred and time passed. She was blessed with a son, Eric, who has been an entrepreneur since the ripe old age of three. He now resides in Los Angeles and, of course, has his own company.

Married to Duke Ayers, Susan says, "Duke has taught me more about unconditional love than any other human I've ever met." Sharing their love and their adventures in Arizona, she credits Duke with the fact that she is writing again.

If you would like to learn more, please visit her website at:

WWW.SUSANMACIVER.COM

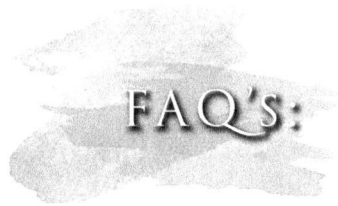

# FAQ'S:

*Why did you start writing?*

I wanted to try something different, something creative. While sharing wine one night with my sister, she read two paragraphs I had written about a girl diving off a cliff. She looked up, eyes wide, and said, "It should be about Atlantis." Suddenly, a magical puzzle fell into place.

Writing a whole book was not anything I had ever considered (much less three) and I have to say, ignorance is bliss. If I'd known just how challenging this eighteen year journey would be, I might never have jumped off that particular cliff!

*Where do you get your characters?*

I know you've heard this before but the characters in this book were just tapping their feet, waiting for their story to be told... Why they chose me, I'm not entirely sure. However, they didn't give me a lot of choice. Maybe their thought-forms compelled me to write!

*Are your characters based on real life people?*

There are traits they have in common with people I know but the Atlanteans I wrote about exist on another plane…

*Which character are you most like?*

Except for my love of the ocean, I don't think I resemble any one of them. However, I can recognize pieces of myself in each character. I think we would all like to have Marik's strength of character, Ni-Cio's need for adventure and the selfless love that Daria exhibits…and sometimes, I just feel meaner than a snake. Why, I probably make Travlor look nice!

*Which character do you wish you were most like?*

Well, I wouldn't want to be like Kyla because I *really* don't like to cook. Travlor is too ornery and Daria is too beautiful…I guess I would choose Mer-An. She's got that tomboy aura yet still is female enough to appreciate a very deep love for her man…not to mention the fact that she gets to swim with dolphins and play with the children!

*Why did you choose a trilogy?*

Once I started writing the first book, I realized the story was too big to be contained in just one novel. A trilogy goes beyond a sequel and takes us into the adventures of an epic. I felt that the very idea of Atlantis deserved the respect of an epic.

*What interested you about the Atlantis legend?*

The sheer mystery and myth surrounding Atlantis is as engaging, to me, as Camelot. I think our hearts always yearn for that perfect Utopian society…I know mine does. Because of that aspect, I wanted to explore the possibilities that a small band of people could have endured a tremendous cataclysm and that perhaps their society could have survived through the ages with their ideals and way of life intact.